In the Eyes of the Earl

KRISTIN VAYDEN

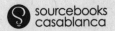

Published by Sourcebooks Casablanca, an imprint of Sourcebooks
P.O. Box 4410, Naperville, Illinois 60567–4410
(630) 961-3900
sourcebooks.com

Printed and bound in Canada.
MBP 10 9 8 7 6 5 4 3 2 1

One

The coward calls the brave man rash; the rash man calls him a coward.

—Aristotle, *Nicomachean Ethics*

"You do realize you've been holding that glass of champagne for over an hour. It's likely gone flat." Rowles Haywind, the Duke of Westmore, used his empty flute to gesture to Collin's still-full one. "And if you keep looking at it with such concentration, the mamas of the *ton* will see it as a sign of your deep loneliness and send their daughters over en masse to ease your heartache."

The last statement startled Collin out of his apathy, and he gave his best friend a glare.

"Ah, welcome back to the party, Collin." Rowles smirked. "Pleasure to have your attention at last."

Collin fought to keep a frustrated expression on his face but lost the battle. It was too much effort. Collin Morgan, Earl of Penderdale, was quite certain that the only emotions he had left were boredom and anger. Odd how the two feelings could coexist. After all, one would think anger would lead to action, but all he had left was apathy—which led to the boredom.

His attention was directed to his champagne as a gentleman misjudged the distance between himself and the wall. Collin lifted the glass slightly, avoiding direct contact with the other man's shoulder as he righted himself. Huffing faintly, the man gave a curt nod before he disappeared into the sea of silk and black evening kits of the *ton*.

"Nearly wore that stale champagne," Rowles commented as he gave a warning expression in the direction of the retreating man's back. "Already deep in his cups and it's not even midnight."

"Perhaps he's the lonely one. However, I don't see the matchmaking mamas sending their hordes in his direction," Collin noted dryly.

"He's not worth their time. You, however, are." Rowles frowned. "What are you now, three and thirty? Practically an old man."

Collin shifted his attention from the sea of humanity to his friend. "I'm the same age as you, or do you not recall such information as a result of our age?"

"Just making sure I still have your attention."

"Why is my attention so deuced important?" Collin asked with irritation.

Rowles considered him. "Because if I don't continually pester you, you'll retreat into that fortress in your mind that you've constructed, and if that happens, I might as well carry on a conversation with this wall." He nodded to the white plaster beside him.

"I'm not that bad," Collin replied, defending himself.

"Tell that to your sister, if you want to try to convince someone. See how that works out for you." Rowles gave a low chuckle.

Collin bit back an ungentlemanly word. It wasn't like him to curse, but he hadn't felt like himself in any way as of late. And he was quite certain his sister, who happened to be married to Rowles, was aware of that as well and had made more than a passing mention to her husband.

Who now was pestering Collin with it.

Brilliant.

"Speaking of my sister, where is she and shouldn't you go and find her?" Collin gave a dismissive wave of his hand.

"First, Joan doesn't need me to look after her, and second, I doubt she'd appreciate me trying to." Rowles raised a brow. "Woman is more dangerous than any man I know, present company included." Rowles lifted his glass in a salute and brought it to his lips before remembering that it was empty.

Collin narrowed his eyes in a disappointed expression as Rowles lowered his glass but didn't remark on his friend's words. They were far too accurate for amusement. Rowles was one of the few who knew about Collin and his sister's work for the War Office. But as Collin thought of his profession, the gray cloud of apathy and anger once again blurred his thoughts.

As if sensing this relapse, Rowles asked in a voice barely above a whisper, "Have they uncovered anything further?"

The words were innocent enough. Anyone overhearing them wouldn't be certain of their context, but they were loaded words for Collin.

"I was given a possible location, nothing more," he said tonelessly.

"And?" Rowles asked, waiting.

Collin sighed, his bones aching with the weight of indecision. "And that's all."

"All?" Rowles asked, his tone incredulous.

Collin turned to him. "Are you going to repeat everything I say? If so, I should say something worth hearing again." He paused. "The Earl of Penderdale is a gift to humanity."

"The Earl of Penderdale has lost his courage if he's not pursuing every course of action." Rowles took a deep breath and looked around the Penninghams' ballroom as if remembering the eyes and ears around him. "This is not the time or place but soon it will be, and you'll have more than me to contend with." He gave Collin a meaningful stare.

Joan. Collin nearly groaned out loud at the implication of all his sister would have to say on the matter. Still, as soon as the emotion rose within him, it dissipated like fog in the sunshine, leaving nothing.

Nothing.

Collin lifted his glass and took a sip.

Flat, just as Rowles had predicted, and it was warm as well. His lips twitched in disgust as he glared at the offending liquid in the glass.

"I warned you."

"I never said you didn't," Collin replied.

"Just making sure to keep my name clear," Rowles added, a little of his merriment returning.

"A fine evening!" Collin quelled a startled jump as a booming voice rang out next to his left ear.

"Fine indeed, Lord Woolworth." Rowles offered a smile as the older viscount nodded with respect.

"Fine," Collin echoed, hoping the quite deaf gentleman would moderate his volume for any further conversation.

The viscount turned to Collin. "Wanted to pay my respects but didn't make it earlier." He patted Collin's back once. His tone softened. "He was a good man, a good man. Gone far too soon, while the old stubborn ones like me live on. I'll never understand it all. There's not a day I don't miss him."

Collin froze; all that remained moving was his heart, which seemed to pick up an accelerated beat as his mind caught up with all that the Viscount Woolworth was implying.

How could he have forgotten?

How could he have let it slip by?

And why the hell didn't Joan drag his ass to the grave site? There was no way she'd forgotten as well.

Just him.

The shock thawed enough for his scrutiny to flicker to Rowles, whose expression said more than any words could have conveyed.

He knew too.

The son-in-law of a man he'd never met had remembered…while the man's own son forgot.

"Never a day goes by… I remember when Eloise passed, your father said, 'Life is colorless until you find love.' He was right. Hell, he usually was." The viscount chuckled. "Regardless, wanted to pay my respects to you and, of course, your lovely wife as well, Your Grace."

"Thank you," Rowles replied.

As the viscount left, Collin turned on his heel as well. He could feel Rowles's stare at his back, watching his hasty retreat, but it wasn't enough to make him hesitate. It was only a quarter-hour ride to the Penderdale house from the party, and the moment Collin darkened his own doorstep, he tugged his cravat loose and tossed it on a table lining the hall. As he took the next step toward his study, he ran his fingers through his hair, tugging, feeling the minor pain, needing to feel something other than the intense shame coursing through him.

He wrenched open the study door and shoved it closed behind him. Shrugging out of his coat, he tossed it on the leather chair beside the flickering fire and braced both hands on the mantel, gripping the wood tightly, his back muscles contracting as he leaned down. The fire crackled, and each snap echoed inside of him until he slowly knelt before the fire and glanced back to his desk, his father's desk. It was the place he remembered his father most clearly, where the majority of his memories took place, and where he'd learned that the weight of the title had passed from his father's shoulders to his brother's and finally to his.

It was the place where he'd learned of his twin brother's death in the fire, and the long-ago loss of his mother during her fight with pneumonia.

It was the same place he'd been given the news that someone was using his name to commit crimes against the Crown.

The same name that his father had carried when he worked for the War Office, the same name with which he carried the legacy, now dragged through the mud. It didn't matter that the War Office was aware it wasn't Collin.

It was still his name.

His. Name.

His father's name.

His brother's name.

His family's name.

He'd been carrying the anger and frustration of the problem for weeks, doing nothing as it ate his soul alive, and he'd let it go too far.

He'd forgotten that ten years ago today he'd lost the reason the name had value.

And for the first time in weeks, Collin felt an emotion other than anger and apathy.

He mourned.

And took action.

Two

The roots of education are bitter, but the fruit is sweet.

—Aristotle, *Nicomachean Ethics*

ELIZABETH ESSEX HELD THE FRAME OF THE BEE-hive so that the sunlight illuminated the fresh, white honeycomb. "Ah, there you are." She studied the eggs at the base of the wax comb, their little rice shape a welcome indicator that the queen was in residence and busy doing her job. She placed the frame back in the box. "You may be shy; nonetheless, you're a good queen," she whispered to the frames, noting the way the bees ignored her presence unless they used her for a momentary resting place before carrying on with their flight.

With care, she placed the lid on the hive and walked away, brushing off the few bees that were riding on her skirt.

"Off you go." Her long, lean fingers brushed the bees' bodies gently, and her smile widened as they caught flight and disappeared back toward the hive.

As she moved through the open field, she closed her eyes, savoring the warm sunshine after many days of rain. Likely it wouldn't last the afternoon. However, one must enjoy the fleeting moments of sunshine when they happened.

Her chestnut mare nickered as she approached.

"Enjoying the grass, Winifred?" Elizabeth asked, untying the leather reins from a fat, low branch. Caressing the mare's neck, she took a deep breath and slung herself onto the side saddle. After adjusting her skirts, she gave a soft click of her tongue to urge the horse to move.

The countryside spread open before her as she took the small deer path toward the main road that led to Cambridge. She ducked under a low branch as the well-used road came into view. The sound of a carriage made her pause before she glanced to the left, watching as a luxurious conveyance with four blood bays raced up the road. Drawing her mare farther back from the road, she watched as the black carriage with an unfamiliar crest passed by. Her mare tossed her head and huffed, as if impatient to move quickly as well. Elizabeth patted her neck once more and urged the mare onto the road, following far behind the rapidly moving carriage.

The apiary wasn't far from the town and was her favorite place to retreat to when the halls of the university got too stifling. It was difficult to be at the university often but not a part of it, excluded. She breathed deeply of the country air and steeled herself to prepare for the next few hours. As she entered the town, she turned toward the River Cam. The bridge would lead to Trinity College, one of the many colleges of Cambridge. She dismounted and took a side street that led to the mews. After handing Winifred off to a groom, she headed toward a little-known entrance to Christ's College.

The ancient door opened silently, and she stepped through, closing it behind her. As she waited for her eyes to adjust to the darkness of the hall, the scent of old books and stored furniture smelled like home. She navigated in the dim light until she reached another door. Smoothing her skirt, she tucked an errant strand of hair behind her ear with her other hand and inhaled a deep breath. The door pushed open effortlessly, and in a moment, the world was transformed. Keeping the door mostly closed, she watched, staying out of view.

Light spilled onto the gleaming floor of Christ's College. Students walked purposefully toward the various lecture halls, giving wide berth to the professors who taught in them. The air was thick with expectation and also a hushed reverence. She'd have to wait to sneak from the doorway to the library unnoticed. It was a miracle she was allowed on campus at all. However, after the untimely death of her mother, Elizabeth had been allowed to be near her father, as long as she was unseen. But though she was older, she refused to give up the opportunity to visit the library and help her father research. It filled her with a purpose and completed that unrelenting desire for learning she couldn't satisfy anywhere else.

Professor Goodary gave her a fleeting nod as he spotted her peeking into the hall. He was an old friend of her father's and had pleaded her case before the board many years ago. She closed the door an inch more, waiting. After a few minutes, the hall cleared and gave her an opportunity to dash across the way to the library, which was usually vacant this time of day.

Taking a deep breath, she opened the door and skirted along the edge of the hallway, head down, lifting her eyes only enough to see ahead a few steps so she wouldn't miss the correct door to the library. The brass handle for the entrance swung toward her just as she was about to grasp it. Jumping back, she waited as two men barreled out into the hall, their focus farther down the corridor. She'd ducked behind the swinging doors and thankfully escaped notice. *Late.* She cast judgment as they disappeared down the hall.

She quickly escaped into the library. The door closed behind her, walling off the hallway, and peace flooded her. The space was illuminated by windows along one wall, casting the sun's glow on the rows of bookshelves that lined the opposite wall, with neat little alcoves dotted between them, some empty, some occupied by a student deep in thought or study. Elizabeth's shoulders relaxed, and she held her head higher as she moved freely into the one place in Cambridge University where she felt like she belonged.

Even if no one else agreed with her sentiment.

She made her way to the back of the library and smiled to herself at the sight of a familiar gray head bent over a leather-bound tome of some ancient era.

"Papa," she greeted, earning a bleary upward glance from her father and a delayed smile.

"Ah. There you are. How are the bees?" he asked, returning his focus to his book.

"Well enough. What are you studying?" Elizabeth asked, then answered her own question as she lifted the front of the book to study the title. "Socrates?"

"In philosophy, one must always question, and questioning comes from constant study, my dear."

Elizabeth's heart warmed at her father's words; he'd repeated the same phrase often. She returned with a quote from Galileo she'd often heard him say as well. "'You cannot teach a man anything, you can only help him to find it within himself...' Right, Papa?" she said with a confident tone and took a seat beside him.

"Yes, indeed." He gave her a quick smile. His teeth were as straight as his back, even after all these years of bending over books. The scent of peppermint and tobacco clung to his tweed coat as she leaned over his shoulder to study the Greek text, translating it silently.

"Dear." He paused and cast her an irritated glance.

She leaned back. "Sorry, I know you do not appreciate me reading over your shoulder, but if you were to share the book, I wouldn't be tempted to resort to such measures." She reached up and slid the book toward her.

"You're more and more like your mother each day," he said with a sigh. Nonetheless, he didn't stop her as she moved the book over an inch closer.

Words like that used to hurt, to reopen the wound left when her mother passed away. But her father had made a habit of repeating them, remind-ing her—and himself—of the truth. Her mother lived on in their loving memory of her. And rather than sorrow, a coil of love for her family bloomed inside Elizabeth.

The Fellows hadn't liked that the somewhat eccentric professor of philosophy had pleaded to bring his daughter to work. But here Papa was far too respected and impossible to fight in an argu-ment, so she had worked hard always to stay out of everyone's way. Thus, making it her goal to melt into the woodwork as much as she could, she became all but invisible to them. While other girls her age were learning the waltz and the finer aspects of needlepoint, she was studying Greek, devouring books in the library, and sneaking into closets beside lecture halls to listen through the grates.

If she looked like her mother, her voracious appetite for knowledge was all her father's influence. And he'd encouraged her, rather than condemned her for the lack of ladylike behavior. When she had a question, he'd answer it and teach her how to find the answer for herself. Still in all this, she understood one truth: Cambridge wasn't for her, not because she wasn't smart enough, or quick-witted, or of the right social standing. It was because of something she couldn't change: she was a woman.

And she was proud of herself. She didn't wish she was a man; she wished she could be educated as the equal of one. However, that wasn't to be, so she resolved to be present but invisible and to learn all she could and pass it along.

Because learning was only half the joy. The other half was in teaching. And she carried that particular character trait of her father's: she loved to teach. If Cambridge wouldn't allow women to attend, maybe she could bring her piece of Cambridge to the women.

She glanced to her father. He was blissfully unaware of the little secret society of women she taught. It wasn't a crime. Nonetheless, it wouldn't be appreciated by the Fellows at the university, and she'd not put her father in that position. So, silent she kept. Turning back to the book, she studied the Greek and remembered a quote from Plutarch: "The mind is not a vessel that needs filling, but wood that needs igniting."

With a smile, she allowed the words to kindle a flame of knowledge in her mind, thrilled that she'd be able to pass the fire to others, not merely filling them with empty words, but igniting something powerful—the power to think.

Three

It is not the possessions but the desires of mankind which require to be equalized.

—Aristotle, *Politics*

COLLIN STOOD OUTSIDE THE STONE ENTRANCE to Christ's College at Cambridge. Hands on hips, he breathed out a sigh of long suffering. He hadn't darkened the door of the college since he graduated years ago, but memories made at the university were some of his best. The friends he'd made had become his family when those who were family passed away.

He studied the students as they avoided the grass and took the cobbled paths, staring in quiet awe when a Fellow walked across the lawn, as was their honor and due as a respected professor of the college. Collin remembered the awe and also the irritation that he'd felt at taking the long way around via the cobbles and being forbidden to use the grass. He'd wager several others felt the same now.

A familiar gray head caught his attention, and

he strode forward. "Professor Essex," he greeted as he approached the tall gentleman. The man halted comically quickly and turned to Collin, his stoic expression melting into a welcoming smile. "Penderdale, why you are possibly the last person I expected to see today."

"Less expected than the Prince Regent himself?" Collin asked, injecting a hint of mischief in his tone as he shook hands with his former professor.

The gentleman tightened his eyes fractionally and nodded. "Yes, even less expected than the Prince Regent. If I remember correctly, while your friends all worked to remain at university and eventually became professors, you swore never to return." He steepled his fingers.

"And still, here I am." Collin spread open his arms as if that was the precursor to a magnificent bow.

"And here you are," Professor Essex agreed. "What brings you back? Wait, no need to stand out here and discuss private matters. Would you like to come to my office for a moment, or do you have pressing plans?"

Collin's plans were far more important but less enticing than a conversation with an old mentor, so he simply said, "Lead the way."

"You know the way. You've been there often enough," huffed the professor, cracking a laugh afterward.

"I've given up most of my mischievous ways."

"Most." Professor Essex released a soft chuckle. "You know that merely means you still have plenty to choose from." He took the cobbled path to a small door beside the large Christ's College building. "Here we go." He opened the door and led Collin down a small hallway to the room at the far left.

"Just as I remember it," Collin commented as the professor swung open the door and gestured to a leather chair opposite a well-worn desk piled with books and manuscripts of various languages and antiquity.

"Some things don't change as much as others," Professor Essex said.

"That is a comforting statement," Collin remarked without thought.

"And that is a telling one. What brings you to Cambridge?"

Collin resisted the urge to shift in his chair. Old habits died hard, and he'd sat in that very chair too often, listening to the lecture of "If you'd only apply yourself..."

He cleared his head. "It's a personal matter. I'm searching for someone who has a...connection... with my name." He left it at that.

"I see." The professor leaned back, studying Collin with the intensity that had once had him struggling to fill the silence with words, any words.

But Collin was older, wiser, and far more experienced than when he'd been a lad at university.

The silence stretched on.

Collin waited, a twinge of some unnamed emotion willing him to fill the void. However, he ignored it, and like all the other feelings he'd had recently, it disappeared and left the void within.

"Hmmm," Professor Essex remarked. "A practicing stoic."

"Says the professor of philosophy…" Collin replied, trying to make his tone lighthearted. He hadn't thought his words or manner were anything but normal. Yet as he considered the thought, he wondered if perhaps the apathy, the boredom and lack of feeling he'd been wallowing in, had seeped through his skin without him knowing.

The thought was sobering.

And still, he didn't feel the inclination to change, but rather just to accept it, if that was indeed the case.

Anything else was far too difficult.

And he'd dealt with enough difficulty in his life that he wasn't about to welcome any more, even if it was to better himself.

"It's not in your words," Professor Essex commented, frowning.

Collin wasn't sure how to reply. He'd forgotten just how perceptive the older gentleman was, and it was unnerving.

"I prefer world-wizened," Collin replied after a moment. "I assume you're still confounding young minds with your philosophical questions?"

Professor Essex nodded as if he understood the unspoken request for a subject change. "I enjoy broadening their minds. If I can teach you, I can teach anyone," he remarked with a dry laugh.

"Touché," Collin replied just as the door to the office swung open.

"Oh!" a feminine voice stated in a startled tone. "Papa, forgive me, I thought you'd be out of your office."

Collin immediately stood out of honor for the lady who'd just entered and turned to bow. She was taller than most women of his acquaintance, with pale-as-alabaster skin and freckles she didn't strive to hide. Her strawberry-blond hair was nearly orange, and her eyes were dark brown, not light as her features would suggest. Her hands were clasping several books to her chest, her long, lean fingers tightening their grip as she studied him, not glancing away but evaluating him—just as he was evaluating her. For a fleeting moment, Collin wondered what conclusions she was drawing about his person.

"It is not unwelcome, dear. Allow me to introduce you to a former student who is in town visiting." Professor Essex stood as well. "Lord Penderdale, allow me to introduce my daughter, Miss Elizabeth Essex."

Collin bowed. "A pleasure." He turned to Professor Essex, one brow lifted in query. "I wasn't aware that Cambridge allowed female students."

"They do not," Elizabeth replied, answering the question meant for her father. Collin turned back to her.

Her pale skin was tinged with a bit of pink on her cheeks. If they'd been in a London ballroom, he'd have assumed she was blushing. But given her expression of restrained hostility, he'd wager the heightened color was from anger.

"It's not common practice. However, I'm not a common man—or so I've been told on multiple occasions," Professor Essex replied with a cough. "My daughter accompanies me at the school and has since she was only ten, when her mother passed."

"I'm sorry for your loss," Collin said, merely out of habit. Wasn't that what one said when a family member's death was mentioned? Wasn't that what he'd heard thousands of times regarding his own losses? It was what was expected—regardless of whether it meant less than half a bloody fig.

"Thank you. I'll take those from you." Professor Essex approached his daughter and lifted the books from her grasp.

She cast a guarded expression at Collin and spoke to her father. "I took notes on the aspects you'll need for the upcoming lecture. They are from the newer manuscript."

"Thank you, dear." He laid the books on the desk. Collin quickly read the titles, then stopped, since he wasn't able to read Greek and his Latin was abominable.

"*Nicomachean Ethics* and Lucretius, Lord Penderdale," Elizabeth stated with a bit of a smirk.

Collin froze, but recovered smoothly as he turned to address Miss Essex. "Ah, thank you. My Latin has never been excellent."

"A pleasure to assist," she replied, and offered a rebellious smile. "They are rather difficult languages to master."

Collin rose to the bait. "Indeed. Yet you've mastered them."

Her chin lifted a little, showing defiance. "Yes, among several others."

"Oh? Quite an accomplished woman." He lifted his chin vaguely, mimicking her expression, curious to see how she'd reply.

"And still far to go. I'll take my leave back to the library." She curtsied prettily, her tone light but her expression steely, as if daring him to question her right to the library's contents.

"A pleasure, Miss Essex." Collin bowed.

Elizabeth's eyes narrowed, as if questioning his honesty with the statement, and in a flutter of skirts, she left the office.

"Pardon the interruption, Lord Penderdale," Professor Essex said as he opened the top book given him by his daughter and quickly scanned the notes within.

"I must say, I'm shocked she has such freedom within the university," Collin stated, still contemplating their short conversation.

"Oh, it's not that she's given freedom, Lord Penderdale. It's that she's talented at blending in and not ruffling feathers, so to speak. Has been since the first few weeks she came to the university with me."

Collin had a difficult time believing that she blended in anywhere, not with that hair, and not with that glint in her eyes.

"It would have been the conventional route to hire a governess, but…" The professor's pause brought Collin's attention back to his bowed gray head as he closed the book on his desk. "I couldn't. She's all I have left, so, here we are." He nodded with a sage expression. "We must, at times, go against the traditional pathways to make new ones. After all…" He gave a small grin. "Isn't that what all the ancient philosophers did? Challenged what was known to gain something new? Knowledge? Truth? Understanding? I like to think I do a little of that on my own, in my own way."

Collin nodded, deep in thought. "I would never have thought you one to question convention. However, people surprise me more than I ever expected them to, so I suppose it's not shocking at all."

"Ah, spoken like a philosophy student. Perhaps some of what I taught you took root in that mind of yours."

"Or maybe I've just grown wise in my old age," Collin returned with a half-hearted smile.

"I believe my postulation is far more plausible," the professor answered with a light tone. "But either one is irrelevant, since the end result is the same—growth. Is it not?"

"As usual, you're correct."

"I do love hearing that," Professor Essex replied. "Well, how long will you be in Cambridge?"

Collin shrugged. "I'm not certain. I'll be residing in His Grace's town house."

"I see. Well, stop by whenever you wish. It's a delight to see old friends." The professor held out his hand, and Collin shook it, then took his leave.

The hall was dimly lit, and as he made his way toward the exit door, he paused as a tall feminine form rounded the corner, her shoulders curved inward, head down and eyes on the floor.

It took Collin half a moment to realize this was the same woman who had quickly humbled him with her intelligence and candor. In her current state, she was anything but confident and challenging. Only a few seconds had passed as Collin made this connection, confusion on his face just as she glanced up to meet his regard.

"Oh." She halted, then as if feeling the need to

explain herself, she added, "There was a parchment I needed to include that somehow was left behind."

"By all means." He bowed and stepped aside for her.

"Thank you." Her back stiffened as if she was no longer trying to blend into the wallpaper as she continued down the hall.

He should have gone on his way.

He should have kept his mouth shut.

But something burned in him that was stronger than good sense.

Curiosity.

So, with a quick turn on his heel, he posed the question that he regretted the moment it slipped from his lips.

"Why?"

As she turned and studied him, he realized that one small three-letter word was exactly the same reason there were full libraries.

Why, indeed.

Four

In order to seek truth, it is necessary that at least once in your life you doubt, as far as possible, all things.

—René Descartes, *Principles of Philosophy*

ELIZABETH REGARDED THE GENTLEMAN BEFORE her. *Why* was such an ambiguous word. Still, she felt quite certain she understood the context behind his query.

"Pardon, my lord?" she asked, part of her hoping he'd retract his question and go on his way, and the other half hoping he'd stand by it and be brave enough to ask. Still, with that courage usually came the next step: judgment and sentencing. As if all the men in her acquaintance, save her father, were the magistrates of her life. Good Lord, it got tedious.

Which was another reason to blend in. For some reason, he still saw her, acknowledged her, though she was trying to be easily disregarded.

Blast the man.

"I asked, why?" He shrugged, as if the question wasn't weighted down with the condemnation of higher education for her sex.

"I did hear the question the first time. I was merely requesting clarification. It's a rather broad inquiry," she replied, feeling the steel in her blood rise to the challenge. Make him say it, not imply anything. If he were to judge her, let it be directly. A frontal assault, no flanking the subject.

He glanced heavenward as if she were taxing him.

Good mercy, he was aggravating, and she'd only just met the man! How was it possible to dislike a person deeply on so short a connection?

"Why do you wish to be part of a community that wants to pretend you don't exist within its walls?" he asked, quite succinctly, if she were giving him credit.

Which she was not.

At least not currently.

"Ah. Well, for many reasons. However, to give an efficient answer to your question, I'll summarize." She tilted her head, awaiting his response.

"Pray, continue."

Elizabeth gave a half smile, then schooled her expression. Pretending she was explaining something to one of her students, she answered. "One, because I enjoy learning, and this is the ideal place for it. Two, because I wish to be with my father, and three, because I can."

Lord Penderdale nodded, his dark brows drawing together somewhat as if considering her question. "All noble reasons, minus the third."

"In what way?" Elizabeth asked, her spine stiffening at his implication.

He gave her a patronizing expression, one that set her blood to boiling. "Come now, Miss Essex. You're clearly an intelligent woman. Your third reason is purely selfish. You care not for how your presence impacts others, or if it makes them uncomfortable. It's for your own enrichment, and let's be further honest... That enrichment is noble but at the same time will not lead to the same end as it would if you were a man."

Elizabeth froze, her heart hammering in her ears as she replayed the words. It wasn't as if she'd never heard them before, except they hit fresh today. "Pardon?"

She couldn't very well tell him that she taught others, shared her knowledge, poured herself out for the women who couldn't attend university but wanted more than their governesses and tutors could give. He'd flatly stated her education was useless since she was of the fairer sex.

He didn't know her at all. However, she couldn't divulge any information about what she did to enrich those ladies' lives, since her father didn't know. So, she was stuck with his judgment, just as she'd expected, without the ability to justify her actions or defend herself.

"I'm not saying you're wrong," he continued with a quirk of his lips. "I'm merely saying you deceive yourself if you believe all your ambitions are noble. But then, my opinion matters little to you."

"Very little," she couldn't resist adding.

He barked a laugh, his smile wide and unguarded. The force of it was stunning, and she gathered her wits to collect herself. Drat the man for being both beautiful and a pain in the neck.

"Be that as it may, I hold no ill will toward you for it. Just thought it…interesting. Good day, Miss Essex." He tipped his hat, bowed, and departed, leaving her in a muddle of her own annoyed attraction and irritation. She watched his back retreat, ignoring the fine figure he cut in the greatcoat as he disappeared through the door in a halo of light.

Light. She snorted to herself. The devil himself could appear as an angel of light, and clearly men could as well.

Her fingers tingled with the frustration of the conversation, its words opening an old wound, one she wished would heal but that nevertheless stubbornly remained. With a straightening of her shoulders, she returned to her father's office. "Papa, this was left behind…" She placed the parchment on the desk and hesitated as he studied her. "Yes?"

"I'm proud of you. You stood up for yourself." He nodded once, removed his spectacles, and rubbed the bridge of his nose. "I think…I've gotten used to it. And I shouldn't have but seeing you today… unafraid as you rose to the challenge a peer of the realm laid before you with rhetoric, I realized my error."

Elizabeth frowned. "What error, Papa? If anything, you've allowed me license that other women can only dream about, and for that I'm deeply thankful."

He waved her off. "No, that too often you try to be invisible, and you, my dear, were meant to be seen... and heard. I'm sorry that I can't give that to you, in this place." He took a deep breath. "But selfishly, I am glad you do it, so that you may remain for at least a little while longer. You're a far better researcher than any other students." He gave a soft chuckle.

"Papa?" Elizabeth questioned, taking a small step toward the desk. "What do you mean, a little while longer?"

Her father's expression furrowed. "Surely you understand." His tone took on professorial phrasing as he regarded her. "You are of age, and soon, likely very soon, you'll need more than these dusty books and halls in your life. You need more than your bees. You'll want a family, won't you? You're not going to find one here, or perhaps you will, but that would be a scandal all its own, which I know you wish to avoid." He sighed. "Life happens in seasons, my dear, and you're in a shifting. Surely I'm only telling you what you already know." He gave a dismissive wave of his hand, paused, and regarded her as if questioning if she truly did understand.

Elizabeth's chest tightened, squeezing the air in her lungs as she replayed her father's words. She forced her thoughts to take a logical route, rather than being ruled by an emotional response, and she considered what he'd said. Logically, there was nothing wrong with his statement. It was a linear thought, however emotionally she resisted it with every fiber of her being.

"Ah..." Her father nodded once.

How she hated when he got that expression on his face, the one that meant he was about to say something annoyingly accurate. She braced herself.

"Humanity...we hate change. Do we not? Still we are constantly forced to embrace it. So, while you resist any sort of change, my dear, remember that it's our destiny. And a delightful thing happens—we grow." He turned back to his research, signaling that the conversation was finished.

She opened her mouth, then closed it. What could she say? He was right. A bloody irritating truth of having a father who was a renowned philosophy professor—hard truths and all.

With a sigh, she turned on her heel and left the office. Rather than take the regular route back to the library, she paused and glanced out the window. Normally when she wanted to think through a dilemma, she'd sequester herself in a forgotten alcove, but she needed air. More air than the library held for her, so with a determined step, she advanced into the bright sunshine. And wondered if maybe her father was more correct than she originally thought.

Change.

Maybe Cambridge had become more than her sanctuary. Maybe it had also become her prison. The place where she was constantly reminded that what she wanted was out of reach. Maybe she wanted more…needed more than that. With a sigh, she headed for the nearest bridge over the River Cam and decided that a walk was what was needed to get her thoughts in order.

If there ever was such a thing.

The bridge led into a small marketplace in the village of Cambridge. The scent of scones lured her to a small tea shop owned by the family of one of her students. As she walked into the shop, she was welcomed by a friendly smile from the man behind the counter.

"Good afternoon, Miss Essex."

Elizabeth greeted her student's father, Mr. Smith, with a warm smile. "A good afternoon it is indeed. But I must say I do think it can be improved further with a spot of tea and one of your wife's scones."

"Clotted cream?" he asked.

"Always," Elizabeth answered as she held out her coins.

"It'll be out directly, miss."

Elizabeth turned to the nearly empty shop and

took a place near the window, then stood, frowned, and took one of the few seats outside instead. The warm breeze of the autumn air swirled around her skirts, lifting them faintly as if teasing her with its antics. She watched the people as they milled about the village marketplace, her attention hesitating at the shire house—the local courthouse—as a familiar face paused before the door and entered into it.

It took her just a moment, but recollection hit her with understanding as she immediately recognized him—Lord Penderdale. Odd, why would he be visiting the local magistrate and watchman facility?

An impish thought brought a smile to her face as she considered that perhaps he was paying off a debt to society in some form or another due to his mischievous ways.

"Tea, scone, and clotted cream." The man set the dishes on the small table beside her and left with a quick bow.

"Thank you," Elizabeth called out, then lifted the teacup, her eyes flickering back to the office, determined to sit a while and wait. Sometimes patience paid off, and she hoped her curiosity would be satisfied a little as she took a sip of the hot liquid in her cup.

She had eaten nearly half her scone when the person in question emerged from the shire house. She didn't know him well, but his expression warned that whatever he'd sought hadn't been found, or he'd been dealt additional consequences for whatever action had him visiting the magistrate in the first place. As if sensing her evaluation of him, his eyes met hers, and his frustration melted into a colder expression as he crossed the street toward her.

"Ah, we meet again, Miss Essex." He bowed and studied her with a calculating expression.

"Lord Penderdale." She nodded, unsure how to continue. Perhaps he'd just leave.

As luck would have it, he didn't, instead pulling out the chair opposite to her. However, before he could sit, the shopkeeper came out.

Small favors, she thought to herself. Perhaps now the lord would take his leave.

"Ah, miss, did you care for a spot of honey? I happen to know it comes from a very highly recommended source." The shopkeeper smiled, offering the little jar that she knew all too well.

"Thank you for offering, but I am quite satisfied with just cream at the moment."

He nodded, then turned his attention to Lord Penderdale. "Are you in need of anything, my lord?"

"No." He sighed and helped himself to the seat across from her.

The shopkeeper gave a wary glance to Elizabeth and excused himself.

"No honey? I think it could be used to sweeten you up, no doubt."

Elizabeth just stared, tempted to rise to the bait, yet wondering if deflecting the comment and extricating herself from the situation as quickly as possible was the wiser of the two choices. She hadn't invited him to sit with her; he'd invited himself. She glanced down at her scone, half-eaten, and sighed. It was too good to abandon, and she wasn't going to waste it. Resigned, she lifted a piece to her lips and took a bite.

"Do you know how many bees it takes to make one small spoonful of honey?" she asked after she swallowed, taking the deflection route.

He leaned back in his chair, the portrait of ease, and shrugged. "I have the distinct feeling you're about to tell me."

"I suppose it doesn't surprise me."

"What, that I don't know the exact details of any random creature on earth?" he accused.

She lifted a shoulder, taking a sip from her teacup. "You've already decided you don't care, and that is worse than not knowing, or not wanting to know. Not caring. Because it's beneath you or not important." She set her teacup down with a soft clink.

Lord Penderdale leaned forward, his eyes constricting. "I repeat my first sentiment. Perhaps you should partake of the honey to gain some sweetness, because if I 'don't care,' as you say, then the judgment placed against you is that you are hiding."

Her eyes widened. "Hiding? What? What could

I possibly be hiding from, and why would you care anyway? I'm uninteresting, invisible, and far more intelligent than anyone of my sex should be. Therefore, I'm already written off. Why waste the time in judgment?" She leaned back and folded her arms, not caring if she appeared petulant.

Lord Penderdale smiled, his eyes taking on a light of mischief. Her belly grew warm, and though she wanted to turn away, she couldn't.

"If you would stop your condescension, you might give me a moment to say something revolutionary."

"Of that, I have high doubts."

"You have a low opinion of anyone other than yourself." He shrugged. "But that's because you're naive. I have high hopes that life will educate you in ways the walls of Cambridge have neglected to teach you. And one of those lessons I will give."

"I wait with bated breath," she whispered. She realized that she'd begun leaning forward, inch by inch, until they were far closer than was socially acceptable. However, backing down wasn't in her nature; therefore she waited.

"Turns out, I have a sister who is quite like you. And I was the one who oversaw her education, which means…" He leaned forward one inch further. "I just broke the mold you thought I fit in. Hmmm…how does it feel when your judgment is wrong? Bitter? You should have asked for the honey."

His eyes flickered from hers to a fraction lower. Her lips, she realized, and the traitorous things buzzed as if they were being touched by his gaze.

So rapidly that she blinked and missed it, he leaned back.

A sound distracted her enough that she turned to see the shopkeeper's wife taking a seat in the chair to the left, no doubt keeping an eye on the two of them at the request of her husband.

Lord Penderdale's eyes gaze slid over to the woman, then to Elizabeth as a knowing smile marred his unusually handsome features. "I'll take my leave, Miss Essex. As always, a pleasure." He stood and made a bow.

With a turn on his heel, he started down the street, paused, and turned back to her.

"Twelve bees. In its lifetime, a bee makes just one-twelfth of a teaspoon of honey." With a smirk, he turned and disappeared into the crowd.

Elizabeth leaned back and blew out a frustrated breath.

Because of all the things that she hated in life, being wrong was chief among them.

And she had the sinking suspicion she was indeed wrong about more than one thing.

Drat.

Five

It is not enough to have a good mind. The main thing is to use it well.

—René Descartes, *Discourse on Method*

COLLIN SPOKE SEVERAL WORDS UNDER HIS breath that his sister would scold him for as he walked away from the insufferable woman he'd swear already hated him. And why? What had he done to deserve such venom? He'd known her all of a few hours, and already she'd made herself his judge, jury, and executioner. Of all the insufferable, self-important, and frustrating people… She had to be their queen.

But his lips twitched in glee as he recalled her face when he'd tossed back the very information she'd not expected him to have. It had been a lucky recollection, how much honey a bee made in its lifetime. His mother had kept a hive in their country home, and she'd educated them on the facts of the insect responsible for the sweet, amber-gold honey. Miss Elizabeth Essex's face had registered shock, irritation, and finally resignation all in rapid succession before he'd turned back around and gone on his way. It was a glorious victory, and after the disappointing visit to the shire house, it was a much needed one.

The shire house had been his first hope in finding a source that could help him track down who was using his family name. He'd been given one man's name and address. However, it wasn't a person of interest as much as it was someone who might be able to *help*. And Collin was quite certain they weren't going to be much *help* at all. He paused before his carriage. "Henslow Mews," he directed, then got in.

The carriage moved forward, and he leaned back into the plush velvet of his seat. Logic said that this was likely another false lead, and that thought led to another, which hinted that this was a fool's errand. It was bloody frustrating, exhausting really, how one day he'd finally feel something, a purpose, only to be tempted to wallow in defeat the next. Perhaps it was a good thing he was away from London and could keep his sister and brother-in-law out of the mess that was his life at the moment. He waited as the carriage moved slowly through the streets of Cambridge, finally coming to a stop at the mews.

He took a deep breath, stepped out into the cobbled street, and squinted at the numbers on the houses along the road. He walked to number fifteen and knocked.

After a moment, the door opened to reveal a small-framed man with blond hair so light it was almost white. "Aye?"

"Michael Finch?"

"Who's askin'?" the man inquired, glancing behind Collin and then back to him, his expression calculating.

"Lord Penderdale. I believe you've heard of me. Or rather, the one who is pretending to be me," Collin said with a bored tone.

"Ach, Penderdale. C'mon in. I was expecting you, although I wasn't given to understand you were a...person of quality." He considered Collin, eyes lingering on the fine cut of his coat.

Collin chuckled as he followed the man inside his home. Collin took in his surroundings, and though he had been assured this Michael Finch was trustworthy, his training had taught him never to let his guard down. With a quick glance about the room, he marked the exits, possible weapons, and potential points of interest.

"Have a seat." Michael gestured to the wooden chair at a small table. The furnishings were sparse, but the room was clean and tidy.

"Thank you. I'll not waste your time. I was told you may have a lead or some sort of information on the person, or persons, using my name to commit crimes locally."

"I've run into a few situations where your

name was indeed present, and you were not." He shrugged, then lifted a cigar from the table. After taking a long puff, he tapped the ashes into a dish and leaned forward. "It's mostly petty things, minor offenses, if you will. But you probably know that. It makes me suspect something further is going on, if you gather my meaning."

"The instances in London, before the imposter took flight to Cambridge, were not slight. One situation would label me a traitor to the Crown if I hadn't had a ballroom full of people able to vouch I wasn't anywhere near the crime when it happened."

"So, there's likely more than one person using your name to cover their tracks." Michael tapped his cigar ashes into the dish once more and leaned forward. "Fancy that, a brilliant criminal. Lucky us."

"I take it you're intrigued enough to help me, perhaps?"

"I've no other cases currently. Consequently, I can offer a wee bit of my time to your cause." He set his cigar down. "For the right price."

Collin leaned forward on the table, nodding once. It wasn't anything unexpected, and he'd have suspected Michael if he didn't require payment. "Well, you did work for an agency in London before you moved to Cambridge, so I expect I'll be paying for the element of expertise you bring to the table." Collin knocked on the table with his knuckles, punctuating his words.

"Ah, you've done some research. I'd think fifty pounds would be sufficient compensation for my experience."

Collin gave a snort. "Thirty-five, and you have a deal."

"Forty."

"Thirty-seven. Final offer." Collin held out his hand, waiting.

Michael studied him, then his hand, finally shaking it in agreement. "Half now and half later," he said as he released Collin's hand.

"Of course." Collin withdrew the notes he'd anticipated needing and laid them on the table.

Michael's expression remained unreadable as he lifted the notes, folded them tightly, and tucked them into his pocket.

"Mitch, I'll be going—Oh." The voice halted when a woman nearly tripped over her feet as she stopped just outside the kitchen where Collin was talking with Michael.

"Lord Penderdale, allow me to introduce my sister, Miss Patricia Finch." He waved to the woman. Collin stood and bowed, quickly guessing she was a few years younger than his sister, Joan, and round in all the ways Joan was fine-boned. Her curly blond hair was forcibly pinned into some semblance of a design he didn't understand, and her eyes flashed with curiosity, then wariness.

"He's to be trusted, or at least trusted enough,

Pat. Go ahead and run along to your detrimental education." He chuckled as his sister speared him with an irritated glare.

"It was a pleasure, Lord Penderdale." She curtsied to Collin, quirked her lips as she regarded her brother, and disappeared out the door.

Collin watched her leave and turned to her brother.

Michael held up a hand. "Patricia likely heard nothing, and if she did, the only friend she has is the scholarly type—odd for a woman. But it's companionship for her, which, when all she has is the likes of me around her, is necessary."

"Scholarly?" Collin asked, a suspicious feeling tickling his spine.

"Ach, I'm not supposed to know, but I follow now and then just to make sure she's safe. It's a harmless little club for women who want to learn more than needlepoint. It's borderline heretical, especially if you were to listen to any of the folk from the university, but I see no harm in it. My sister loves the teacher, and they've become fast friends."

Collin shifted on his feet. "Is the teacher a woman?"

"Do you think I'd let my sister go unaccompanied if it wasn't?" Michael Finch twitched his nose and took a deep drag of his cigar. "If we're to work together, you need to have higher expectations of my character."

Collin held up his hands in surrender. "I meant no slight. I was just curious. It's not common for something like this to happen in London; therefore I find myself…fascinated."

Michael studied him, then nodded. "Understood, nor is it common here." He shrugged. "Nevertheless, no harm can come from it."

Collin wanted to ask outright if the teacher was Elizabeth Essex, but rather than give away that he was familiar with her, he went about the question in a different manner. "How do you know this teacher has anything worthwhile to teach? Just curious."

Michael answered. "She's one of the professors' daughters, lives like a bloody ghost at one of the colleges at Cambridge. Poor thing, probably the only social life she'll ever have."

Collin bit his lips to keep from smiling. Of course she taught. He wasn't surprised. He applauded her ingenuity in finding an outlet for all those hours spent in the library. Belatedly, he wondered if her father knew. After a moment's consideration, he decided that she likely didn't tell him the full extent of the truth, but she wasn't one to lie—of that he was certain, even on such a short acquaintance as they shared.

Collin turned his attention to Michael. "I'll return in the morning, and you can go over any details you have regarding the situation."

"I'll be here." Michael lifted his cigar.

"Then I'll take my leave. It was a pleasure, Mr. Finch."

"Michael, or Mitch, either suits, but Mr. Finch was my father and I'm not too keen on being called by his name." There was silent hostility in his expression at the last words.

Collin nodded. "Michael it is." He stepped down from the porch and made his way to the carriage. Part of him wished he could follow Miss Finch to her meeting with Miss Essex. However, showing up unannounced and without invitation would not be helpful.

So instead he told his coachman to take him back to Rowles's town house, where he'd be staying for the foreseeable future. At least he was assured to have a very comfortable residence while he was in Cambridge. A duke as a brother-in-law certainly had its benefits. Though, to be fair, Rowles had been one of Collin's best friends before he became a brother-in-law as well.

The carriage moved forward on the cobbled streets before halting in front of a stone edifice. Collin stepped out, observing that the number on the door was the only differentiating trait from all the other doors on the street belonging to the same building.

"Well, Rowles, I must say I expected a little more than this," he muttered under his breath.

The door opened as he took the last step up,

and a weathered face nodded in deference. "Lord Penderdale." The butler stepped aside, allowing Collin entrance into the dark hall.

As Collin's eyes adjusted, he noted the tasteful furniture, speaking of the wealth of its owner in an understated fashion. He reevaluated his first impression. The duke's residence did not disappoint in the least. He gave a nod to the butler and was greeted by a plump woman who curtsied her welcome.

"Lord Penderdale, it is our pleasure to serve you at His Grace's residence here in Cambridge. If you'll follow me, I'll direct you to your chamber. Would you care for refreshment in the parlor in a quarter hour?" she asked, a hospitable smile on her face.

"That would be delightful."

She nodded her understanding and led the way down the hall and up the stairs to the second floor. Collin noted the open doors as they passed, marking the small library and office, likely piled high with notes and books. His brother-in-law had been a professor at Cambridge before he had inherited the title of duke.

Collin stifled a shiver at the memory of the fire that killed the duke's brother, as well as his own twin.

Odd how the memory of fire made him feel cold. The housekeeper paused in front of double doors, opened them, and stepped aside for him. Collin walked in, approval in his tone as he turned to the housekeeper, thanked her, and made a mental note to write and thank Rowles as well.

"Refreshments will be waiting whenever you are ready, my lord." With a final nod, she closed the door as she left.

Collin sighed deeply, his body aching from the long travel and events of the day. He sank into a wing-backed chair by the low-burning fire and leaned back, closing his eyes. It hadn't been an all-in-all unproductive day, although it wasn't as helpful as he'd hoped. But it was a start. And one had to begin somewhere, he reminded himself.

He glanced about the room, rose, and watched out the window. The windows faced the street where his carriage had arrived, and beyond that he could see down another street toward the river in the distance. But mostly, he saw other buildings, similar to the one he was currently in. He looked down to the street. If necessary, a hasty exit through a broken window would be possible, though less than ideal. It would likely result in some broken bones; however, bones healed. This was a safe place, he told himself.

He took in the rest of his surroundings. Four-poster bed, chairs, desk, the usual. It was comfortable, and he was at ease. All that was missing was a spot of tea, which he thankfully had waiting for him in the parlor downstairs. It was a bright spot in his day, he thought rather sardonically as he started toward the door. As his hand touched the cool brass, he paused. There was another bright spot, and it involved tea as well.

A smirk teased his lips as he walked out into the hall. Verbal sparring with a fascinating woman was always a highlight, and fascinating women in London were few and far between. Beautiful? Yes. Well trained? Yes. Fascinating? No. Most were dull as mud and equally shallow. As he took the stairs to the parlor, he pondered Miss Essex. Her strawberry hair was the color of a sunset with a storm on the horizon, and those dark eyes and long, lean fingers added to her full allure. But if he were honest, her mouth and the words she'd spoken were what had him thinking about her long after they'd met.

He took a seat in the parlor and poured himself some tea and watched the steam swirl about as he finished filling the cup. He lifted it to his lips and smiled as he thought of a different set of lips.

And he suppressed a chuckle as he considered just how much she'd hate him thinking about her. That made him like her all the more.

Six

ELIZABETH SCANNED THE SMALL ROOM AT THE
back of the tea shop, meeting the eye of every student before she began with a quote. Her voice rang
clear as she said, "'I found myself beset by so many
doubts and errors that I came to think I had gained
nothing from my attempts to become educated
but increasing recognition of my ignorance.'" She
finished the René Descartes quote from *Discourse*.
"Who remembers who said this?"

A few of the women glanced down. However,
Patricia Finch's eyes held steady as she called out,
"René Descartes."

"Well done," Elizabeth praised. "Well done.
And what can we glean from this quote? Amy?"
Elizabeth turned to another student.

Miss Hasselridge was one of the quietest students, but she had the best attendance record. Though she didn't like to speak out, Elizabeth found Amy always had an intelligent response to her questions.

Amy swallowed and glanced about the area as if searching for courage, or for someone to take the question instead. "I believe it means that the more you learn, the more you realize how much you still don't know."

"Well said," Elizabeth remarked. "But did Descartes stop his education and the furthering of his mind?"

"No," the women murmured.

"No, he did not. Rather, that very question is what spurred him on to greater and deeper understanding. This quote is taken from his *Discourse*, published in 1637. You'll get the opportunity to brush up on your French as you read this. A nice change from the Latin you've been reading." She took a deep breath. "Though the war with Napoleon is finished, I understand there is still some animosity toward the French, and I share it. Nevertheless, I don't wish for it to cloud your judgment as you read this literature."

Elizabeth opened the book and took a seat, turning to the first page and beginning to read in French. When she'd finished several pages, she stood and nodded to another student, who came to the chair before the book and took her place, beginning to read. Elizabeth listened to the words come to life as they were read out loud. It was the best option, under the circumstances. Not every household held a copy of the Descartes *Discourse,* so they read it together. The process was tedious and would take more time than she'd like, but the result was a widened scope of literature, of thinking and understanding. What resulted was education, and that was exactly the goal. Therefore if the process wasn't ideal, the outcome was.

Slowly they rotated until every lady had read a few pages. Elizabeth took one final turn reading and then posed some questions to the class, asking them to consider them for next week. The whole meeting was a little over an hour, which never seemed long enough. However, it was a start, and it was a far cry more than any of the women would ever achieve on their own.

It wasn't that Elizabeth was against more traditionally feminine forms of education; it was just that they were incomplete. Education was education, learning was learning, and whether it was needlepoint or flower arranging, it was still interesting and a learned skill. But education should be more. Women deserved more. Descartes was not on the normal reading list for most young women, and it would be a scandal if she cracked open his *Passions of the Soul.* She'd been scolded soundly when her father discovered she'd begun to read it, and her father was usually quite amenable to whatever she wished to read. *Discourse* was far less scandalous.

The ladies stood from their chairs and chatted for a bit, enjoying the social aspect of the class as well as the education. Elizabeth smiled as she took in the space, glorying in what it encompassed: tradesmen's daughters, shopkeepers' daughters, farmers' daughters, gentlemen's daughters all coming together and disregarding the ways in which society constrained them.

"I'll see you all next week," Elizabeth said as she stacked her books and placed them in her leather satchel.

"Elizabeth?"

Elizabeth met the inquiring face of Patricia Finch. "Yes?"

"May I read ahead?" Patricia asked as she traced her finger along the back of a chair.

Elizabeth paused, then nodded. "Of course. Does your brother have a copy?"

"Yes, he might balk a bit when I ask to borrow it, but he'll let me, especially if I tell him you suggested it." She gave a sly smile.

Elizabeth's cheeks heated at her friend's words. "Your brother would likely let you use the book regardless of who suggests it, Patricia."

"Oh, I don't know..." Patricia drew out the

words. "I can't remember the last time he asked about any woman, and he was certainly asking about you after you visited last week."

"A polite inquiry, but it isn't significant. Besides, I'm quite content to assist my father for the time being." Elizabeth attempted to dodge another matchmaking scheme of her friend.

"Will you still come over for tea tomorrow?" Patricia asked.

Elizabeth held back a sigh. Of course she would go, although she didn't appreciate the connection Patricia was trying to form between her and her brother. It wasn't that she had anything against him. He was adequately handsome to tempt her, but that wasn't enough. She wanted, needed more than attraction. And she wasn't sure he held an interest in her, truly. Patricia likely was seeing only what she wanted to see, what she willed to be.

"Of course I'll be there tomorrow. Two?" Elizabeth answered.

"Indeed. I'll see you tomorrow." Patricia gave a mischievous wink and darted out the door before Elizabeth could say anything more.

Taking a deep breath, Elizabeth left through the back door of the shop and walked briskly across the cobbled alleyway. Her home wasn't far. Nonetheless, as the light faded over the tall buildings of Cambridge, an uneasy feeling tickled her skin. She glanced around her, keeping an eye on her surroundings. She rounded a corner and then released the tension in her shoulders at the sight of her father waiting outside their door, watching for her return. With a smile, she slowed her hurried pace, knowing she was being watched. Her father rocked on his heels, a pipe in his mouth as he watched her progress. She had loved her mother, and her death had been devastating for them both. Her father keeping her nearby and at Cambridge had been her saving grace, and she knew it had cost him. She lifted a hand in a wave as she neared their stoop.

"Evening," her father greeted her as she paused by the stairs.

"Good evening, Papa." She reached up and kissed his rough cheek, a half-day's beard growth scratchy against her lips.

He gestured for her to take the stairs ahead of him. "How was your evening? Miss Finch is doing well, I hope?"

Guilt overcame her as she nodded, swallowing the catch in her throat. She hated lying to her father, but it was better this way. She was protecting him, keeping him in the dark so he didn't know she was secretly teaching women the very things the institution he worked for kept for the men in their halls.

"Patricia is well," she answered, thankful it wasn't a lie. "I'm having tea at her house tomorrow afternoon."

"Good. I'm glad you have some feminine companionship. I worry that you spend so much time with me." He closed the door behind them and started toward his study. "You should invite her over for tea this week, return the gesture," he coached.

Elizabeth smiled to herself. He tried hard to fit both roles, the mother she'd lost and the father he was, and at times it was so transparent it was endearing.

"Of course, thank you for suggesting that."

He paused in the doorway to his study. "I wish I knew more about the social aspects of life. I admit they have always been a source of ambiguity to me, shifting like sands I can never quite hold in my mind. It's times like this I miss your mother even more. She understood those unwritten rules and the written ones." He gave a dry chuckle. "Kept me in line, and no doubt would have nabbed you a first-rate husband."

"I think I'll be able to nab my own husband when the time comes," Elizabeth said with a saucy tone.

Her father's lips spread into an amused grin. "Of that I have no doubt, and I should encourage you to hurry along that process, but I must admit to being selfish and enjoying the fact I have you all to myself."

"I'm thankful we have each other, and someday, when I do marry, it will be to a man who values you just as much as I do. Subsequently you won't ever be alone, Papa," Elizabeth asserted with conviction. How would she love or respect a man if he didn't have respect and affection for her favorite person in the world, her father? Impossible.

"We shall see, but enough of this for tonight. I'm going to read a little before bed. Tomorrow comes early." He gave a small wave before disappearing into his study.

"Night, Papa," Elizabeth called and then turned toward the stairway. She made her way to her room and opened the door, releasing a pent-up breath while sagging onto her bed. The chambermaid had stoked the fire in the hearth, and it glowed cheerily, keeping the room comfortable. With a deep sigh, she rose. It had been a full day, and she considered all its events while she readied herself for bed. When she finally slid under the covers, she closed her eyes. Her earlier irritation with the arrogant Lord Penderdale swelled back into her thoughts, and against her will, as she finally drifted to sleep, the words that filtered through her mind were not those of Descartes but those of Lord Penderdale.

Seven

What is a friend? A single soul dwelling in two bodies.
—Aristotle, *Nicomachean Ethics*

COLLIN'S FIRST APPOINTMENT WAS AT THE SHIRE house, to find out if there'd been any new occurrences of his name's misuse. As he waited to be seen, he considered what actions should be taken next, with Michael Finch's assistance. He trusted the man—at least trusted him not to make a fool of either of them—but wasn't sure how much help he would be. Collin was shown into a small office where two men waited, one seated, one standing. "Lord Penderdale, I'm the clerk for the local watchmen, and this here is Mr. Thudd. He was on duty last night and has some information for you."

Collin shook the hands of each and took a seat, leaning forward as he waited for the watchman to tell his tale.

"I was doing my rounds over by Bridge Street, and I heard a fight brewing, two blokes yelling at one another. I hustled my way over and saw someone in a cap with a stick yelling at another man, trying to rob him, or so I thought. But no sooner had I arrived than the one with the stick ran off. I gave chase, only he was like smoke and disappeared. When I circled back to the first, he wasn't injured too badly but he said something I thought you'd be interested in. Turns out I missed most of the fight. The man who ran off had been cheating at cards at one of the clubs and was called out by the gentleman I was talking with. They'd exchanged a few blows, nothing serious. Turns out, he had been using the name Lord Penderdale while he was playing cards, which raised the first one's suspicions as he didn't dress like a lord. Therefore, he thought if the man was cheating about the name, he would possibly cheat with the cards. He was right, called him out, and when he was about to lose the fist-fight, or so the first guy said, the card cheater picked up the stick, then ran off when I arrived."

"So, the one who ran was playing cards under my name."

"Yes." The watchman nodded.

Collin frowned. "Where was he playing cards? Did you find out?"

"The Hare," the watchman answered. "I had heard you stopped in here yesterday, so when your name was cited, I took special interest. I also have the name of the man who discovered the cheater."

"Excellent." Collin's heart was pounding. Finally, a lead—something, anything that might give him a direction for some answers!

"His name was Luke Morrison, works at the livery down the way."

"Very useful, thank you," Collin answered, committing the name to memory. "I'm working with Michael Finch. If he stops by to ask further questions, would you mind talking with him?" Collin asked.

"Of course not," the clerk answered. "We're familiar with Michael. Good to know you have someone local to assist you."

"Indeed. In fact, I'm to meet him soon. I'll take my leave, and hopefully this information will be of assistance in figuring out what is going on." Collin drew in a deep breath and extended his hand in thanks to each man once more.

"We'll keep our ears open and let you know if we hear more. Would you prefer us to contact you directly or go through Michael?"

"Either. I'm staying at the Duke of Westmore's residence, but if you see Michael, you can pass along the information through him."

"Of course, my lord."

Collin didn't miss the way the men's eyes widened at the mention of the duke's name. Though Rowles had been a professor at Cambridge for a few years and was known in town, things had changed when he inherited the title. One could not carry the title of duke and not have it bear considerable weight.

Collin took his leave and, once he reached the street, directed his coachman to take him to Michael's residence. When he arrived, he rapped on the door a few times and stood back, rocking on his heels as his mind spun in several directions regarding how the new information might be of assistance.

Michael answered the door, then rubbed his chin. "Ach, if you're arriving this early, I hope it's because you've learned some news." He stood back and allowed Collin entrance into the hall.

"Indeed, and though London society would certainly consider eleven o'clock early, I didn't expect that you would," Collin answered with a teasing lilt to his tone.

Michael paused as he led the way to the same small table where they'd conversed yesterday and gave him a sarcastic grin. "I'd agree with you, but I spent most of the night searching out information for a certain gentleman."

Collin nodded. "I appreciate your efforts."

"About time someone appreciates my efforts," Michael said a little too loudly for it to be meant for Collin. As if on cue, Patricia came into the room with a pot of tea. "Your bellyaching doesn't give me pity for you or an appreciative heart," she retorted. "Lord Penderdale." She curtsied.

"Miss Finch." Collin bowed and took the seat Michael gestured toward.

"I'll return with the teacups," Patricia murmured.

"Ach, sure she uses manners around you. I may have to keep you around more often, might improve things a bit around here," Michael grumbled, but Collin noted the tone was anything but resentful. Michael and Patricia's dynamic was a welcome familiarity; it reminded him of his interactions with his own sister and immediately put him more at ease in their presence, though they were still of new acquaintance.

"I say the very same things about my sister. Let me know if you have any better luck than I have had over the years," Collin added with a light tone.

"Here we go." Patricia laid out the teacups and took her leave. Collin appreciated her understanding of the need for privacy.

"So, why don't you start and let me know what you found out, and I'll add in. It may relate," Michael said as he poured the tea.

"Very well," Collin replied, then went into the story given by the night's watchman, carefully laying out every important detail he had learned.

"The Hare... I was there last night too, but didn't stay late. I moved along to the tavern on the outside of town. Should've stayed at The Hare." Michael took a long sip of tea. "And I know Luke, rough fellow but honest. We can head over there next."

"Agreed. Your turn." Collin lifted his teacup and

took a sip of the hot liquid, waiting for Michael to begin.

"As I said, I was at The Hare, where there were several card games going on. I recognized every man in the place, so I decided it wasn't likely your imposter would be present. He must have come by later."

"Why are you assuming it's not one of the local men?" Collin asked.

"It's less likely, and it would cause talk since everyone would already know his name." Michael shrugged. "It's not impossible but less likely. Therefore I'm starting with what would give us the greatest success rate."

"I understand. Carry on."

Michael nodded. "So, using that same theory, I thought that the taverns outside of town would be more likely to be visited by those not local. I was correct in that assumption—knew less than half— and kept my eye on several for most of the night. Nothing came of it, but I did notice that *my* notice was taken into account."

"They noticed you were watching them."

"Yes, and I'm not obvious enough for that to be the case unless they know what to look for...which made me suspicious. I asked after them of the barkeep, who's an old acquaintance of mine. He's going to keep an eye out as well. I didn't tell him why, and he didn't ask. Good man, and he trusts me enough to know if I ask him to keep an eye out, there's a good reason for it."

Collin set his teacup down. "Thank you. Sounds like you laid some good groundwork for us last night."

"It's a step." Michael shrugged. "I'd suggest we go visit Luke next."

Collin nodded in agreement. He took a final drink of his tea and set the cup aside. Standing, he shook out his coat a bit and waited for Michael. "Should we take my carriage or walk?"

Michael stood, his forehead knitting as he considered Collin's question. "The less suspicion, the better. So, let's do this: walk to the livery, have a drink at the tavern, and return and regroup back here. Here's my thought on all this…" He paused and took a slow breath. "If those we're trying to ferret out discover that you're here, trying to ferret them out, I doubt they'll be as easy to find. Best to blend in a little."

"It's a good plan," Collin agreed.

"Pat? We're headed to the livery," Michael called out, and then led the way to the door.

Collin followed him as they took a left onto the street and started down toward the market where the shire house was located. Collin studied the streets and the buildings and gathered his bearings. It had been a while since he'd roamed Cambridge, and some things had changed, but much had stayed the same. The streets were crowded with people going about their business, the scent of animals and bread wafting through the air as vendors meandered around a few stalls selling wares.

Michael nodded at a building ahead, and Collin tipped his chin in understanding. A shingle with the word *Livery* was hanging ahead.

The scent of linseed oil and leather permeated the air as Collin entered through the stable door. Michael lifted a hand in greeting as he called out, "Luke!"

The beast of a man turned, and his weathered face broke into an almost smile as he approached Michael. "Good day to you, Mitch." His dark eyes shifted to Collin, no doubt taking in the fine cut of his coat and the fact he was certainly not a local gentleman.

"This is Lord Penderdale," Michael said with a significant tone. "The real one."

Luke's brows shot up and he nodded once. "Ah, been talking to the watchmen, eh? Well, it was a tussle last night, for sure."

Collin held out his hand in greeting. "I'd be very appreciative to hear your take on what transpired last night."

The man took a deep breath, and Collin had a hard time understanding why anyone would pick a fight with him, other than desperation.

"I haven't met too many people of quality in my life, but I know one when I see one, and last night the man saying he was you didn't appear to be a titled gentleman."

"Can you describe what he was wearing? What he looked like?" Michael asked.

"Same height as you, Mitch. London accent when he spoke, cockney. His clothes weren't the same quality as your friend's here, but they weren't rags either." He paused as if filtering the mental image for more detail. "His eyes were shifty too, like he was not at ease."

"Well, if he was cheating, that makes sense."

"Yeah, but he came in that way, checking over his shoulder. I was already playing with some friends, and he joined in the game."

"I saw you there last night, so he came after I left. When would you say he arrived?" Michael asked.

Luke replied, "Yeah, you left about ten. I'd say he arrived a half hour after that."

"And when did you call him out for cheating?" Collin asked.

"Well, I was suspicious right away because he wasn't a good cheat. I'd say maybe a quarter hour into the game I called him out, and we took it out back. 'Tisn't polite to fight in the bar, plus I like the place, don't want to cause a mess because of some stupid fellow."

"How generous of you," Collin said, and meant it. How often he had seen fights at gentlemen's clubs, the men not concerned if they broke furniture or harmed others. The fact that Luke had the foresight to consider those things spoke highly of him.

"Thank you, my lord," Luke answered. "Well, I took him out back, and he got real scared real quick. He picked up this stick and came at me. I blocked the stick, which gave me one hell of a bruise on my arm, and gave him a solid facer. So, I'd reckon you'd just need to be searching for a man who took a facer and is sporting a purple bruise."

"Excellent," Michael told him. "Very helpful, Luke."

"I try," Luke replied with a smirk. "The watchman came over, the cheater ran away, and that was it. I went back in to my card game."

Michael leaned forward with an amused expression. "Did you win?"

Luke blew out a breath. "Indeed, I did. Cleaned up real well."

Michael slapped his shoulder with approval. "I'll have to try and humble you later this week."

"You can sure try," Luke replied good-naturedly.

Collin listened to the two men as they bantered back and forth, setting a date for another card game. "May I join?" Collin asked, thinking of a plan.

Luke sized him up, and Michael narrowed his eyes, then offered a nod. "That's not a bad idea, you know. Luke, set it out about town that there's a gentleman in town who has money to lose and a weak game."

"I would be insulted except that's exactly what we need. If we lay a trap, maybe I'll be able to see one of these bastards face-to-face and find some answers," Collin said.

"I'll be sure to spread the word. When would it be?"

"Yeah, might as well. But don't use his name. It will scare off those trying to make work of it."

"Understood," Luke agreed. "Well, I'd best return to my work. Michael, I'll send word if I hear of anything else, and if not, I'll see you at the game tonight." Luke reached out his hand and shook Michael's, then Collin's before taking his leave back into the inner room of the livery.

"Well, that was helpful," Michael stated as they walked back out into the sunshine.

Collin agreed. "It was. Now we have a man with a facer to locate and a game I apparently need to lose."

"Are you any good at the game? Or am I going to need to save you a time or two?" Michael winked.

"Ass." Collin chuckled. "I can hold my own, thank you."

"We'll see." Michael paused at the crossroads. "The taverns will be mostly empty now, but if we go to a few of the boardinghouses, we can inquire if any of the tenants have injuries. I know most of the proprietors. After, I'll take you to the taverns. Since they're on the outskirts, we'll make our way in that direction."

Collin gestured for him to lead the way.

Michael turned down a side street and knocked on a wooden door that, like so many in Cambridge, was similar to the one beside it.

Collin waited as Michael spoke with the proprietor of the boardinghouse, nodding when introduced as a gentleman from out of town. The same process repeated itself at various boardinghouses across Cambridge, all with the same result: no current boarder with a black eye.

"It makes me think the man is local, or local enough that he doesn't need lodgings," Michael said as they made their way out of town to the tavern he had visited last night.

"Or they're staying with someone local," Collin added, his mind continuing to work on the problem at hand.

"That's certainly a possibility as well. I'd wager that we need to make the rounds at the taverns tonight to see if we notice anyone with that black eye from Luke."

"If the cheater shows his face again soon."

"Aye," Michael agreed.

They visited the tavern and had a quick pint as they took a moment's rest. Michael checked his pocket watch and straightened. "Time to go."

Collin took a last long draw of his pint and set it on the counter. "Have an appointment?"

Michael stood and waved to the barkeep. Collin

noted the way Michael's ears turned faintly red at the question and filed the information away for later reference in his memory.

"You could say that." Michael avoided the question.

Collin's curiosity was piqued. "Oh?" Then he smirked.

"Well, since you'll just try to ferret it out of me, I'll tell you. My sister has a friend coming to tea this afternoon, and let's just say she's not hard on the eyes."

"Oh...I see." Collin nodded his approval. "Well, I suggest we make our way back to your residence. Wouldn't want you to miss an opportunity."

"Let it never be said that Michael Finch missed an opportunity." He chuckled. "The lady won't give me the time of day, but that just makes the challenge more irresistible."

Collin studied Michael for a moment, considering his words. As an older brother, he was used to monitoring the potential suitors for his sister, making sure that anyone with less than pure motives was removed immediately. Though his sister was happily married now, the instinct still remained, but as he studied Michael, he didn't pick up any of the warning signs that he would be less than honorable in his pursuit of whatever woman this was. Sometimes a challenge was only that, a bit of extra work that was worthwhile, and his instinct said that this was the case for Michael. He wasn't one to prey on women, Collin didn't think. And usually his instincts were correct.

"We should have taken my carriage," Collin said when they were about halfway back to Michael's home.

"It would have drawn too much attention. Plus, if any other people of quality were visiting from London, they could recognize your crest on the carriage. Better to play it safe and keep your anonymity."

"Very well," Collin agreed, tugging at his collar. It was still warm for fall.

"Don't tell me you're so soft that you can't handle a little walking, my lord," Michael goaded him.

"Work smarter, not harder," Collin returned. "If one has a luxurious conveyance, one would be amiss not to use it."

Michael gave him a disbelieving expression but straightened as they came around the corner and saw his house.

Collin enjoyed watching his new friend grow more anxious as they approached the dwelling. There were little signs, but ones that Collin picked up on nonetheless. Michael started tapping his fingers against his breeches as they walked. Next, he rubbed his nose, then tugged his earlobe. For one who was usually so collected and had a history of facing down criminals, he certainly seemed a bit agitated, and it was deeply amusing to watch him grow more and more unsure as they took the final steps to the house.

"Are you well?" Collin asked quietly.

Michael gave him a glare and whispered a word under his breath that made Collin's grin widen.

Michael opened the door and stepped into the hall.

Collin followed, freezing behind Michael as he heard a familiar voice.

"Ah, Mr. Finch."

It was Elizabeth Essex. He would bet his life on it. He hadn't seen her, but the voice… He knew the voice far better than he should for such a short acquaintance. It had haunted him, beckoned him, and clearly he wasn't the only one on whom it had that effect.

Swallowing his surprise, he followed after Michael and paused as he gave a wide, knowing grin to Elizabeth. Her eyes shifted from Michael to him, widening in shock before her chest constricted with words she dared not speak out loud.

"Good afternoon, Miss Essex. We meet again. It is, indeed, your lucky day."

Eight

*Some men are just as sure of the truth of their opinions
as are others of what they know.*

—Aristotle, *Nicomachean Ethics*

ELIZABETH CHOSE NOT TO SAY THE WORDS THAT
were on the edge of her tongue and decided to
take the higher road. But it was difficult. Her body
revolted against her choice as she studied the handsome and very irritating smirk on Lord Penderdale's
face. Lucky day? She thought not.

"Good afternoon to you as well, Lord Penderdale,"
she said sweetly, perhaps too sweetly, because
her tone brought Patricia's attention full on her
immediately, as well as Michael's. She could feel
her friend's curiosity, as well as her would-be suit-
or's curiosity like a tangible presence in the room
beside her, but she ignored them. Lord Penderdale's
expression held a challenge, and she wasn't about
to be the first to look away. If he wanted a battle of
wits, it was a pity she was the only one who had
come armed.

Lord Penderdale's eyes crinkled as his grin

widened. "Tell me, Miss Essex, are you having honey with your tea?"

Her eyes widened, and she twisted her lips before she lost the battle with the smile. "I'm plenty sweet on my own, wouldn't you agree, Mr. Finch?" She turned to Michael.

Michael blinked, his eyes flickering between her and Lord Penderdale before he nodded. "You're as sweet as can be, Miss Essex."

At his words, Lord Penderdale coughed a laugh. "Forgive me, something in my throat. Road dust." He coughed again, his eyes not leaving hers.

"Pity you don't have tea yourself to help rid you of the malady. But I'm sure you'll be…leaving?" Elizabeth bit out the words as she lifted her own teacup, taking a long sip.

"Leaving? Wherever could I find better company?" Lord Penderdale asked with an innocent expression.

An expression that Elizabeth wanted to forcibly remove from his face. The man was infuriating. "Where indeed?" she answered. "I was more or less implying that you may wish to find those with whom you have more in common. Those who believe women should have their feet shackled to their needlepoint and pianoforte."

At her words, Michael choked on a laugh he tried to cover with a cough, less successfully than Lord Penderdale. But as her eyes darted over to him, she noted that while he was certainly amused, he was eyeing Lord Penderdale with a hint of suspicion.

Collin's laughter interrupted her study of Mr. Finch, and she regarded him once more.

"Ahh, Miss Essex, you are delightful when you're mistaken. As I've said a few times before—I'll have to start keeping track—if you knew my sister, you'd have a much different opinion of what you assume, I believe…trust me."

"That's the problem. I find I can't…believe you, that is," she said in a clipped monotone.

"I'll simply have to prove you wrong, which, if I'm being honest, hasn't been too difficult to do," Lord Penderdale said with a cheeky tone.

"Honesty is always welcome but rarely found," she returned, her hands fisted on her lap as she resisted the urge to stand and go toe-to-toe with the frustrating man. She was about to address Mr. Finch. However, Lord Penderdale spoke before she could get the words out.

"But opinion and truth are different, wouldn't you agree, Miss Finch?"

Elizabeth's attention shifted to her friend, watching as Patricia's eyes shifted between Lord Penderdale and herself, as if searching for salvation from the evident fight she'd somehow been dragged into.

"Well, I believe I've been told that is the case, Lord Penderdale," Patricia answered after a moment.

Elizabeth turned a disbelieving glance on her friend. "You believe?" When had Patricia ever stated something weakly? She was a woman of deep and loud opinions, one of the reasons she was a fearless and devoted friend. And now, suddenly in the presence of Lord Penderdale, she was all soft-spoken? Elizabeth just stared mutely at her friend, trying to figure out how the world had just turned on its ear.

"I'm going to go on instinct here, but who perhaps told you, Miss Finch?" he asked in a charming voice.

Elizabeth's attention snapped to him at the tone of his words. "Are you sincerely using your charm—"

"You find me charming? Delightful. The feeling is mutual, I assure you. But you interrupted my question to Miss Finch." He waved a hand. He'd dismissed her.

Dismissed her after scolding her. Elizabeth's face flamed with frustration.

"Well, that is…" Patricia took a deep breath. "Miss Essex."

Elizabeth closed her eyes, waiting for the nightmare to end. Was this truly happening? She was having afternoon tea with her delightful friend, discussing various topics, only for it all to be hijacked by the most infuriating man ever born.

She opened her eyes and met his scrutiny, not willing to back down a centimeter.

He regarded her, prolonging the moment with far too much delight, if his expression was any indicator. "Well, Miss Essex, which is it?"

She took a deep breath through her nose. "Well, if you wish to have a debate, Lord Penderdale, we need more tea. Because I assure you, even in our short acquaintance, I've noticed you tend to use a lot of words, many of which are unnecessary, and thus you'll need some tea to keep your voice working if we're to dive deeply into the information you're seeking," she answered.

"Well." Collin shrugged. "If my flaw is waxing poetic on answers, yours is in avoiding them entirely."

She blinked. The problem was, she was no longer certain what the actual question was. She forced her thoughts into neat ranks as she reviewed the conversation and desperately searched for whatever morsel of a question they were circling about. Her frustration had made her an utter ninny.

She had to master it, the anger. She took a slow breath and stalled as she considered their conversation by taking another sip from her nearly empty teacup.

"Miss Essex, I'll remind you of the question you seem to have forgotten." He addressed her once more.

She opened her mouth to reply but inhaled tea instead. She held up her napkin just in time to prevent herself from coughing the tea onto the table in front of her. Her throat itched with the need to cough, but thankfully the urge subsided as quickly as it had come on.

"Are you well?"

She nodded, then turned toward the voice, realizing it was much closer than she remembered. Lord Penderdale had moved closer and was watching her with what appeared to be concern.

As if he cared.

Which he didn't. She knew that.

But part of her wished he did.

Silencing that small voice in her head, she nodded again. "I'm well." She swallowed. "Truth and opinion are different, yes. However it's not as simple as black and white. Only a fool will base his life on opinion, but it's also foolish to base your life on truth without context."

"Well said," Lord Penderdale conceded and took a step back.

Elizabeth watched his movements, an odd curiosity swirling about her belly as he held her gaze. His eyes were green and difficult to read. She suspected he wished to be that way, finding it safer to keep distance from people. Odd they could have that character flaw in common. Actually, having anything in common was miraculous. However, suspecting that commonality was just a hunch. Nonetheless she wanted to know, not just assume, but ask him, dive deeper, *know* him.

Curiosity was a dangerous thing.

"I wasn't aware you two were acquainted."

Michael's voice interrupted her thoughts and she nearly jumped. Setting her teacup down, she used the moment to gather her thoughts.

"We aren't really—" Elizabeth started just as Lord Penderdale said loudly, "Actually I'm old friends—"

"We are not." Elizabeth turned her attention back to him. "I've known you a short three days, if that, and it's been the most unpleasant three days of my life."

Lord Penderdale bit his lips as if struggling to restrain his laughter. "Ah, the compliments keep coming. Allow me to clarify." He gave a chiding expression. "I'm old friends with her father, one of my former professors. He taught alongside my brother-in-law and best friend who recently stepped down from teaching at Cambridge."

"I wasn't aware—" Elizabeth started, then paused. No, it wasn't her business. "Pardon me, never mind." She held up a hand.

"See, Miss Essex, you do not know as much about me as you assume," Lord Penderdale said and turned to Michael. "I do have a short and somewhat antagonistic friendship with Miss Essex."

"I see." Michael nodded. "Well, if you're staying for tea, I can have the cook refresh the ladies' pot."

"I believe I've interrupted your party long enough," Lord Penderdale said. "However, I thank you for the kind offer. I have some errands to see to. But I'll see you later tonight, correct?"

"Aye, nine o'clock?" Michael asked.

Collin agreed. "Yes."

Elizabeth watched as he turned his attention to her.

"Thank you for the delicious conversation, Miss Finch, Miss Essex. I look forward to seeing you both again soon." He bowed and then walked to the door.

As he disappeared onto the street, Elizabeth turned to notice both Patricia and Mr. Finch staring at her with openly disbelieving expressions. It was at times like this that she noted how similar they were as siblings. Their expressions were nearly identical, only one was decidedly feminine and the other masculine.

"Well?" Patricia said, breaking the silence.

Elizabeth glanced down to her empty teacup. "Well, what?"

Patricia let out a long sigh. "What do you mean, what? How do you know him and when did you start the second Waterloo? I haven't seen aggression like that since…well, ever actually. But it wasn't really aggression, was it?"

Elizabeth turned to her friend. "Pardon?"

"Nothing, never mind. Disregard what I said." Patricia waved her hand. "Well, Michael, what do you think?"

Michael rubbed the back of his neck as he took a seat at the table with them. "I'm not certain what exactly to think, but if I wasn't so bewildered, the whole exchange would have been quite entertaining," he admitted.

"Entertaining," Elizabeth stated. "That's not the word I'd use."

"Of that I'm certain." Patricia giggled. "You'd use far more descriptive words, but entertaining is exactly what it was. Now…" Patricia addressed her brother. "Is Lord Penderdale married?"

"Good Lord, Pat, I didn't ask nor will I."

"He's old enough to be married…"

"So am I, but I'm not," Michael stated, his gaze flicking to Elizabeth before darting back to his sister.

It was an expression Elizabeth didn't miss, and she still wasn't certain how she felt about it. If they were all being honest, each of them was old enough to be married. As if everyone understood that at once, the room fell silent. Elizabeth lifted her teacup and glanced into it. Still empty. She set it back down and turned to Michael as another question came to mind.

"How do *you* know Lord Penderdale?"

Michael shrugged. "We're in a bit of a business partnership for the time being."

"Helpful, Mitch," Patricia replied with sarcasm, then turned to Elizabeth. "He showed up yesterday, and they've been working together since. I don't know anything else, sorry." Patricia gave an apologetic expression. "However, it stands to reason that he will be around my brother often enough for the time being."

Michael shifted in his seat. "I can be sure that the times we work together do not interfere with your visits, Miss Essex."

Elizabeth smiled her thanks but waved off the offer. "I appreciate the sentiment. However, I can fight my own battles, if need be. I won't restrict myself simply because of his presence. He's irritating, not dangerous."

Michael coughed a laugh, then stood. "At that, I'll take my leave, ladies. I believe you were in the middle of a conversation before we interrupted."

Elizabeth said goodbye, and no sooner was Michael out of the room than Patricia grabbed her arm. "I didn't want to say anything in front of my brother, but…" She paused and glanced about the area, indecision in her expression. "Mitch, we're going to go for a walk!" she called out. Releasing Elizabeth's arm, she stood and started toward the door. "Come."

Elizabeth stood, smoothed her skirts, and prepared herself for whatever conversation Patricia thought required privacy. She had the sinking suspicion it revolved around Lord Penderdale.

Sure enough, as Elizabeth met her on the street, Patricia began her query.

"When did you meet him?"

Elizabeth sighed. "Who?" Though she knew very well who Patricia was inquiring about, she was disinclined to talk about him.

"Don't be contrary," Patricia chided. "Lord Penderdale, of course! At first I fancied him… He is decidedly handsome, and that voice…" She sighed. "But we are from very separate spheres socially, so it was merely a delightful daydream. However, you…" She shrugged her shoulders. "Your father is a gentleman, a knight, and you are therefore a gentleman's daughter…"

Elizabeth stopped her. "My father is not titled."

"He's the lowest of the ranks for titles, that's true, but you're missing the point. He's titled. It wouldn't be an unequal match."

"Stop." Elizabeth held her hands out in front of her friend and faced her fully. "There is no need to discuss this because, one, there will be no match, and, two—"

"You have a lot of reasons," Patricia interrupted.

"Because, two," Elizabeth continued in a firm tone, "I am not interested in him, nor is he interested in me."

Patricia raised an eyebrow.

Elizabeth met her stare, daring her to question her words.

Patricia's eyes tightened and she tipped her chin as she spoke. "I've never been to Vauxhall Gardens, but I've heard about the fireworks that they send off at the parties. And I honestly can't imagine they are more explosive than whatever was going on between you two in our little house back there," Patricia stated flatly. "And there's nothing you can say that will change my mind, because unlike being at Vauxhall, I did witness this event." She shrugged, stepped around Elizabeth and continued. "Besides, I think he likes you."

Elizabeth counted silently to three before following her friend, keeping her temper in check. Did no one listen to her? It was infuriating! There were no fireworks, no attraction—perhaps a little attraction—but nothing of consequence between them but venom and a very different opinion about what a woman's education should entail. As she thought of the last point, her wretched conscience checked her. If he was speaking the truth about his sister, that last disagreeing point may be moot.

"Elizabeth?" Patricia turned, waiting.

"Coming." Elizabeth caught up with her friend. "Can we please talk about anything else? The man infuriates me and has from the moment I saw him. I'd rather talk about anything else."

"Anything?" Patricia asked, a smile playing on her lips.

"Anything is a broad answer, agreed. But please…"

"Very well, I'll set the topic of Lord Penderdale aside for the moment. So, tell me, if you are not interested in 'the one we shall not name,' does that mean you may fancy my brother?" Patricia's grin widened mischievously.

"You don't stop, do you?" Elizabeth couldn't help but return her friend's smile. She supposed it was her penance to have a friend as stubborn as she was.

"He'll be slow but steady and win you over. Just you watch," Patricia promised, "and then we will be sisters-in-law."

"You're already my sister in my heart, Pat. I both love you and find you as irritating as I imagine a sibling would be," she teased.

Patricia swatted at her. "I don't know if I should be honored or insulted."

"Both, make it fair," Elizabeth said lightheartedly.

Patricia laughed. "Well, on that note, have you decided if you'll travel with your father to London next month? I know you were debating it, but I think it would be lovely, even if it's just for a few days."

"I haven't decided. It's rather…populated."

Patricia glanced heavenward as if praying for patience. "Exactly."

"Well, what you find as a positive aspect, I find less enticing. But I'll likely go."

"Good. You need to get out of that stuffy library. You're paler than usual."

Elizabeth lifted her arm and studied her skin. "I'm always pale. And besides, isn't that the London fashion? Heaven forbid that a lady should be outside." She placed her hand on her forehead as if she might swoon at the thought.

"Tell that to your bees. By the way, we need more honey," Patricia added.

Elizabeth made the mental note. "I have a few jars left. I'll bring one to our next class."

"Thank you. I love the honey, although I'm still trepidatious about the bees."

"They don't sting unless you hurt or threaten them. Sometimes I don't wear gloves," she added.

"You're braver than I am. Although we already knew that."

"On this we disagree, but it's an old argument I won't resurrect. I should head back to my father. I need to finish some research." She twisted her lips, her mind already back at the library, thinking about which book she'd need next.

"Very well."

Patricia accompanied her toward the college and, as if sensing Elizabeth's inner musings, didn't prattle on as usual. As Elizabeth crossed one of the stone bridges over the River Cam, she paused in the middle. Her attention on the water, she watched it lazily flow under the shadow of the bridge. Her chest was tight with anxiety as she considered how the river just kept moving, so much like life, never giving a person a choice to stop and stay in the moment. It was always pushing them forward.

As a teacher, she understood the concept and

logically was able to applaud it. After all, if one had the choice to stand still in time, one likely would, since humanity resists change. Yet it is the very thing needed because the constant change and adaptation facilitate growth. But like physical growth that results in growing pains, growth in experiencing life could also be painful. And that's what wound around her heart and made it ache. Because she couldn't always stay where she was. She knew that, and if she had her way, her father would live forever and she'd never stop helping him research as she hid away at Cambridge.

But that wasn't growing. It was…stagnation. She didn't want that, nor did she want to face an uncertain future. And all futures were uncertain. Her mother's untimely death was proof of that.

She blinked at the water and forced herself to leave the thoughts that plagued her on the bridge as she walked toward Christ's College. Patricia shared a small smile with her, but it didn't reach her eyes. Elizabeth considered that maybe her friend had many of the same questions as she did.

After bidding farewell to Patricia, Elizabeth took a side entrance to the library, vowing to find the darkest corner and melt into the shadows. She'd face the difficult problem of the future another day. The greatest philosophers didn't answer all their questions in a lifetime, so she could take another day to try to sort through her own heart.

Nine

*Revolutions are not about trifles, but they spring
from trifles.*

—Aristotle, *Politics*

AS THE HOUR APPROACHED FOR COLLIN TO MEET
with Michael, a tightness cinched his chest. This
was the first real lead they'd had in unraveling the
mystery of who was using his name. The hope of
finding information was tempered by the realistic
understanding that it could be all for naught. They
might find nothing, and this might lead nowhere,
and as Collin considered that possibility, he nearly
sent a missive to Michael to cancel their appointment. Why try if failure was the likely outcome?

He went so far as to sit at his desk and retrieve a
piece of parchment, but he didn't follow through.
He'd given up too often in London, all for things far
less important. No, he'd try regardless of whether
his efforts were likely to end in failure. With a determined step, he went and dressed for the evening. He
was careful to select clothes that were of quality but
didn't imply his titled status. Earlier he'd studied

Michael's clothing and went for a similar appearance, much to his valet's chagrin. He believed his valet was more pretentious than a duke.

That amusing thought followed him into the night as he hired a hack to take him to Michael's residence. He stepped from the carriage and was starting up the steps when the door opened.

"Good evening, you ready?" Michael asked, tugging on his coat and adjusting his sleeves.

"Yes," Collin replied and gestured to the hack.

Michael nodded and then spoke with the driver, giving him several names before stepping into the hack.

Once Collin was seated, Michael addressed him. "I gave the instructions to the driver."

"Good."

Michael tugged at his sleeve again, and this time Collin noticed the movement spoke of fidgets. Curious, Collin searched for other indications Michael was agitated.

The man's knee bobbed a little, and his attention was fixed out the window, his expression knit.

"Do you have concerns about tonight's plan?" Collin asked, searching for a reason his new friend seemed ill at ease.

Michael turned to him with a perplexed expression. "No, it's pretty straightforward. Do you?"

Collin shook his head. "No, but you seem… unsettled. I was merely curious."

Michael nodded, his eyes looking to the floor of the carriage and then back up to Collin. "That was some debate you and Miss Essex held earlier today."

Understanding slammed into Collin like a right hook. With clarity and slight chagrin, he understood the situation at hand. "I'm not a contender for her affections, my friend. I'm no rival."

Michael shrugged off the words, but his foot stilled. "It's no' of my business."

"I'm informing you anyway." Collin shrugged. He found Miss Essex attractive, and she was far too fascinating for his own good, but he wasn't about to offer for her. He chuckled as he thought the word *marriage*.

"Something funny?" Michael asked with a relaxed grin.

"Just my own thoughts," Collin answered. "Now, where are we headed first?"

Michael snapped into business mode and outlined their evening, with their first stop being at The Hare with Luke. "You ready to lose at cards? Because I'm hoping I'll be the one winning," Michael taunted.

"Indeed, though I thought it better if I didn't dress like a peer of the realm, so I took a page out of your book of fashion," Collin responded with a bit of goading.

"Never thought I'd have a lord think I had anything to do with fashion, although miracles do happen," Michael replied with a smile. "You can't hide quality, and you still appear the part."

Collin snorted. "Tell that to my valet. You'd have thought I asked him to clothe me in something inappropriate. I think I offended his sensibilities."

"Seems like rank isn't the only seat of prejudice," Michael added.

"Indeed."

The hack rolled to a stop before The Hare, and Collin took in a deep breath.

"If Luke was able to spread the word, there should be quite a few opportunistic men inside hoping you'll show your face and lose your wallet," Michael said.

"Lucky me," Collin replied, then alighted from the hack.

Michael followed him.

When Collin opened the tavern door, he restrained a smile. Luke had done his job well. He mentally thanked the man as he noted the full tavern and the attention he drew as he entered the area.

Collin sidled up to the bar and ordered pints for each of them. As he did, Michael caught his eye as he widened his and blew out a little breath as if impressed. Collin nodded once, showing he understood the silent communication.

The barkeep set their pints on the bar, and Collin scanned the space as he took a few sips, taking notes. Michael was doing the same, but unlike Collin, he knew the town well and would be able to spot those who didn't belong or who were strangers—like Collin.

Michael turned toward Collin and murmured just before he lifted his pint to his lips. "The faro table, three men I don't know." He took a long drink.

"How's faro sound?" Collin said a little loudly as he regarded the room and found the table that Michael had quietly mentioned.

"Of course, Sir Oxley," Michael said, then withheld a grin at the name he'd just made up.

Collin gave a slight roll of his eyes but followed him to the table.

Michael approached the men. "Next hand, will you deal me and my friend in? He's visiting from London, and I told him we'd have some fun tonight."

The men at the table nodded, their stares collectively sizing up the new additions.

Next hand, Collin took a seat across from Michael, giving each of them a better view of the table and the area around them. As the cards were dealt, Collin sighed. The banker turned two cards over, the winning and losing card. Collin placed his bet on the card he thought would win and waited for the turn the end. He won the first round and the second. By the third, the men at the table were eyeing him with suspicion. In that round, he purposefully placed a bet on the card he thought had the lowest chance of winning the round. The mood at the table lightened when he lost.

"So, you're from London?" one of the men asked, placing his bet on the ten of spades.

Collin nodded, setting down his bet on a different card. "Indeed, traveling for business. I have a friend who teaches at Cambridge."

"Aye, not surprising," another man added.

"What's your business?" the first man asked, then groaned when he lost the round, watching as another collected the chips.

Collin glanced at his rapidly decreasing stack of chips and prepared to attempt to lose again. "Textiles," he answered. It was an easy answer to a telling question, one that wouldn't raise suspicion.

The dealer laid out the cards, and the group went silent as everyone made their bets and then the high and low cards were turned. "You in town for long?" an older man to Collin's left asked, eyeing him quickly before studying the dealer.

Collin took a sip of his pint. "A few weeks or until my business is concluded." He tried to think of a way to lead the conversation toward more significant topics that might ferret out information. "Heard there was a bit of a scrape last night around here. I must say, when my friend suggested this place, I was skeptical."

"I told you it doesn't happen often, and the cheater got his clock cleaned by Luke. Speaking of which, anyone seen him about? I'd like a piece of him myself," Michael added after his quiet spell at the table.

The man beside Collin shook his head. "Nah, he ran off right away. Knew we'd all have taken after him if Luke hadn't scared him off. But I don't think he'll stay away for long. Cheaters can't resist a game."

"True," another murmured.

"I saw him," the first man said as he placed a bet. "He saw me and ran. I was playing last night with Luke, so he recognized me. Quite the purple ring around his eye. Luke's right hook is deserving of respect, that I'll say."

"Where did you see him?" Michael asked, lighting a cheroot.

Collin placed a bet, keeping his eye on the table as he pretended to count his chips.

"He was walking down the market street, then ducked behind a cart when he saw me. When he saw me watching him, he ran away. I was tempted to chase him down, give him a piece of my mind and fist, but the missus was waiting for me at home, and I'd get an earful there if I was late. You pick your battles." He chuckled.

The men around the table echoed the sentiment with quiet guffaws and laughter.

"Had he played before? Or was this the first time you'd seen him? I'm guessing he's not from around here," Collin pressed, knowing he only had one or two more questions before his inquiry into the topic gained interest at the table, thus defeating the purpose.

"He was new, but it's an old name he used. I'd heard it before, different man though."

Collin schooled his features into passive interest. "You don't say. What was the name?"

"Penderdale. Earl, I think. Lord Penderdale. I haven't seen too many peers of the realm, but I'll eat my hat if he was one of them."

Collin laughed with the rest of the group at the statement. As he was formulating his next question. Michael jumped in with his own query. "I've heard it too. I wonder why it's being circulated."

"Probably a made-up name," a rotund individual said, jerking his chin to the cards as if reminding them their focus should be on the game at hand.

Collin placed his bet and added a comment. "I'm from London, and I've heard the name. It's not made up."

"Interesting," mumbled a slender man with a well-trimmed beard as he placed a chip on a card.

"It's only recently I've heard it, so someone is trying to cover their own tracks, cheating their way through the countryside with some borrowed name. Charlatan," the man beside Collin stated, leaning back in his chair. "The point is, I care little. I do, however, care that I don't lose this hand," he added with a grin.

There was a low rumble of agreement at the table as the topic shifted.

Collin placed three more rounds, then stood. Michael followed suit, and they excused themselves from the table and game. As they left The Hare, Luke nodded once in their direction, as if saying he was staying and would keep his eye out.

"Well, that was both helpful and not. I don't think we're any closer than we were when we arrived, but we did confirm that multiple people are using the name," Collin said. "Which I already knew, but it's still good to confirm."

Michael pointed down the street. "This way to the next one. And I agree, but we also know the guy Luke decked is still in town and has a shiner. So, I say tomorrow we put our efforts into tracking him down."

"Agreed."

As they entered the next tavern, Collin took a deep breath. Trying to lose went against every instinct in his body, and he had to steel himself against the sensation of throwing a game. *It's like paying for information,* he told himself, but that didn't make it easier. When Michael found their targets, they joined the whist game and Collin settled in to listen, lose, and hopefully in the end win information.

The rest of the evening followed similarly to their first stop at The Hare, and as the working men retired for the night, Collin parted ways with Michael, with a plan to reconvene on the morrow at midday.

That night, Collin slept fitfully, a recurring dream plaguing him. He was climbing a cliff, heaven only knew why, and a rope was lowered from the top, promising a safer alternative to scaling the rock's face. But every time he reached for the rope, it drifted just out of reach. His fingers would touch the edge, teasing him, and he would reach farther, sure salvation was at hand. Still he'd miss, and in his efforts, his other hand would slip, sending him plummeting to the darkness below. It was always then he'd wake up, cold as if he'd been in a room walled by ice. He awoke this time from the dream to sunshine bright and warm outside his window, though his skin was still chilly from the realistic dream. He closed his eyes and sank back into the pillows, eyes closed but very awake. With a deep sigh, he opened his eyes once more and rose from bed.

After he dressed and broke his fast, he used what was left of the morning to catch up on correspondence and business. A letter from his sister had arrived, and he hadn't replied. He'd certainly get a tongue-lashing for his tardy reply, but reply he must.

Collin,

You're no doubt making progress, and I continue to wish you well with it. Everything in London is as it was when you left, so you're not missing anything thrilling. I do miss you, and Rowles sends his regards as well. I can't believe I'm going to say it, but I miss your dry humor, as pitiful as it became. You know I'm telling the truth, and I hope that you've recovered some of your purpose and joy. I could give you all the on-dits for the happenings in London, but as you'd ignore that, I'll simply say, write back and tell me any interesting details from your adventure.

With love,
Joan

Collin reread the letter, smiling and chuckling by turns as he came to various lines. How like his sister to call him out, but do it with unmistakable affection. He withdrew a sheet of parchment and began to reply, wishing he had more information to share. The reply didn't take much time, but it had a cheering effect. His sister was all the family, save her husband, that he had in the world. It was sobering, that. After his twin had passed away in the fire that left all of London rocked, he and Joan had grown close. Before, he'd always had his twin brother, the very mirror image of himself in thought and appearance. They would finish each other's sentences and, with a glance, knew the other's thoughts.

Collin though back to that disastrous fire—which he had escaped by the merest chance. Collin and his twin had been among the guests invited to a celebration of the Duke of Wesley's nuptials. But duty called, and Collin was unable to attend. His brother Percy did go, and it was the last thing he'd ever done. So many of London's elite had been lost that day. The duke had invited many friends, and no one had survived the fire or its smoke, which filled the hunting lodge that fateful night. Titles were passed to second sons, Collin being one of them, along with his two best friends, one of whom was now married to Joan. A friend had become a brother-in-law, but no one could ever replace Percy.

It was a painful memory. Still, it had forced a bond between him and Joan that he did not regret. The memories seemed to linger in the room. With a determined movement, Collin stood and took his correspondence with him. In a few minutes, he'd dispatched a servant with the missives and was on to the next task. He had about an hour before he was to meet Michael and, after a moment's consideration, decided to leave early and take a more circuitous route on foot, to check the village marketplace and several other places for the man with the black eye.

Though he and Michael would likely go back over the same ground that afternoon, one could never be too thorough. And if he were being honest with himself, he knew he needed something to do, regardless of whether it was going to prove redundant. He wanted a distraction from his sister's letter, from the memories it brought back into focus, and from the problem at hand that still had no solution or solid leads. He wanted to move and be active as if it mattered, though he full well knew that activity might prove fruitless.

He donned his coat and stepped out of the house. A footman followed him carrying a black umbrella, which he opened and handed to Collin to shield him against the light rain starting to fall. Collin took the umbrella and started toward the marketplace.

Keeping his attention on people's faces, he tried to block out the memory of a different face, one that was just as irritating as that haunting dream he kept having. He wouldn't think of her. But trying not to think of her only made it impossible not to think of her. His memory conjured up a perfect recollection of her strawberry hair, creamy skin, and intelligent eyes. They'd had quite the row yesterday, but he'd not been angry, not for a moment; rather, he'd loved the challenge. It brought to life some part of his soul that he'd thought had already died of apathy. It was a delicious sensation, and he craved a little more. With an effort, he forced his attention to the men around him. Men in shops, men striding down the cobbled street, men on horses, men on foot, but none of them sporting a black eye. Collin twisted his lips in frustration, but continued on his way to Michael's house, arriving only slightly earlier than they'd arranged yesterday.

"Afternoon." Michael nodded, grabbing his coat as he answered the door. "You're early, but it's just as well." He stepped out into the street and adjusted his collar. "Miss Essex has her class tonight and normally doesn't stop by. However, just in case, it's best to have some distance between the two of you," he said.

"Afraid of the fireworks?"

Michael chuckled. "No, afraid I'll get roped into the argument and I'll ruin my chances with the lady."

"Ah, I see, that's the rub, isn't it?" Collin responded.

"Indeed, it is." Michael's tone was light, but something in his expression seemed like a warning, as if he wasn't sure the lady returned the sentiment, or maybe he viewed Collin as a rival for that same affection.

Collin took a deep breath. It was laughable, except it also was not. He wasn't interested, and they'd never stop fighting if they were forced to keep company for more than a quarter hour at a time. Still, something about that was exciting, challenging, and alluring. It was enough to give him pause when he should have simply waved away his friend's unspoken concern.

"Best of luck taming the shrew."

"I won't tell her you said that," Michael replied, wincing. He recovered quickly. "It's a part of her charm, the frankness of her character."

"In London, we don't regard that as charm," Collin replied. "And 'frank' is a polite way of describing her."

"It may be sprinkling sugar on the situation, but seeing as she's a beekeeper, I'd stick with being sweet with my words. The lady likes her honey, and I'm hoping any sweet words I can say will attract her."

Collin paused. "She's a beekeeper? Well, doesn't that make sense." He shook his head. "Blasted woman and her questions," he whispered under his breath, just enough ahead of Michael that hopefully his companion didn't overhear the words. He didn't want to explain his second interaction with Miss Essex. But it was clear she wasn't playing fair. It rubbed against him wrong, the idea that she knew the subject matter well and had set him up for failure. That he answered her well-placed question correctly was a source of triumph, and his lips quirked in a grin at the memory. Still, she hadn't played fair.

Something for which he'd make sure she'd pay.

"Let the games begin."

"That's an odd expression. Should I be concerned?" Michael asked warily as he caught up with Collin and matched his stride down the road.

"No, no concern. Just thinking." Collin changed the subject. "I came through here earlier to keep an eye out for any men with a black eye but saw nothing. I thought with Cambridge being much smaller than London it would be easy to find a particular person. However, I'm discovering it's every bit as difficult as in a larger city."

"Vermin like to hide in the dark shadows."

"Indeed, they do," Collin agreed. "So, if we don't see him in the obvious places, what do you suggest?"

"We start one place and comb through. It's going to take time, but turns out, that is what we have to give. So, we'd best get started." Michael shrugged as he walked purposefully toward the market center, where they would presumably start.

If only they hadn't started those many other times with the same lack of progress, Collin might be able to muster some hope. As it was, he fully expected they would find absolutely nothing.

Meaning that tomorrow they'd have to start again.

And again.

It began to feel like a miserable circle: starting,

going nowhere, and repeating the process. Maybe he should have stayed in London, let the criminals keep his name and use it until they tired of it and found a new one. For all the bloody good it did to leave London, he could be home, judging all the peers and drinking good brandy. Not that the duke's Cambridge residence had poor brandy by any stretch. But it was frustrating, going nowhere.

As Michael rounded a corner and disappeared, Collin thought perhaps he should just do the same. Joan would miss him, and Rowles. His other best friend, Quin, the Duke of Wesley, would miss him as well, but they'd all survive. Maybe what he needed was to get away from England entirely. No one could use his name for crime if he was out of the country.

Michael came back around the corner. "You coming?"

Collin shook himself from the depressing thoughts and nodded. "Right behind you."

Ten

The young have exalted notions, because they have not been humbled by life or learned its necessary limitations; moreover, their hopeful disposition makes them think themselves equal to great things.

—Aristotle, *Rhetoric*

ELIZABETH CLOSED THE BOOK AND LEANED BACK in the wooden chair. She rotated her neck and sighed deeply as she woke her body up from the nearly frozen position she'd been in while she reviewed the pages of *Discourse* by Descartes. She was familiar with the text but wanted to reacquaint herself with the subject matter that she would be covering tonight with her students. For years she'd watched her father pour himself into the same books over and over as he strove for deeper understanding of the material he was devoted to teaching. *There's always something deeper if you take the time to look.* His words echoed in her mind. And he was correct.

She'd read *Discourse* enough times to be quite familiar with the subject matter, but as she studied, aspects of it would shine differently, and she'd consider them in a light she hadn't seen before. If one wished to teach, one must first be an insatiable learner. She could think of nothing more delightful than seeing something new in a book, or researching a question to find out the answer, or better, finding a new question she hadn't considered. Her books were her friends, providing long, thoughtful conversations that never seemed to fully end.

She smiled to herself as she stacked the books carefully and placed them back on their proper shelves. She was alone in the library, the light fading as the room took on the shadow from the sun arching lower in the sky. As she scooted her chair back under the table, the scratching sound was overly loud and irreverent in the quiet room, but since she was alone, she didn't worry about it being disruptive to others.

She picked up her parchment notes and placed them in a leather reticule, then walked away from the table and toward the door. The college would be quiet, with most classes already dismissed. Those who lingered in the halls would either be professors or academically focused students who regularly used the library, such as herself. But she wasn't a student, and the mental reminder stung. She paused a moment before opening the door to the hall, hoping it was deserted.

After opening the door silently, she scanned the

corridor beyond. It was empty. Breathing a sigh of relief, she relaxed her rigid posture and walked down the hall, not taking the more hidden route she'd usually use when it was crowded. For a moment, she closed her eyes and pretended she belonged, that it was acceptable, normal, for her to be walking down these halls with other peers, other women and men, all joining in the journey of education. A smile tipped her lips as the familiar daydream filtered through her mind with each step she took. She opened her eyes and was continuing toward the door when she heard footsteps behind her. Quickly, she moved to the far side of the hall, her shoulders rounding as she tried to blend in as much as possible.

The footsteps slowed as they neared her. Heart racing, she steeled herself as she glanced behind.

"Your father is gone home," the older man, Professor Greybeck, said. His eyes were hard as flint as he regarded her as if she were a mess left behind by someone reckless. "You shouldn't be here ever, but especially if your father isn't here on campus. And so I'd suggest you run your skirts out that door and head home." He barked the words softly.

Elizabeth nodded. "My apologies," she whispered and started on her way.

"Women don't belong here, and you're only proving that fact. Not the opposite, Miss Essex. Your presence does a disservice to women. You are not championing them, nor are you proving that you can be equal to the men in these halls. You're simply existing against anyone's will, save your father's. And all the respect I've had for him over the years has seeped away with every day that he's weak enough to allow you to remain here. Go."

Elizabeth didn't turn back when he spoke, and his last words were punctuated by the closing of the door behind her as she quit the building. It took all her power not to run, or, conversely, turn and vehemently defend herself. Neither would work, nor would they shift the man's opinion. And truthfully, she could take whatever insults and maligning he threw in her direction. She'd developed some tough skin during her time in the college, but it was when they attacked her father that it shattered her heart. Because deep down, she knew it was true. Her father could say he didn't care, didn't mind, and he likely didn't. He wasn't one to lie to her; nevertheless the fact remained that she cared. She cared about the ostracism her father was dealt because of her, because she stubbornly remained somewhere she wasn't wanted. However, the other option available to her was to be at home…and do what? Learn another melody on the pianoforte? Practice her needlepoint? Gossip with some friends? She'd rather rot. Unfortunately, as she grew older, it seemed the only respectable option for her, but more importantly, for her father.

She should have told her father she was at the

library so he could have escorted her. However, again she'd refused to use good sense and now had to walk home alone. Thankfully, Cambridge didn't have the same strict social constraints as London, where a woman's reputation could be questioned if she were alone in public, but being alone still wasn't wise. She should hurry, but she paused as she crossed a bridge into the market square toward the tea shop where she taught in the back room. She needed a moment to herself, to collect her thoughts and release the tension that dug into her back with each step.

She had a decision to make. Staying at Cambridge wasn't an option. If she was honest, she had to admit she'd outgrown that a few years ago, but she'd stubbornly lingered. What now? She had to decide, and soon. But maybe not tonight. There had to be another option, or else there would be too many women miserable in life. She leaned against the stone railing of the bridge and pinched her nose with her gloved hand. Drawing one deep breath after another, she released her nose and opened her eyes, losing her focus in the relaxing flow of the water beneath her. She lingered a few more moments, waiting for the tension to drain and for her mind to take on some of the required clarity needed to approach the lesson for the night.

Determined, she pushed back from the stone rail and walked toward the tea shop. It was time for teaching her ladies' society, and the tea shop where the class was held was now closed for the evening. Squaring her shoulders, she walked around back of the building and knocked on the door, smiling as she inhaled the sweet scent of tea cakes and other delicious things lingering in the air around the shop.

"Good evening, Miss Essex!" Mrs. Smith said cheerily as she set down a dish she'd been washing. "Mary is already in the back and several others have arrived as well."

"Good evening to you and thank you!" Elizabeth walked through the kitchen and into the small space between the kitchen and the tea sitting room. It was a bit smaller than the front of the store, but it was far more private, which was necessary. Elizabeth greeted her students and waved when Patricia came in and slid into a chair beside Mary.

What remained of Elizabeth's previous stress melted away as she took in the eager faces of her students. This…this was what a calling felt like. That sense of rightness, of providence that it came to pass, and the idea that she was giving them something good and tangible. It filled her.

"Shall we begin?" she asked and opened her leather satchel to withdraw her notes. "I hope everyone reviewed the material?"

She watched as several nodded and some glanced away. She bit back a grin at that. "Today we will continue reading, but I wanted to give you several important aspects to think about as we read." She began to walk around the room as she considered her notes.

"In *Discourse on Method*, René Descartes lays out four clear methodologies for studying and learning. We will address three of the four. These are fundamental to understanding how to break apart more difficult problems, but also in recognizing the small pieces of the whole picture in a situation. Allow me to list them." She paused and regarded her students, making sure she had their full attention.

"The first point I want you to consider is this rule, in which he states: *Never believe anything unless you can prove it yourself.* Now, can someone tell me what he's referring to as far as subject matter?"

This was an important question, clarifying the direction they would take on the concept.

Mary spoke up. "Mathematics?"

Elizabeth nodded. "Indeed, geometry to be specific, along with algebra and logic."

Mary beamed, clearly proud of her correct answer.

Acknowledging Mary's smile with one of her own, Elizabeth continued. "The next rule he lays out is to reduce every problem to its simplest parts." Elizabeth swallowed hard as she considered this. Wasn't this the very thing she should apply to her own life? Break down the issue into its smallest parts and better understand them. She'd been approaching it all wrong, trying to see and solve the bigger picture, but it was too big. That was the problem. She had to break it down, study it in pieces, and piece those smaller parts together to get that bigger picture. Then she'd understand it further, deeper.

"This is especially helpful in mathematics since some problems require us to dissect the issue to find the solution," she said after a moment's reflection. "But it is also a methodology applicable to life. One we can implement when faced with a large problem that seems too big to surmount. We can break it down, find its simplest parts, and address them individually."

Elizabeth moved on to the next point. "Finally, we come to the third rule: Be orderly in your thoughts. Go from simplest to most difficult when solving a problem. This should seem like common sense, but how often do we dismiss the small issues in light of the larger ones, thinking them more important?" She grinned, watching the ladies nod in understanding.

Patricia spoke up. "It's true. I never thought of it that way though."

"That's exactly the goal—to think differently, wider, broader, and understand things better because we have learned how to learn. That may sound redundant, but part of education is understanding how to digest the information, filter it in our mind, and use it property. Turns out, that doesn't always happen naturally. We have to train ourselves to do it."

Elizabeth shifted her papers and set them aside. Withdrawing her book from the bag, she took a seat and settled in to read. "I'll take my turn first, and then we'll go around the room as usual." She opened the book and began to read.

After everyone had taken her turn, Elizabeth dismissed the class. She collected the book and parchments and placed them back in her satchel and turned to face Patricia, who had come to stand beside her.

"I think my brother and your friend, Lord Penderdale, could use your information on problem-solving. I don't think they are doing mathematics, but whatever they're doing, it's not been successful, if my brother's glum countenance is any indication." She leaned against the wall. "They left this afternoon and came back just as I was headed out the door. Michael was cross, and Lord Penderdale's handsome face was twisted in frustration as well. Though he was still handsome. Is that breeding? Or just luck?" she mused.

Elizabeth laughed. "I wouldn't know since I don't find him terribly handsome." Her gut twisted at the half-truth she had just told, but if she interpreted attractiveness as an inward attribute, then she was being honest. If it was purely outward, then she was a liar. Because Lord Penderdale was not hard to look at, not at all.

"You're daft if you think him anything less than an Adonis."

"I hope he never hears you say that. His already grand opinion of himself will only grow," Elizabeth replied dryly.

"I doubt he's still at my house. You want to come over for a bit?" Patricia invited.

Elizabeth considered it. She didn't have much to tend to at home, but she was hesitant. She didn't want to encourage Michael, which could likely happen if she showed up at their house. Her heart was undecided on the man, and that should be her answer. Thinking of her recent lesson, she decided to put it into practice. "I'll follow you home."

Don't believe anything you can't prove yourself. Descartes was referring to mathematics, but she could use the concept on a wider scope, couldn't she? She was fairly certain that Michael fancied her, but he'd never said it, and she'd never asked. This could all be for naught, and perhaps he was merely being very kind to her as Patricia's friend. With that consideration, some of the tension she'd started to harbor in her chest began to unwind. Once she was there, perhaps she'd simply ask Patricia. But that would also be indirect and not as accurate. Sighing, she collected her things and followed her friend out the door and toward her home.

"You've gone quiet," Patricia mused as she matched Elizabeth's stride.

Elizabeth twisted her lips. "Just thinking about the three rules we spoke about during class and debating how well they will work when applied to other situations."

Patricia blew out a long-suffering breath. "Do you ever stop thinking? Wait, no, let me rephrase that." She paused. "Do you ever stop being so academic? Not everything or everyone can be analyzed and studied."

Elizabeth regarded her friend. "I understand that, but I also find much of human nature fascinating. What's wrong with wishing to understand it further?"

Patricia eyed her and afterward turned back toward the street. "Nothing, I suppose, but it isn't a relaxed demeanor that you portray, so it doesn't seem much fun, that's all."

"I'm fun," Elizabeth stated flatly, then realized her answer proved her wrong. She softened her tone. "I do many interesting things that don't relate to academics."

"Like?" Patricia asked, her lips pursed as if withholding a smile.

Elizabeth glared as she answered. "I tend to bees, I can ride well, and my pianoforte is improving."

"I didn't say you weren't accomplished, but it wouldn't harm you to find more reasons to laugh. That is all I'm saying," Patricia countered and promptly changed the subject. "My brother will be happy you're coming over."

Elizabeth groaned. "You can't be certain of that."

Patricia broke into a loud giggle. "Oh, I'm certain."

"He's said nothing to me; therefore it's not a certainty at all."

"Why would he say anything to you and risk your rejection before he's befriended you? For being brilliant, you're quite obtuse regarding men," Patricia stated in a wry tone.

"He's kind to me, but he's kind to everyone. That doesn't signify—"

"There's a difference between being kind and being intentionally attentive," Patricia replied with a patient tone. "You don't know the difference but…watch tonight. If he's there, which I think he will be, watch how he tries to converse with you on topics you'd like to talk about, little things like that. And you know he'll be the one who insists on accompanying me when we take you home."

"There are only two options: you and him. He can't very well take me alone, and you would walk back home alone if you came with me. Either way, it's more of a formality than a mark of preference," Elizabeth pointed out.

"Very well, don't believe me. Just use your powers of observation to make your own judgments," Patricia answered. "And we made the conclusion just in time." She swung open the door and called out, "I'm home, Mitch."

"About time. I'm headed out in about a half hour, and I…" He paused as he came into the hall. His eyes widened, and his ears turned vaguely pink as his attention landed on Elizabeth.

"Pardon, Miss Essex. Good evening."

"Good evening, Mr. Finch."

The silence carried on for a moment before Michael addressed his sister. "I'll be out later tonight. Be sure you bolt the door while I'm away."

"As always, Mitch. You coddle me so. I'll be quite fine." Patricia moved into the parlor. Elizabeth followed and set down her satchel on the table.

Michael followed them into the room. "How was your class this evening, Miss Essex?" He gestured to the chairs, and once they were seated, took a seat himself.

Elizabeth met his brown eyes and smiled. "It went quite well. We're studying René Descartes and how to apply his rules for mathematics to other areas in life."

He nodded. "Ah, *Discourse*, my sister tells me."

"Indeed. Have you read it?"

Michael nodded once. "It was a while ago, and I can't say I finished the book, but I studied the concepts."

"Did you enjoy it?" Elizabeth asked, truly curious for the answer.

He shrugged. "I read it at a time when academics were less palatable than fishing in the river." He gave a boyish grin, his eyes crinkling at the corners, his smile revealing a small gap between his front two teeth.

Elizabeth waited for her body to react to him. She listened as he addressed his sister for a moment and studied her own emotions. Did she feel attraction? Friendship? Interest? He was easy to converse with and truly a kind man, but she didn't feel any difference with him than with any other friend. Odd, shouldn't she feel something?

Reduce the problem to its simplest form. As she thought the words, she considered the problem at hand...herself. The simplest part was understanding herself, and, if truth be told, she wasn't certain she knew the answer.

"I won't be able to escort you home, Miss Essex." Michael turned to her.

Elizabeth's attention snapped back into place as she gathered her wayward thoughts and waved him off. "It's of no consequence. I'll make my way home now." She stood.

"I can see you halfway, and I'm sure your father will be out watching for you as well," Mr. Finch stated as he stood.

"Thank you, but it's not far, and my father will indeed be out waiting for me. Therefore, I'm perfectly safe."

Mr. Finch seemed to deliberate but nodded after a moment. "I'll still escort you a ways, and Patricia can come with me partway as well."

Elizabeth nodded and followed Patricia to the door, satchel in hand. Patricia's subtle wink didn't give her a comforting feeling, but she proceeded anyway. Perhaps it wasn't a bad idea to have some additional time with Mr. Finch. It would give her a few moments of his undivided attention in a very public place. No doubt Patricia would linger behind and pretend to study other things to give her time with her brother. Elizabeth pressed her lips together, unsure if she was thankful or irritated with her friend.

"Miss Essex." He offered his arm, and they started toward her home. His warm smile hinted that he was happy to have a few moments with her as well. As expected, Patricia lingered behind. "I'll be just behind you, Mitch, I'm terribly slow today. My ankle has been bothering me."

Elizabeth resisted the urge to shoot her a disbelieving look, but decided against it.

"That's unfortunate, Pats." Michael cast a glance at his sister, as if assuring himself she wasn't in too much discomfort, and carried on, offering Elizabeth a shy smile.

Logically, she took a moment to think about how she felt about that. Did it please her? She found that it did, in fact. "Do you have a busy evening ahead of you, Mr. Finch?" she asked, initiating some conversation as they walked.

"Somewhat. Turns out I'll be with your dear old friend, Lord Penderdale."

"Why must you bring him up?" she teased—flirted, actually.

He gave a self-deprecating smile. "I knew it would get a reaction, and it's amusing."

"So, I am to be your entertainment?" she asked with a soft laugh.

"Is that such a bad thing? It's always a goal of mine, to get you to smile. If I must tease you a bit, it's for a worthy cause," he answered, his expression more sincere than his words seemed.

"Well." Elizabeth smiled, unsure of how to navigate the conversation further. She'd certainly achieved one goal. He did harbor an interest in her. Now she simply had to determine if she shared that interest or merely felt friendship.

Descartes's rules weren't as simple as she'd first expected. Then again, when had any human emotion been uncomplicated?

"Did I offend you?" he asked, his forehead furrowing with concern.

She shook her head. "No, not at all, Mr. Finch," she answered truthfully. And with further frankness she added, "I am merely struggling to identify my own feelings regarding what seem to be yours." She hazarded a peek up at him.

His eyes widened, and his lips bent into an amused grin as he glanced away momentarily. "I do appreciate your forthright words. It's part of your charm."

"Is that a good thing? It seems like most people aren't as appreciative of that aspect of my character." She noted that they had arrived at the spot where they'd likely separate for the evening—him to whatever plans he had with Lord Penderdale and her to her own home.

"People struggle with honesty, which can be harder to swallow than a lie. I've dealt with far too many liars in my day, Miss Essex. Consequently, honesty is something I appreciate deeply. I certainly find it part of your charm, and I hope that perhaps you may give me an opportunity to prove that." He halted his steps and regarded her fully, his expression hopeful and still guarded.

"I'll consider that," she answered, unable to give him more of an answer.

He nodded. "That is fair, Miss Essex. And unfortunately, this is where I must leave you. I'll watch until you're out of sight, and it should only be a short walk to your home from here."

"Thank you for your kind escort, Mr. Finch. Have a good evening." She slipped her arm from his. "Hope your ankle improves, Patricia," she said sweetly, narrowing her eyes when her friend's met them.

Patricia grinned unrepentantly. "I'm sure I'll be much improved tomorrow."

"I'm sure you will too," Elizabeth muttered under her breath. She waved goodbye and proceeded down the street. Before she rounded the corner, she glanced back and met Mr. Finch's regard, an odd stirring of emotion swirling inside her. It felt good to be watched over, even if it was by someone she considered more friend than lover. He nodded and waited, his attention not wavering.

Taking a deep breath, she rounded the corner. Her attention was on the ground while she lost herself in thought for a moment as she hurried on. Abruptly, she hit something hard. Her satchel dropped from her hand immediately as she stumbled to right herself.

"Pardon." A man spoke swiftly. He grabbed her satchel and ran, but not before she was able to get a good look at him.

He wasn't overly tall, with modest dress and cap, but the defining feature was the heavily bruised left eye. He gave one final glance before running down the road away from her, leaving her on the ground and fuming.

She watched his retreat, contemplating what to do next. She couldn't very well follow him, though it wasn't doing any good to sit here on her bottom either. Sighing, she started to stand, but upon hearing rapid footsteps, she glanced up in concern. Was there another criminal about? She'd walked along these streets for years and never before had she been accosted! What was the world coming to? She tightened her eyes, studying the rapidly approaching figure, then groaning when she recognized the face.

"Good evening," she called out, finding her footing and dusting off her skirts.

"Good God, Elizabeth—Miss Essex." Lord Penderdale came to a halt before her, immediately and quite tenderly grasping her shoulder as his other hand cupped her chin, tilting it to the side. "Are you well? What happened?" His green eyes traveled over her face as he gently tilted it one way, then the other, studying her carefully. His other hand, at her shoulder, traveled down her arm and supported her elbow, as if worried she might be unsteady on her feet.

Her heart beat out a ragged rhythm, her skin prickling with flashes of heat, then cool, cresting like waves over her as goose bumps settled on her skin. She tried to find her voice, but it was gone. Her mouth opened and then closed.

"Are you injured?" he asked, searching for injuries, and though she understood what was going on, she struggled to react, to do anything. He released her chin and carefully moved his fingers through her hair.

She flinched when he touched a tender spot.

"Ah, I'm sure that's painful," he whispered softly, and gentled his touch as he seemed to determine the size of the bump. She didn't remember hitting her head, but well, she was upright, and then was not, so it wasn't a surprise that she didn't remember all of what happened.

"Lord Penderdale." She spoke finally, mentally chastising herself for the momentary muteness.

He met her eyes and smiled as if hearing his name pleased him. "The one and only. I'm glad you don't seem too much the worse for wear."

Elizabeth blinked, needing to do something. He was too close. His hand was still cupping her elbow, her body tucked indecently close to his as his other hand cupped the back of her head. For all the world, someone would think they were about to kiss, in public. Yet though she understood this, she didn't move. She didn't step away and tell him it wasn't proper, that even if he was just trying to help her, he shouldn't be so close.

But her voice wouldn't work. All she could do was stare at his warm look and savor that odd feeling of safety as he held her close.

His gaze dipped to her lips and traveled back up to her eyes, and his expression darkened with something she couldn't identify but she could feel. To the bottom of her toes, she could feel that nameless emotion. His attention darted back to her lips, and she licked them slightly. She didn't think about doing it; it was instinctual. He noticed and his gaze darkened further, sending heat pooling in her belly as her heart picked up its jagged rhythm. He leaned forward, and his eyes narrowed as if he was just as confused by all of this as she was.

Elizabeth couldn't help it.

She laughed.

It was a nervous sound, one that grated in her ears as Lord Penderdale released her with gentle care. Immediately, she noticed the loss of his touch, and against her will, her body mourned it.

"You are well?" he asked, for the second or third time. She'd lost track.

"Yes, as well as can be," she answered, proud of herself for stringing together a full sentence. Dear Lord, her wits must have been addled.

His scrutiny sharpened. "Can you tell me what happened?"

She took a deep breath. "I was coming home from the Finches' when I rounded the corner and some man ran into me, sending me backwards, and then he ran off with my satchel. He'll be disappointed when he finds only parchment notes and a book within it, but it's valuable to me," she said dejectedly.

"What did he look like?" Lord Penderdale asked.

"He was of medium height, modest dress and cap, and a bruised left eye, purple-ringed."

Lord Penderdale eyed her curiously. "You gathered all that information and remembered it?"

She gave him a withering glare. "I want my satchel back, and he has it. If I'm to help the authorities find the knave, they need to know who they are searching for."

He nodded once. "Yes, but that was rather descriptive. I'm impressed is all."

"Oh." She relaxed her glare. "Were you chasing him? Is that why you were running? I must say I've never seen a peer of the realm in a sprint before."

He eyed her with a bemused expression. "Yes, I was pursuing him, and I'm terribly sorry he not only injured you but stole your satchel. I'll do my best to recover it for you. And I'll have you know, I'm quite swift on my feet."

"I believe you," she answered. However, that left her with one question. "Why were you chasing him?"

Lord Penderdale glanced behind her and around as if expecting the rogue to come back to the scene of the crime. "He has something of mine as well."

Elizabeth tipped her chin. "Oh?"

Lord Penderdale regarded her unrelentingly, his expression holding her captive as he said, "Yes, he has my name."

Eleven

Everything that deceives may be said to enchant.

—Plato, *The Republic*

COLLIN'S HEART FINALLY SLOWED TO A NORMAL cadence. When he'd rounded the corner and seen a woman struggling to her feet, he'd leapt into action. When he'd heard his name and seen Elizabeth's face, his blood had gone cold.

Elizabeth. He'd used her Christian name, and it had been far too natural. He hadn't obeyed any rules of propriety; he'd have cheerfully hanged them all in that moment. All he could think was: *not her.* He'd canvassed every inch of her in observation, making sure there was no lasting damage, no injuries seen or unseen. His mind had been a flurry, forgetting about his single-minded purpose to chase the man and only concerned that Elizabeth was unharmed. He'd cataloged her features, supported her as he drew her in, gently probed her head and found that one small bump that gave him a momentary panic until she'd finally responded, reminding him that she was well or, at least, well enough.

But then everything shifted. He was aware of how close she stood, of how she smelled like beeswax candles and lemons, of how perfectly she fit into the lee of his body and how perfectly tempting her lips were to kiss.

And he'd eat his left boot if she hadn't felt the same thing. Those intelligent, logical, and maddening eyes had seared through him, bewitching him until all he could do was lose himself in the moment.

He'd never wanted to kiss a woman this badly in all his life.

And he would have, if not for that one single sound that still echoed in his mind.

Laughter.

Nervous laughter that sounded anything but amused, more a terrified noise that he understood the moment he heard it.

He felt it too.

Because this was Elizabeth Essex. He was more likely to verbally assault her than kiss her.

Maybe it was the confusion of the moment, maybe his wits were still addled by her touch, but when she'd asked the question, he didn't think about any answer but the truth.

Elizabeth tipped her chin. "That's why you're in Cambridge and why you're working with Mr. Finch."

"Yes," he answered, realizing he didn't want to

keep any secrets from her. They'd been honest, likely too honest, from the beginning. He'd continue that trend, for better or worse.

"I see. Well, can you tell me more?"

Collin shifted on his feet. "I can, nonetheless I'd feel better if we got you home first." He offered his arm, waiting for her to take it.

Her small hand wrapped around his arm and rested on top. His soul calmed at her touch, as if finding something it had needed all along. It was a confusing sensation, but he filed it away to be studied later.

"You know, I was about to say I could make it home on my own, but I think we can both agree that would be foolish of me, given the circumstances." She chuckled to herself.

Her laughter was delightful, not abrasive and loud, but soft and feminine. He'd never noticed how a woman's laughter was such a vital part of her allure, a reflection of her personality.

"Yes, given the circumstances, I think it's best you have company," he agreed. "If you wish, I can give you the short version of this whole sordid mess."

"It's sordid, is it?" she asked, a light teasing tone to her voice.

He gave her a sarcastic grin. "Depends on your definition. Simply put, my name has been used by a man committing petty crimes in the greater

London area, but what I discovered in my investigation is that it began here in Cambridge."

"So, you believe that since it originated here, you can find who started it here."

"Yes. Exactly."

"It seems like a good plan, but I'm assuming that based on Patricia's information on her brother's moods, you've had little luck."

Collin sighed. "You're far more observant than you let on, and yes."

"Except tonight..." She paused, waiting for him to pick up the story.

He shrugged. "A few nights ago, we learned of a situation where a man used my name and then was promptly called out for cheating and given a black eye. We've been searching for him for the past few days—"

"And you found him."

"As did you."

Elizabeth winced. "Only to have him lost again."

Collin paused their walk. "You were far more important."

Elizabeth's deep-brown eyes widened, then her gaze softened. "Thank you, although I'm sorry he got away. I'll be sure to keep my eye out for him—"

"No," Collin stated flatly.

"Pardon?" She frowned and regarded him with indignation. He swore her hair sparked.

"No, don't keep an eye out for him. We have no idea how he is involved in any of this, but it's likely he's not the leader, if there is one. However, he's possibly dangerous, and I don't wish for you to be hurt."

"Thank you for your concern, but I want my satchel—"

"I'll take care of it."

She sighed. "I'm not going to go after this man by myself, Lord Penderdale. I'm not that daft."

He eyed her, as if questioning her words and not fully believing them.

"I won't. You have my word. Is that enough for you?" She resisted the urge to place a hand on her hip for emphasis.

"Would my word be enough for you, if the situation was reversed?" he challenged.

Elizabeth considered his question. Lord Penderdale was a great many things, but he was trustworthy, of that she was confident. So with a nod, she answered, "Yes."

"Is this..." He paused, stepped back, and regarded her. "Did we just become friends?" Collin placed a hand on his heart as if startled. "You did after all, just imply that you trusted me."

"Don't let it go to your head. I'm sure I'll find a reason to battle wits with you upon our next meeting. This is not a truce."

"I certainly hope so. Otherwise, I'd think that tumble addled your wits."

"I'm happy to report my wits are not the least bit addled," she stated with a grin.

"I'm very pleased to hear it. I happen to find those wits gloriously entertaining, if not somewhat irritating."

"Then we understand one another." She grinned.

Collin nodded, not trusting himself to speak at the moment. Her smile was powerful, tempting, and he'd be damned if he let her know just how effective it was. His heart pounded in his chest, and he glanced away from the force of her smile, gathering his own addled wits. He'd never met a woman who turned him inside out, and he wasn't certain if he hated the feeling or craved it.

He turned his attention back to her, watching as she lowered her eyes, then peeked up through her lashes.

His body responded approvingly to her flirtatious glance, though he'd bet his last pound she didn't realize what she was doing.

Which made it all the more powerful.

She was temptation personified. And he was not immune.

He offered his arm once more and continued on. "Will your father be worried?" he asked, needing to distract himself. Thinking of her father would certainly be helpful.

"He's accustomed to my evenings out," she answered with a shrug.

Collin could feel the tension in her body as she

answered, her smile gone. Her light brows furrowed as she halted their steps. "He doesn't know," she blurted out.

He blinked, trying to follow her train of thought. "You'll have to explain," he said after a moment.

She sighed and bit her lip. "I'm pretty sure Mr. Finch said something to you about his sister's classes, and you're smart enough to make the connection, or maybe he told you that I'm the one who teaches them," she said rather inarticulately.

Collin nodded. "I see. He doesn't know you teach women in the evenings."

"No, he does not, and I don't wish him to know either. He… It's hard enough as it is, to have me at the college." She glanced up, her eyes narrowing as if daring him, challenging him to say anything about it.

He held up a hand in surrender.

After a sigh, she continued. "It's…complicated…but I don't wish for this to add to what he already must endure for my sake. Please, don't mention it."

Collin gave a succinct nod. "Your secret is safe with me, Miss Essex." He bowed.

"Ah, so now you're being proper." She dusted off her skirts, needing to do something with her hands.

Lord Penderdale's answering grin was anything but repentant. "Caught that, did you?"

"I'm quite observant," she replied.

"To be honest, I didn't exactly plan on using

your Christian name, Miss Essex, though now that I've taken the liberty, I find I'm quite reluctant to relinquish it," he said, his tone gentle.

She studied his face, trying to read his unspoken meaning. "I don't remember giving you permission."

"You didn't. However, this is me asking for permission now."

"Permission, not forgiveness for taking the liberty," she clarified.

"I only ask for forgiveness when I regret something… This I have no regrets over," he said openly.

"At least you're honest."

"I'm nothing if not honest, Miss Essex…" He let her name linger, drawing it out slightly, longingly.

"You did just come to my rescue." Elizabeth struggled to find her resolve to refuse him, but found she wished to hear her name from his lips again. The words came out in a rush. "Only if it is just the two of us. Already this is against my better judgment and is not proper."

"So…never?" he teased. "So rarely is it only the two of us. However, I accept your terms."

"Well, it's currently just you and me, so 'never' wouldn't be an accurate statement, would it?" Elizabeth replied, her muddled thoughts adding an indignant tone to her voice as she struggled to gain control of herself.

Collin huffed impatiently. "Do you ever tire of attempting to be right?"

"Do you?" she asked sweetly, too sweetly. There was steel under that sugar.

"No."

"Me either," she answered.

"Well, then, Elizabeth—" He grinned. "I must use the privilege while I can."

She shook her head with a bemused expression.

"I am to meet Mr. Finch after I see you home safely. Do you wish me to tell him that it was you the black-eyed bandit assaulted? Or would you rather keep that between us?"

She was thankful for the change of subject, then paused as she recollected his words. "Black-eyed bandit?" she asked with derision.

"I thought that a clever name," he answered.

She frowned. "Very well." Her lips curved into a small smile. "No, don't tell him. He'll…worry and blame himself. You see, he was just walking me halfway home. He was to meet you, and I insisted I was safe…" She bit her lip and didn't finish.

"I see." Collin sighed. "I apologize."

"For? What could you have possibly done differently? Not chase the man who is using your name for evil? I think not." She shrugged.

"Regardless, I feel somewhat responsible. Mr. Finch should have ignored your insistence and walked you home, meeting with me be hanged." He growled the last part. "You're far more important."

"Regardless, I'm quite well, considering all things, and you were there to assist me almost immediately."

"I was the one chasing him... Again, I apologize—"

She held up a hand. "We've gone over this. No need." She paused. "Please don't tell Mr. Finch or Patricia. Let this just be between us."

"I was right. We did become friends, a secret and all."

He earned a giggle at that statement, and then a smile as well. If he didn't find the "black-eyed bandit" tonight, he'd still consider the entire evening a victory.

"Friend." She held out her hand.

He took it and shook it twice, noticing how her small hand fit perfectly in his. He reluctantly released her.

She glanced away, and he noted the way she stretched her hand a few times, as if his handshake was lingering with her.

It was certainly lingering with him.

How was it possible to be infuriated by and also attracted to a person? They continued walking toward her home.

"Friendship or truce?" Elizabeth asked suddenly, as if the thought just occurred to her.

Collin turned to Elizabeth and nodded with a smile, regarding her as a worthy opponent, or ally, depending on the occasion.

"Both, why limit ourselves?" he replied.

She nodded. "Why indeed, Lor—Collin." A tinge of pink highlighted the pale skin of her cheeks.

Collin watched the color bloom and soon fade, noting that he enjoyed the display far too much, as well as the sound of his name on her lips.

"I'm glad you agree, but to be a gentleman, I must disclose that I will still spar with you whenever the occasion arises. I find I cannot help myself. You're quite fetching when indignant."

Elizabeth blinked, blushed again, and struggled to collect herself, faster than he expected. "Then we have an understanding, since I'll certainly do the same."

"Agreed."

Elizabeth glanced ahead as they rounded the corner and released his arm quickly. "My father is waiting. I'm sure I'll see you later. After all, you are searching for something that belongs to me." She grimaced.

"You don't want to explain to your father why I'm walking you home?" he asked.

"The very last thing I'd like to do."

"I rather thought it would be the second-to-last thing."

She glared. "Very well." She met his gaze. "Thank you. I don't think I said that earlier."

"No need for thanks. I'm happy I was able to be of service. I'll see you soon, Elizabeth." He reached down and lifted her hand, perfectly fitting within his own, to his lips and kissed the air above her wrist. His lips tingled as if he'd touched her skin.

"Good night." Her tone was deep, as if unable to trust her voice, and she slowly withdrew her hand. After she crossed the street and disappeared inside her house, he released a long breath.

He was in trouble.

And it wasn't about the person stealing his name.

It was with the woman who could easily be stealing his heart.

Twelve

Mankind censure injustice, fearing that they may be the victims of it and not because they shrink from committing it.

—Plato, *The Republic*

COLLIN WATCHED AS ELIZABETH CROSSED THE street, heading toward a corner. Not wanting to lose sight of her, he quickly moved down the street so he could see her round the bend. In typical Elizabeth fashion, she jogged across the next street before pausing at a stoop with a black door. Collin watched as her father stepped down from the stoop, indeed keeping an eye out for his daughter, and then ushered her inside.

Safe. Collin released his tight shoulders and turned on his heel, his focus on finding Michael. It would be easy enough to keep Elizabeth out of the story, and he agreed with her sentiment on why she wished to be left out. Michael did fancy her, and Patricia was a dear friend. They'd both be concerned, and since there was nothing to be concerned over… Yet as he considered the words, he knew he wasn't being entirely truthful.

He didn't want Michael to know. Collin liked that he and Elizabeth had a secret. Liked it a little more than was safe. And he'd told Michael he held no interest in Elizabeth. As he thought it, he grinned at how delicious her name had tasted on his tongue. He'd used it without thinking, and he'd use it again. He was already thinking of delightful ways to get away with using her Christian name, all causing her to chastise him. He could hardly wait.

He focused back on the road and crossed several streets until he found the meeting spot prearranged with Michael. Sure enough, Michael was resting against a wall, looking at his timepiece.

Collin was more than a little late.

Michael tossed a cheroot from his mouth and glanced up. Upon seeing Collin, he pushed back from the wall and started toward him. "Evening," he stated, his irritation clear.

"My apologies. There was a bit of a situation," Collin answered, waving Michael forward. "On my way to meet you, I came across a man with a black eye."

Michael's attention cut to him. "And?"

"And he ran down the street and knocked into someone and darted away. I stayed a moment to check on the poor lady, and by then, he was gone," Collin explained with a sigh. "But he went down this way, which may or may not mean anything, but we can certainly try."

Michael nodded. "Too bad you had to stop for the woman. It's the best shot we've had."

Collin shrugged. He didn't exactly agree—after all, the woman he'd helped was Elizabeth—but a shrug wouldn't raise suspicion about his true feelings. "What's down this way?" Collin asked as they followed the direction the man had taken.

"A pub a little ways down and a lower-rent district for shops."

"Let's try the pub first. Maybe he's in need of a pint."

Michael agreed. "Maybe I am too." He smiled. "Why don't we split up? I'll start in the pub, and you can search the streets. We'll cover more area that way."

"You just want that pint," Collin accused good-naturedly.

"I do. It's been a night for me as well. Laid out my intentions for Miss Essex and all." He breathed out a long breath. "It's been a long time coming, and I don't have time to beat around the bush, so to say." He shrugged as he turned to Collin.

Collin schooled his features and nodded, then slapped his friend on the back. "The pub is yours, friend," he said by way of answering.

"I'll check the back as well and ask around."

"I'll return in half an hour," Collin stated as they paused in front of the Horsehair Pub. Michael went in, and Collin took a moment to reflect on what had just been said. He'd had no idea, and Elizabeth hadn't said a word, not that she would, but he rather thought she'd have acted differently if she was planning to allow Michael to court her formally.

How well did he truly know her? Would she choose to disclose that kind of information to him? Likely not, which left him in a fog of confusion. It forced him to think of his own intentions, his own feelings.

And he'd really rather not.

Odd, a few weeks ago, he'd felt nothing. Apathy was his constant companion, and now he was fending off pesky emotions with a proverbial stick. All because of a woman.

But wasn't it always because of a woman? It was a tale as old as time.

And he was no more immune than the next man.

But that did beg the question: What was he going to do about it? He wasn't about to court her. He had no intention of marrying, and even if he did, they'd be at each other's throats constantly.

However, part of that concept was alluring, because Elizabeth was passionate, persistent, and thorough, all good aspects of lovemaking, and he could quite easily imagine those traits put to good use.

But he wanted more than passion. He wanted...

He stopped his thoughts. What was wrong with him? He was in Cambridge to find a criminal, not a wife. And most certainly not Miss Essex, who was a bluestocking to the core and unsuited for him in nature.

But all those facts didn't cool his warming to her or squelch his desire to see her again and soon.

He'd just made a friend in Michael, and now he was fighting interest in the woman Michael was actively pursuing.

Good Lord, he was a cad.

And currently a pathetic investigator. He shook his shoulders and focused on the job at hand. Find the man with the black eye, question him, and recover Elizabeth's satchel.

He made a mental note to keep the satchel out of sight if he did indeed find it. He traveled down the road, searching alleyways and studying the various men in the street with a little too much interest. He earned a few questioning glares as he passed. He was looking down an alley when he noted a rumpled dark object. Curious, he strode forward and picked it up, recognizing it immediately.

Elizabeth's words came back to him. "They'll be sorely disappointed when they discover it's only parchments and a book."

Apparently the fiend found the satchel more trouble than it was worth for the contents. Collin lifted the leather bag and rifled through it, noting the book was present, but no parchments. A quick scan of the alley revealed a crumpled wad of written pages, and he carefully retrieved them and smoothed them out. He slipped them into the satchel and fastened it closed. Well, at least he was able to find something. Moreover, its presence here meant that he was going the right direction in searching for the man who had stolen it. He wrapped the satchel's strap around his shoulder and followed the alleyway into a different street where it spread out. There were a few closed storefronts, a few cheap boardinghouses Michael had already visited. Nothing to catch Collin's attention. He decided to wait and leaned against the stone wall, kicking a foot up behind him.

After a while, a boy about eight or nine started down the road in his direction. Collin waved the boy over and held up a shilling. "Have you seen a man with a black eye?" he asked.

The boy eyed the shilling and then Collin. "Aye."

Collin handed over the shilling, and withdrew another. "Where?"

The boy held up two fingers.

A chuckle bubbled from Collin's throat as he held up two shillings at that. "Where?"

The boy nodded toward a building that had a shingle reading "Apothecary."

Collin repeated the word, earning a nod from the boy, and he paid him. "Did he go in there? And when?"

The boy waited, and Collin dug in his pocket and withdrew a few more coins.

"A few hours ago. I live down the street and don't like that place. People go in the front, afterward go out the back. Odd."

"So, he could have gone out the back?"

"That would be my guess." He shrugged, took the coins, and then ran off.

"Apothecary," Collin whispered under his breath. He walked over to the building and stood under the shingle, studying the door. No windows on the front of the store to let in light, not like any apothecary he'd seen in London. Odd indeed.

He checked the doorknob and found it open. After swinging the door inward, he entered slowly. The dim room came into focus after a moment, a few candles on the wooden countertop casting a vague glow in the room.

"Can I help you?"

Collin turned toward the voice and nodded, quickly taking in the details of the man who spoke. He was of middle age, with an immaculately trimmed mustache and clothing that spoke of quality. The man rested his hands on the well-worn countertop and waited.

"Yes, I'm searching for a headache remedy," Collin answered. It was a common reason to visit an apothecary.

"I'm afraid I'm about to close," the man answered swiftly.

Collin's suspicions grew. What apothecary worth

their salt didn't have any willow bark or other sort of remedy on hand for a headache? Testing his theory, he waved a hand and said, "I'll come back tomorrow." He turned to leave.

The man's voice halted him. "I'm sold out until I receive more. You may want to try the apothecary near Trinity Street."

Collin thanked him and went out the door, thinking over the details he was able to gather while inside.

The shop boasted apothecary paraphernalia and tools, with a brass scale on the counter collecting dust. It had certainly been some time since its last use. All the other apothecaries he'd ever visited held glass jars of various contents used for healing remedies, while this shop had bare shelves. But it was the smell that was his first clue. Apothecaries all had a particular scent of dried herbs and lavender, with a minor burning tinge of whatever tincture was just opened. It was a welcoming scent, but was not present there. The shop's air was the same as outside, as if the doors had been opened and closed often—odd for a nonworking apothecary—or there was an open door in the rear as the boy had stated, constantly allowing airflow.

Collin started down the street, taking a longer route than necessary in case he was being watched, and afterward rounded a building that would take him around to the back of the apothecary in a block or two. The boy had said that men went into the apothecary through the front but left through the back, and Collin was going to see for himself. If the man who had received him when he'd entered the apothecary was present, Collin would be recognized immediately. He glanced both ways and crossed to the other side of the street. His clothes were not conspicuous—it was common to have a dark-brown overcoat—and he pulled his hat down further on his face as he drew closer.

The street was quiet, and that also struck him as odd. It wasn't so late that there wouldn't be other people milling about, but he shrugged off the detail and focused on the building ahead and across the street. A wagon with a team of old bays waited as it was loaded up with a few crates. Several men made short work of the crates and then disappeared into the back of the building. The driver headed down the road ahead of Collin. He made the decision to follow the wagon rather than linger behind the apothecary and risk being seen. At least the driver of the wagon wouldn't recognize him.

The horses were not in rush as they continued down the road, and Collin could easily keep them in sight. After a few blocks, they turned down another street that would lead out of Cambridge. Collin jogged a few steps to catch up a little. The driver scanned the street, his scrutiny landing on Collin, who ducked his head and turned at the next road to ward off suspicion. He waited around the corner until he could see the wagon pass along the original street, and he once again followed, only this time he kept a slender building between them, using the alleyways between to keep an eye on the wagon. As he passed the third alleyway, he lost track of the wagon, so he backtracked to the previous alleyway and crept forward, carefully checking the street for his quarry. When he didn't see it, he stepped onto the street and noted the directions possibly taken.

He selected a tight alley, and darted down cautiously, hearing the sound of echoing hooves. When the sound stopped, Collin paused and listened. The stone walls of the alleyway allowed the sound of men's voices to echo. The sound was far too muddled for him to grasp the words, but he carefully inched forward. The alley ended in another street, and he leaned against the wall. After taking a deep breath, he removed his hat and peeked around, just enough to see. The driver of the wagon was shaking the hand of another man. As the second man turned toward the back of the wagon, Collin's eyes widened. It was their mystery man with the black eye! He withdrew from the corner.

He needed a plan.

And not one that would see him overcome because he was outnumbered. The fellow bandit would recognize him, so sauntering across the street to get a clearer view was out of the question.

But he needed to determine what was being hauled in those crates; clearly somehow it was all related.

Too bad Michael wasn't present. He'd have a better chance at going unnoticed and thus getting closer. Collin sighed. If he was foolish, he'd just hang the consequences and dare to be recognized as he got a closer look, but as it was, they would likely just move the operation somewhere else, and he'd have to start over in his search. No, he'd be wise and note the location to come back later. He noted the street names and then went off to find Michael.

Before he could meet with Michael, he had to take care to hide Elizabeth's satchel. He couldn't exactly wear it into the pub, that was for certain. Collin crossed several blocks to a more populated street and hired a hack to take him back home. He would deposit Elizabeth's satchel there and return to Michael to communicate what he'd found.

In short order, the satchel was taken care of, and the hack was rolling to a stop in front of the Horsehair Pub. Collin stepped out and paid the driver, then went into the well-lit building. The sound of conversation and laughter eased some of his tension. After scanning the crowd, he spotted Michael talking with a gray-haired man at the edge of the bar. He approached them, waving at the bar-keeper for a pint as he closed the distance.

"Michael." He nodded, then turned to the other man. "Oxley," Collin said, introducing himself.

"Thomas." The man took Collin's offered hand.

"Tom was talking to me about an odd situation that I found interesting," Michael said, lifting his pint to his lips.

Collin ignored his own thirst and turned to Thomas. "Oh?"

Thomas lifted his cup sloppily, as if he'd had too many before that one, and dove into the conversation with gusto. "Aye, I was sayin' to my friend here"—he gestured to Michael—"that I was visiting my sister. She lives outside of Cambridge by a small creek that feeds into the River Cam."

A barmaid set down a pint in front of Collin, and he lifted it to his lips, listening to Tom's story.

"And she was complaining something fierce. She usually does, but this time she had a reason. She gets her water for washing and such from the creek, and the other day, when she went to collect water, it was all tea brown-yellow. Stained everything, she said. Well, I had to go and check it out myself. She's a widow, so I try to help her manage things where I can, and so I went to the creek. Nothing seemed odd, but I followed it up a ways and found a crate."

Collin's attention snapped into focus when the man said a crate. "Go on."

"It was tea."

"Smuggled tea," Collin guessed.

"I'm thinking so. Someone was trying to hide the evidence and dumped it in the creek, thinking the water would do its job. It did, to a certain extent, but the smuggler wasn't a smart one. Everyone knows you need to dump the tea." He glanced skyward.

"Interesting," Collin stated. "I have a friend who works for the War Office. Do you think your sister would mind if we went and had a look?"

He shrugged. "Likely not, but it's no use. I picked it up and burned the crate. No need for that to make her clothes all tea-stained."

"I see." Michael eyed Collin. "Was there anything remarkable about the crate? Or the tea?"

The man seemed to think. "Just a wooden crate, like a million others."

Michael finished off his pint and nodded to the man. "Thank you."

Collin followed suit, polishing off his pint as well, and then followed Michael out the door of the pub.

"Well, that certainly goes hand in hand with my findings," Collin stated as they walked down the street.

When Michael turned curious eyes to him, Collin told him about his evening.

"So, it would seem that somehow your name is mixed up with tea smugglers."

"It would seem so. Which boils down to evading taxes due to the Crown, a wonderful offense," Collin said with sarcasm. "Tomorrow let's travel down to where I saw the wagon unloaded, see if we can uncover any information. If I'm lucky, maybe our old friend with the black eye will still be there."

Michael chuckled. "So, tomorrow?"

"Tomorrow." And with a nod, Collin headed home.

Now, if he could only figure out how best to return Elizabeth's satchel, without anyone the wiser.

Thirteen

ELIZABETH AWOKE THE NEXT MORNING WITH A mild headache. As she reached behind her head and tenderly touched the bump, she understood why her head throbbed. It wasn't a large bump, but it certainly was tender. It would be a good day to stay at home, and she would be wise to take a day to recover. Her body itched as if already revolting against the concept of inactivity. The breakfast table was set, and her father was reading the two-day old *London Times* as he drank his tea.

"Good morning." He lowered the newspaper and welcomed her with a smile.

Elizabeth returned the welcome. "Good morning, Papa." She sat across from him and poured herself some tea.

"It's times like this I'm thankful we don't live in a larger city." Her father folded the newspaper and lifted a section, showing a bold-print headline regarding a crime.

"It is a little calmer here in Cambridge," Elizabeth agreed, but her mind flickered back to last night. She thought over her studies and how they had pertained to human nature. Plato had believed that evil was a result of ignorance. She didn't agree with that statement. Ignorance could certainly be part of the whole, but there was also a willful choice, as in the case of Lord Penderdale. The knave impersonating him chose to blame another by using a false name, so that wasn't ignorance.

"You're deep in thought this morning," her father commented, setting his teacup down.

"Woolgathering," she answered. "I think today I'll visit the bees. It's been over a week, and I'd like to inspect the colony. Then I'll take a ride."

"So, I won't see you at the college?" her father asked.

She shook her head. "No, I'll stay close to home after that."

Her father's shoulders relaxed, as if…relieved? She hadn't noticed that before. Perhaps her presence at the college did cause him some anxiety. He'd never tell her or admit it, she was sure of it, but maybe she was being overly determined to do something that might not be in the best interest of those she cared about most.

It was a conundrum.

And her head hurt more just considering it.

Why did change have to occur? Better yet, why

was it human nature to resist it so? She lifted a piece of toast from a plate and began to slather it with marmalade. "I need to harvest some more honey. I had several frames that appeared nearly ready last week, so they should be abundant today."

"It sounds like you have your day's work planned," her father commented as he pushed away from the table and stood. "I'll be on my way. I'll see you this evening." He walked over and kissed her head tenderly.

Elizabeth patted his hand and wished him a good day. After she broke her fast, she donned an old dress that she often used for beekeeping and that already had a few beeswax stains on the skirts. After buttoning up her sturdiest boots, she stepped out back and collected her smoker and a basket that would carry the frames of capped honey back to the house for harvesting.

In short order, she was riding out toward the hives, passing through the streets of Cambridge until she reached the outskirts of town where they blended into the farm country and small woods. Winifred, her mare, plodded along without a second thought to the slight bustle around her, but Elizabeth scanned the street, searching for the rogue with a black eye.

She had purposely resisted the temptation to think too much about last night's events. Not because they had frightened her, but because they were very confusing and she wasn't sure how to sort through them. Descartes's methodology be hanged. She didn't want to break down the problem into simple parts, because every part she dared to consider was not at all simple.

She had started the night with the intention of deciphering Mr. Finch's attentions and her own reaction. She had partly accomplished that goal; he was certainly interested in her. The problem was understanding her own heart. It was true that he was kind, brave, and generous, but when she met his gaze, her heart didn't pound and her belly didn't grow warm.

And as fate would have it, immediately after her confusion with Mr. Finch, she had found herself with Lord…with Collin. And it was different and wrong.

Wrong in every way. Nonetheless, her heart couldn't beat a steady rhythm in his presence, and when he looked at her, all her many thoughts evaporated. At one point, she'd thought she'd stop breathing, for heaven's sake!

She would be lying to herself if she denied the attraction, the strong desire to be around him again though she was likely to lose her temper, but the emotions were also deep, and that was the rub.

With Mr. Finch, it was about what she wanted to feel or should feel.

With Collin, it was what she was powerless to stop feeling.

Which should be her answer. The problem was, she didn't like the answer. And she wasn't sure Collin held any interest or, more importantly, any lasting interest in her. All this musing was likely for naught, she chastised herself as she guided her mare onto a deep path from the road.

Enough, she scolded herself. There would be plenty of time to digest her emotions and reactions later, to lay them out in little logical lines, but thinking about them now was making her head pound.

She ducked under a low branch and listened to the soft hum of the bees working around her on the last flowers of autumn. Soon they would be finishing all their honey-making and preparing for winter.

When she drew closer, she dismounted from her mare and tied her to a low branch far out of view of the hive. She'd never known her bees to be aggressive, but she wasn't going to risk harming her horse, who was tethered. She took down the bucket and tools she'd strapped to the saddle and removed the items she needed first. She slid on thicker gloves and put a veil over her small hat to cover her face and neck. Withdrawing her smoker, she collected some dry debris from the woods and placed these in the small can, lighting it and watching as the smoke curled up.

With the smoker in one hand and a bucket and small metal bar in the other, she walked to the hive, approaching from the back. It was a round hive, with a single entrance and a removable lid. She set down her smoker and lifted the lid of the hive, the humming sound of tens of thousands of bees filling her ears. The hive was warm to the touch, another miracle of nature, and she waited a moment to let the bees settle. She slowly reached down to her smoker and puffed it a few times to calm the bees hovering around the top of the hive. They distanced themselves from the smoke, and she got to work.

She searched through each piece of honeycomb, noting the patterns of the brood, and selecting a few frames that were fully capped with golden honey. She took the metal tool and slowly scraped along the side of the attached honeycomb to loosen it. Honey broke out of a few of the capped cells, and the bees immediately flocked to it, their little tongues devouring the dehydrated nectar. They'd store it in their honey stomach and deposit it back in the hive later, wasting nothing. She continued working and withdrew a full comb of capped honey, gilded in the sunlight and sticky. She could only remove two frames of the honey. The rest would need to be saved for the bees so they would have adequate food to survive the winter. They shared, and it was important she always leave them enough for their own use.

Setting the honeycomb inside the bucket she'd brought along, she went to work on the next one to harvest. In short order, she'd removed the honeycomb and placed it beside the first. The removal of the comb granted her a deeper view into the hive and a better view of the remaining comb, where some cells were filled with honey, some with larvae waiting to hatch, and some appearing empty but likely filled with eggs from the queen.

The queen was vital to the hive's survival. Without her, there would be no continual source of bees to work in the hive and collect the nectar and pollen. The queen's one job was to lay eggs, and she took it seriously.

Elizabeth twisted her lips. If only all of humanity had such determination, she mused. She carefully placed the lid back on the hive and dusted the lingering bees from the honeycomb before she took it back to where her horse waited. Winifred usually ignored any bees that tried to ride on Elizabeth's skirts or the bucket, but Elizabeth was cautious. One sting could spook a horse easily enough, even one with as gentle a temper as Winifred, and that could end badly for both of them.

She attached the bucket to the saddle and then unwound the reins from the branch. Leading her horse through the woods and back to the path was the best choice for both of them. A few bees followed the scent of their honey, and a few rode on Winifred's rump, but thankfully none felt threatened enough to sting. As the road came back into view, Elizabeth dusted off the last bee and checked her mare for stragglers before mounting up.

She realized, belatedly, she should have taken Winifred for a ride before visiting the bees, since she couldn't do that now. That was unfortunate, but at least she had her honey. The road wound around slowly, and Elizabeth relaxed as the rhythmic pace of her horse lulled her into a peaceful state. The sunshine was warm on her skin, and with only a few puffy clouds littering the sky, the area might make it a whole morning without rain. That was another good reason to collect the honey today, since bees didn't appreciate foul weather.

As Winifred sauntered into town, Elizabeth's attention snapped back into focus, and she scanned the faces of any men in the street. It wasn't as if she had a plan of action if she did see the criminal, but at least she could tell Collin when and where she'd seen him and possibly use that to pinpoint where he called home.

She navigated the streets without any sight of the man and eventually slowed her mare as she reached home. After caring for Winifred, she took the bucket into the kitchens in the lower part of the house and began working, much to the chagrin of her cook and scullery maid. She ignored them and proceeded to take care of the honey. It was a slow process, extracting. First she took a clean bucket and set it on the countertop. Next, she held the honeycomb above the bucket, then took a long knife and began scraping off the wax caps of each honey cell, careful not to cut deeply but just scrape the top off the cells. The golden honey began to ooze out slowly, catching the light as it flowed into the bucket.

When she'd finished opening all the cells, she turned the honeycomb to the other side and performed the same process. She scraped the wax from the knife onto a nearby dish for later use and watched as the honey slowly collected in the bottom of the bucket. Eventually, she'd need to hold the comb on a string over the bucket, allowing the final drops to make their way into the bottom. When the comb was empty of the honey, she would save half for the wax and then return the other half to the hive for them to reuse. They'd likely disassemble it and rebuild new comb with it, but she'd deposit it back into the hive to discourage bees from other hives from trying to take it.

Bees were amazing and used all their resources— and then reused them all for the betterment of their collective.

She picked up a spoon and dipped it into the honey, lifting it to her lips. It was delightful, sweet and warm. All she needed was a biscuit.

Elizabeth quit the kitchens, leaving the scullery maid and cook in charge of keeping an eye on the honey. They were accustomed to the process and waved her off as soon as was acceptable. She took the stairs to the second floor and was about to head to her room to change when she heard a familiar voice from the direction of the front door. Usually, her father would answer the door if he was home, as they didn't employ a butler, just a few maids and a cook, but when her father wasn't home, one of the servants often answered.

Elizabeth made her way to the front door, her eyes taking in what her ears had suspected. Lord Penderdale—Collin—was standing on the threshold, her satchel in hand.

Warmth coursed through her, and she felt her cheeks heat when he noticed her approach. "Miss Essex." He bowed.

"Lord Penderdale," she answered. "Won't you please come in?" She turned to Molly, who had answered the door, and smiled.

"Thank you." He crossed the threshold and removed his hat, following her into a small parlor to the left. Molly took a seat as well, a mindful chaperone.

He glanced to the servant and set the satchel down on a chair.

"Molly, would you please ask the cook for tea to be brought up?" Elizabeth said, watching as the servant reluctantly left the room. The room had no door to close and was open to the rest of the house, but Molly was quite observant of propriety.

As soon as Molly was out of earshot, Elizabeth turned to Collin. "How did you find it?" she asked and went over to the chair to retrieve her satchel. She had doubted she'd ever see it again and opened the flap to find her book and now-rumpled parchment notes. "Apparently he didn't appreciate my take on Descartes's methods," she added with a smile aimed at Collin.

He returned the smile and shook his head. "Not everyone can be taught to appreciate higher education. Our rogue discarded it in an alley where I found it. Very uneventful, I assure you."

"I think I've had enough excitement for a while, thank you." The memory of her tender bump added emphasis to her words.

"I wanted to make sure I returned it as soon as possible. That way, you could use it if needed," Collin stated, his voice softer than she'd expected.

Looking up, she met his warm regard. "Thank you. Sincerely."

He took a step closer, lowering his voice. "And you'll be pleased to know that I was able to communicate the needed information to Mr. Finch without including you in the details," he added but watched her reaction closely.

Elizabeth's belly fluttered like it was being tickled from the inside out. "I appreciate that. I'm sure you had much to explain due to how late you were for your meeting."

"It was nothing. It worked out just fine." He stepped back.

Elizabeth frowned. Something was off, different. And she couldn't place her finger on it. She glanced down and then groaned. "Good mercy."

"What?" Collin asked, stepping close to her and lifting the satchel, clearly assuming her exclamation was regarding it.

"Oh no, the satchel is fine. I'm…merely being vain." She twisted her lips.

"Vain?" he asked, his gaze flickering across her features before darting down to her dress. "Ah, let me guess." He tapped his lips with a finger.

Elizabeth's face was still flushed with warmth from the expression he'd given her as he studied her. She needed to stop reacting so! It was… confusing.

"You were visiting your bees," he announced.

"Yes, and I was extracting honey, which explains the several smudges. I'd suggest not getting too close to me, else your fine coat will be far less fine."

His eyes crinkled in a smile. "Were you expecting me to get that close to you, Elizabeth?" he asked teasingly.

Elizabeth saw the bait and tried to resist it. "No, but in case you brushed against me—"

"Ah, you want me to make it appear like an accident." His smile widened into a challenging grin. "I can work with that."

"No, I said nothing of the sort—"

"Actually, you most certainly did," he corrected, "ten seconds ago." He proceeded to quote her.

"I take it back," she replied tightly, trying to keep herself from smiling.

"You can't. That's the beauty and the curse of words," he stated. "You should know that with all your study. After all, who can tame the tongue? It has both life and death—"

"I know my Bible, Lord Penderdale," Elizabeth cut in, wanting to flirt, but resisting. Was that all she did around this man? Resist? *Don't capitulate or lose your temper. Don't fall for his charm…resist.*

"Collin," he chided softly. "After all, I'm going to be shameless in my use of your name, whenever possible."

She glanced heavenward. "I regret giving you leave to use it."

"And nevertheless, you can't take it back, can you?"

"According to you, no. Words apparently take on a life of their own once released into the wild."

"I'm glad you understand," he said with an approving tone.

"Don't talk down to me," she retorted with a glare.

"I wouldn't dare."

"That I don't believe," she snapped back, but she couldn't resist the grin that broke across her lips.

"How about…" He paused and mused for a

second. "I wouldn't dare talk down to you unless it was in a flirtatious manner?"

Elizabeth studied him, words about to tumble from her mouth, but she held them back. Flirtatious? Was he flirting?

Was she flirting?

Yes. Yes she was. Good Lord, she was openly flirting in her father's parlor. What had become of her?

"I do believe I've left you speechless. A first, I'm sure."

She glared. "Not a first, but I am more cautious with my words than others," she said, pointedly accusing him.

"Or you simply restrict your words based on the emotions you don't wish to consider," he countered. "Ah, tea." He stepped back and regarded her, his eyes sparkling with challenge and mischief, flaunting that he'd won the moment.

She couldn't very well give a smart rebuttal with Molly's eagle eyes on her.

"Touché," she whispered, earning a gloating smile from Collin.

"To be continued later?" he asked a little too hopefully.

How could she say no? She didn't back down from a challenge, but her verbal sparring with Collin was…fun, exciting. He made her think, study herself, and articulate her thoughts concisely.

She'd never met anyone like that.

And it was addicting.

"Miss, here's some of your fresh honey for the biscuits as well," Molly pointed out before stepping back to allow Elizabeth to pour the tea.

"Thank you, Molly," she replied and then turned to Collin. "How would you like your tea?"

"No cream, but I'd love a little honey," he added. "I rather like sweet things."

Elizabeth's contemplation cut to him, and she narrowed her eyes.

He merely smiled wider, as if proud of himself.

"You can certainly use the sweetening up," she noted, using his own words against him.

He winced playfully. "Touché."

She arched a brow and poured the tea. She lifted a lid to a small dish and stirred in a bit of honey before handing the tea to Collin.

"Thank you." He took a small sip. His forehead furrowed for a moment before asking a question. "Where do you procure your tea?"

Elizabeth frowned a moment, then turned to Molly. "Isn't it the shop down by Trinity?"

"Yes, Miss Essex," Molly said. "We only buy our tea there, not from anyplace less reputable and certainly not from those urchins that sell in the alleyways." Molly eyed Lord Penderdale, as if judging him for asking.

"What do you mean, 'less reputable'?" he asked Molly.

Elizabeth noted the way his body had tightened with tension at her servant's words, and she knew they must hold a deeper meaning for him. Interesting.

"Aye, there's a few shops that are known for selling the used tea leaves and heaven knows what, but they also have a small amount of quality tea under lock—but it's not aboveboard, if you gather my meaning. It's risky business that, no tax. King and country must be blooming mad, but if you peep at them sideways, they usher you out the door real quick."

"Hmm," Collin stated. "That's interesting. You say you know which shops?"

"Aye, and a few have set up small stalls in the market area, but they are for the poor. Their leaves are the char sold by the cooks and added to. However, if you look like you're worth more than a shilling, they'll try to sell you higher-quality stuff. Mostly black tea though." She added, "It's been going on for a few months. I told the watchmen, and the professor sent to the magistrate to be aware, but I don't know much more. They likely can't prove anything."

"I see. Well, this tea is delightful, clearly purchased somewhere reputable," he added, and Molly settled her ruffled feathers a bit.

Elizabeth watched the exchange silently, studying the information and how Collin received it, deducing that perhaps the men who were using his name might be in the tea smuggling business.

After all, it was a huge problem. She'd read an article in the *Times* about it a year ago. During the war, smuggling had been rampant. Brandy, tea, lace… All were in high demand, and criminals worked with vigor to supply that demand. Adding in that the French imports were illegal only made the situation more volatile. She'd read that only about fifteen percent of the tea used in Britain in the past year was legally imported, and the rest was illegal. Everyone she knew drank tea regularly. That meant that eighty-five percent of the tea was contraband. It was an astounding number. How could the War Office and any sort of law enforcement agency address such a large problem? It seemed insurmountable, which was likely why the street boys could easily peddle the stuff without getting caught. If they were, someone would take their place the next day.

There had to be a root.

And good Lord, it was likely a taproot that went down forever. She wondered if perhaps the issue with criminals using Collin's name was far more involved than she, or maybe he, expected.

Elizabeth poured herself some tea and added a drop of cream and some honey, then sipped slowly.

"So, this honey is quite fresh. Is it from today?" Collin asked, ending her woolgathering.

She nodded and set her teacup down. "Yes, today, thus my sticky self." She waved at her rather unappealing dress.

"Or your sweet self. However you wish to look at it." He took a sip of his tea. "Will you be visiting Miss Finch today?" he asked, but his expression made the question seem weighted, as if there was something she was not privy to.

"Why?" she countered, curiosity making her narrow her eyes. "Trying to avoid me? Are you wanting a rematch for that conversation earlier?"

"First off, I won that battle." He set his teacup down and rested his arms on his knees. "And second, no."

"No…" She waited.

"I'm not avoiding you. Did you already forget your question? I'm disappointed, Miss Essex." He made a *tsk* sound with his tongue as if chiding her.

"You're insufferable."

"Why, thank you," he replied. "You're evasive."

She resisted the urge to roll her eyes. "I wasn't planning to visit Patricia today, no."

He nodded, his expression tightening for just a moment. "If you don't mind me asking, what are your engagements for the rest of the afternoon?"

Elizabeth turned her attention to her teacup and sipped slowly. She was using the moment to think about her answer. She didn't have plans. She was going to read at home, check the honey every once in a while, nothing terribly exciting. But if she said she didn't have any plans, would he invite her to make some with him? Did she want that?

Break down the problem into its simplest parts.

Yes. She did want that.

Setting the teacup down, she shrugged. "I've nothing pressing. I was going to read and check the progress of the honey extraction every once and a while."

"I see." He nodded once, then regarded her with a twinkle in his eye. "At the risk of starting a war, would you perhaps like to take a walk with me? I promise to behave," he said sweetly, innocently. Too innocently.

Elizabeth narrowed her eyes. "When you act like that, it makes me more suspicious."

"Act like what?" he asked, a gentle smile lifting his lips.

"Like you're not a proverbial thorn in my flesh," she explained with false sweetness.

He chuckled at her words. "Don't hold back your true emotions, Miss Essex."

"I won't, which should be fair warning," she said, offering a smile.

He nodded once. "I understand and willingly take on the risk of your company."

She bit back a giggle. "And what of me? What if I don't wish to take on the risk of your company, as you put it?"

"Then you're not as brave as I thought," he

challenged, leaning back and waiting, watching for her reaction.

Her eyes narrowed into slits at the gauntlet thrown. "Very well, I suppose I can tolerate your company for a few more minutes this afternoon."

"A glowing compliment if I've ever received one."

Elizabeth arched a brow but turned to Molly. "Would you accompany me this afternoon with Lord Penderdale? I'm sure he'd love to see where the questionable tea sellers hide," she added, and directed her attention back to Lord Penderdale, curiously watching his reaction.

He studied her for a moment and then smiled approvingly. "Delightful."

"And observant. Don't forget that," she complimented herself.

He shook his head good-naturedly, and she thought she heard him whisper, "Too observant," but she wasn't sure.

"I'll be ready in a quarter hour. Will that be acceptable?" she asked as she stood.

"I'll wait with bated breath, Miss Essex." He lifted his teacup and then selected a biscuit from the plate. "And I'll be sure to appreciate the honey you recently procured."

Elizabeth quit the room after asking Molly to follow her and assist with finding a cleaner, more presentable dress. As Molly helped her change her clothing, Elizabeth's mind wandered and her chest constricted.

Mr. Finch had all but declared himself last night. She still hadn't sorted through her feelings with any finality, and yet today she was spending an afternoon, or at least part of it, with a man she normally couldn't stand—by her own choice. She glanced in the long oval mirror, wondering who she had become in the past few weeks. *Blend in, keep quiet, head down* was her usual practice. However, the words chafed against her soul, as if she'd outgrown them and they now constricted her. But abandoning her invisibility would keep her from assisting her father at the college. She had to be invisible to be present.

As she considered that, she realized something vital. And that one truth had the power to change everything. She didn't want to be invisible anymore.

Fourteen

The unexamined life is not worth living.

—Socrates

COLLIN ATE THE LAST BITE OF BISCUIT AND licked his fingers clean of the remnants of sticky honey. He savored the sweetness on his tongue. It was amusing, the dichotomy of Elizabeth Essex. She was anything but a simpering, sweet, and demure London debutante, and nonetheless she cared for bees and harvested honey—the sweetest substance. It was a balance, he decided, and rightfully so. He'd seen enough of the calculatingly sweet heiresses in London to note there was an unnatural flavor to their character, counterfeit—in a way. Forced. Elizabeth was unafraid of her thoughts or of speaking them out loud, even if they were less than complimentary. She'd be sorely out of place in a London ballroom, and that was exactly what attracted him. In a word, she was authentic, real and natural. And she offered absolutely no apology for it.

In fact, the only time he'd ever witnessed her intentionally try to blend in was that first meeting at Christ's College. He shook his head as he remembered it. In her rather bad attempt to blend in and be invisible, she did the exact opposite, as if her attempts to remain unnoticed only brought her further into his view. It grated at him, watching her. It was why he couldn't help but say something, rightfully earning her ire. But that fire she'd unleashed with her words was exactly what he'd seen hiding behind her foolish attempt at being invisible.

She was made for more than trying to avoid notice.

He wondered if she knew that.

Or wanted that.

It was a pity, and it also wasn't his problem.

No, his problem had taken on a new twist when he'd learned that some people were peddling smuggled tea, likely all connected with the men using his name. Good Lord, the issue kept spinning out of control. As many answers as he'd found in the past week, he'd tripled the number of new questions raised in response. It was maddening. However, what could he do but keep searching?

He heard a sound in the hall and stood. As expected, Elizabeth came into view, her maid close behind. He remembered how Joan had always required a chaperone in town, and though some social restrictions were less in the country, certain proprieties must be met.

"Miss Essex." He bowed.

"Lord Penderdale, thank you for waiting."

He noted the fine cut of her dress, nipping along her hips and giving just enough of a silhouette of her shape to whet his imagination. Her strawberry hair was twisted into a loose chignon, a tendril of hair curling around her neck and leading his gaze lower. He snapped his attention to her eyes, forcing a gentlemanly manner he'd rather have ignored.

Damn, but she was beautiful.

And tempting.

Perhaps it was a bad idea to take a walk.

He was intentionally walking into an irresistible situation, knowing full well his friend had feelings for the lady.

Nevertheless, he didn't want to listen to the better side of his conscience.

"It was no hardship to wait, Miss Essex. The biscuits were delightful company."

"They usually are. Our cook is excellent," she replied. "But add honey to anything and it improves it."

"On that point, we are in utter agreement. Rare, that." He hinted at a smile.

She twisted her lips, drawing his attention to their pink bow-like shape. "Indeed, shall we go before we find something to disagree about and start the war early?"

He chuckled. "Wise and lovely... How am I so lucky?" He offered his arm, and in a few moments they were taking in the air and directing their steps toward the market streets of Cambridge.

"So, Miss Essex, have you always resided in Cambridge?" he asked. A quick glance behind him afforded an assurance Elizabeth's maid was following behind. He might be a cad for spending time with Elizabeth when his friend's pursuit was clear, but he wasn't a rake.

"Yes. I was born and raised here and have only left once. My father and mother took me to London when I was eight. I don't remember much, just the smell."

He chuckled. "It takes some getting used to."

"I much prefer the country."

"Cambridge isn't a small village," he challenged.

"It is compared to London," she replied. "And the smoke dissipates quicker."

"I suppose you're correct."

She paused and regarded him. "I do love hearing you say those words."

He arched a brow. "Clearly you don't hear them often, and likely won't, so feel free to bask in the moment, Miss Essex."

She narrowed her eyes, then continued. "Has anyone told you that pride comes before a fall?"

"You should hope I don't fall, since I have your arm in mine. If I did take a tumble, you might come along with me."

She tried to slip her arm from his.

He resisted her efforts. "No, you are my anchor. If I do take a fall, it's your penance."

"For what?" she asked, her tone outraged but her lips bending into a smile. It was far too much fun to bait her.

"I haven't decided."

She pursed her lips, irritated. "Truly. You're making me serve penance for an offense I haven't committed?"

"Yes." He met her gaze. He'd already dug himself into a proverbial hole. It was now time to be stubborn about it. And he could be plenty obstinate when he wanted.

"You're daft." She shook her head but didn't try to pull her arm away, merely sighed.

Collin took that as a win.

"Well, Lord Penderdale, where did you grow up? London, I assume?"

"Indeed, smelly ol' London," he answered. "It's not so bad, and I will say there are wonderful benefits to living in a large town. For one, the museums. I'm surprised you haven't visited them."

"My father and mother took me when I was eight, but I don't remember much. I would like to see the British Museum," she answered wistfully. "My father…" She paused and bit her lip.

Collin waited, hoping she'd continue.

"My father doesn't like to travel since my mother passed. Before I was born they traveled a lot, and I think it reminds him too much of her." She gave a single-shoulder shrug, as if trying to downplay the emotion of the moment.

Collin nodded. "I understand. It's difficult to revisit things that you once enjoyed with a loved one." His words haunted him, the truth of them all too fresh for his own comfort.

"Yes. Maybe one day when I'm an old spinster I can travel and see what I wish," she said, her words more musing than statement.

"What makes you think you'll be an old spinster?" He spoke the words before he'd had the time to consider them.

She regarded him curiously. "Well, I suppose I don't."

It was on the tip of his tongue to ask about Michael, but it wasn't his business, and he'd not put her in the position of feeling obligated to give an answer.

But the curiosity burned inside him. If she was considering spinsterhood, then wasn't that answer enough? She had a perfectly acceptable suitor, however deep down she expected to be a spinster. Odd and telling.

"You think you're too much of an eccentric bluestocking," he stated, daring her to disagree.

She regarded him coolly. "Yes, I know I am, but as it turns out, I'm at peace with that. And I don't expect to change to accommodate someone else," she answered with a challenging tone.

"Good." He nodded and paused at the corner of a busy street.

"Good?" she asked, her tone indicating confusion.

"Yes." He carefully gauged traffic and led her across the road. "Why would you change for someone else? If you did, then they wouldn't be loving or appreciating *you*, but who they wanted you to be. Happens enough in London. I'd hate to see it happen to you."

"Oh," she stated somewhat flatly, as if his logic was watertight and unexpectedly so.

"Lord Penderdale?" Molly asked from behind them, and Collin paused and turned.

"Yes?"

She jerked her chin forward. "Up this way is where it is. I'll walk ahead just now and let you know if the store is open."

At his nod, she stepped around them.

Collin gave her a few moments to get ahead, and soon followed.

"So, can you tell me why the tea smugglers are important?" Elizabeth asked softly.

He turned to regard her, those wide brown eyes not missing anything. "Again, you are far too observant."

"Or you're just easy to read. Are you sure you are an officer of the war office?" she asked, teasing him.

"The best you'll ever meet."

"I've only met one, so the odds are in your favor," she responded. "My question stands."

Collin gave her a sarcastic expression but answered her question. "While I was searching for our criminal, I found a curious shop and, upon further inspection, discovered workers loading crates."

Elizabeth blinked slowly, then frowned. "You do realize that there is nothing remarkable about a shop loading crates, right? Certainly they do that in London as well…?" She eyed him skeptically.

He sighed impatiently. "Yes, I'm aware, but it's that combined with the shop not selling what it said it sold, and… Never mind. The crux of the story is that after following the wagon with the crates, I saw our bandit helping unload them."

Her eyes widened as she nodded in understanding. "Now that makes more sense."

"And last night Mr. Finch spoke with a man who had found a broken crate filled with tea not too far from Cambridge."

"Therefore, when you put the puzzle pieces together, it all makes sense. And they are using your name to hide their involvement."

"But it begs the question… Why me?" Collin mused.

"Why you, indeed," Elizabeth echoed.

Molly waved a hand subtly, and Collin shared a glance with Elizabeth before stepping ahead quickly.

"If you peek over there…" Molly pointed

discreetly. "There's a lad, and he's lingering by the alleyway there and a cart near a small shop."

Collin turned and saw, his mind spinning with options. "Molly, would you purchase tea from them for me?" He handed her a few shillings.

She nodded, gave a nod to her mistress, and then ambled through the crowd. Collin took Elizabeth's arm once more and slowly meandered after Molly to keep an eye on her and the transaction.

"When you turn away, I'll watch," Elizabeth murmured, meeting his eye for a fleeting moment before regarding a flower salesman.

Collin watched as Molly spoke to the lad, and he nodded. Collin looked down, studying a lily before hazarding a glance up. He noted that Elizabeth glanced away from Molly when he did so.

It was an odd feeling of teamwork. He didn't study the emotion too deeply; his attention was focused on the transaction twenty yards away. Molly was given a little box, and she ambled away, taking a serpentine route toward them.

"We should walk away and avoid suspicion. She'll follow us," Elizabeth said, then tugged him toward the end of the street.

Collin followed, appreciating her understanding of the situation, and started up the other side of the street.

"It appears as if she was successful," Collin said after a moment.

"Yes, but I'm wondering what information you can glean from it," Elizabeth said as she turned to study him.

"I'm not sure, maybe nothing, but at least that will close that door of possible information," he answered.

"I see." She nodded. "Eliminating prospective information sources. That's quite fascinating. I hadn't considered it that way, hmmm." She knit her forehead in deep thought.

"What is that mind of your concocting?" he asked, bemused.

"Wouldn't you like to know," she quipped. "Nothing, honestly. Just considering how that concept can be applied to other areas of life."

"You remind me of your father when you do that," he said.

"I'll take that as a compliment."

"It was certainly meant that way," he replied.

They had rounded a corner, and Collin paused to wait for Molly to catch up.

In a moment, she reached them and held out the box. "Here you go."

Collin accepted it gratefully. "Can you tell me what was said?"

Molly nodded, stepping closer to a building and further out of the street. "I merely asked if they had any of the quality stuff available."

"Did you say 'tea'?" Collin asked.

Molly shook her head. "No."

"Pray, continue."

"They named their price, and I paid it. I'll say this, it's far less than I find in the shop. That's for certain. They gave me a box and said good day. That's it."

"Simple and to the point," Elizabeth stated.

"Indeed. Hmm." Collin opened the box and fingered the loose leaves of the tea, inhaling the sweet and pungent scent. "It's not bad quality." He opened the box further to let Elizabeth see. "The leaves are curled, nonetheless not fractured into a million pieces, and there's not an overabundance of stems. It's better quality than I expected to find."

"I can agree with that," Molly stated.

"So, they are smuggling quality tea, but from where?" Elizabeth asked.

Collin studied the package; it was brown and nondescript. Nothing about it set it apart. "I'm not sure. That would be helpful to find out. However, I have a feeling they don't wish for anyone to know."

"I'm sure."

"Was there anything different about the lad?"

Molly shook her head. "Nothing I could tell."

Collin twisted his lips.

"You said earlier that there was usually a man or two in the background. Did you see anyone or was the lad alone?" Elizabeth asked Molly.

"I saw one man. He was leaning against the wall

and not paying much attention, but that probably meant he was listening to every word. I eyed him for a second, but his cap covered his face in shadow so I couldn't see anything."

"Just one man?" Elizabeth asked.

Collin glanced to her, curious why she was pressing that detail.

"Yes. One," Molly answered.

"But before, there were two—every time or just occasionally?"

"I–I'm not sure, Miss Essex. My apologies."

"It's of no consequence. I was merely trying to consider if perhaps they always had two men watching and now there was one, they are feeling less threatened by discovery, or they have so many more places to sell that they are spread thin. Like you said, Lord Penderdale, it's the process of eliminating possible information."

Collin smiled. "Well done, Miss Essex. I'm impressed."

"Another compliment? I'm not sure I quite know what to think," she teased.

"I'll try to insult you at least three more times to make up for it," Collin replied, earning a playful glare.

"Good, wouldn't want to think you appreciated intelligence in a woman. The world would have turned on its ear."

"Ah, and here is where I get to insult you," he

scolded. "First, will you honor me with your arm, and I'll escort you back home?"

"If I must." She took his arm, watching as Molly waited a moment, then followed behind.

Collin regarded her. "I'm going to tell you a secret, but you must promise not to tell a soul."

Elizabeth tipped her chin. "Another secret? I'm not sure I wish to have so many in my possession."

"I think this secret will serve you well and may possibly change the way you perceive some things, including me," he said convincingly.

"With potential like that, how could I refuse? Very well, I accept your terms and will not break confidence."

"Thank you," Collin said, then paused, not sure how best to explain. He wanted her to know that of all the things that did irritate him about her, her intelligence and determination to better her mind were not among them. In fact, he deeply respected that about her.

He proceeded cautiously. "As you know, I am the eighth Earl of Penderdale. I was responsible for my sister's education and her come-out into society and eventually had to approve her match."

"Yes, I would deduce those things," Elizabeth replied cautiously. "You've mentioned your sister, and I know you have a duke for a brother-in-law."

He nodded. "What you don't know is that my work…is of a sensitive nature." He left it at that.

"You are involved with the War Office, aren't you?" she asked.

He frowned. "Am I that obvious? I clearly need to polish up my skills."

"Deductive reasoning. I do love Aristotle's methods."

He sighed. "While I appreciate your intelligence, I will admit it's sometimes annoyingly humbling."

She beamed. "I believe that is the nicest thing anyone has ever said to me."

He frowned. "You clearly need to get out more often if that is the case. But I digress."

She waved for him to continue.

"My sister is a student of graphology."

She halted in her steps and turned to him. "What?"

He watched her, enjoying the expression that flickered across her face and echoed in her eyes. "You're a very smart person. You heard me, and you can make your deductions from there." Collin watched as her brows knit, and he could only assume she was piecing together all the implications. Graphology was the study of handwriting and has been used to determine forgeries, specifically during wartime. Collin's sister, Joan, worked for the War Office as well. It wasn't common for a woman to be involved in such matters, but Joan was exceptionally talented, and Collin had made certain her identity was protected. Even her betrothed didn't know until after the match was approved and Collin was certain it wouldn't be an issue between them.

Elizabeth frowned, casting her eyes down, and then regarded him once more. "Perhaps I have... misjudged you."

"Sweeter words have never been spoken." He sighed. "Would you say them again? I swear it's like honey in my ears."

"No, but I am shifting my opinion of you. Your sister... You allowed your sister to help at the—"

"Shh. That's enough. You get the gist of it. She's a very valuable asset, prolifically talented and more stubborn than you. If you ever meet, the world will shudder in fear, of that I'm certain," Collin said in a serious tone, but he grinned at the thought. Yes, Joan and Elizabeth wouldn't run out of words quickly. Rather, he and Rowles would suffer the endlessness of that conversation.

"Thank you," Elizabeth said after a moment. "For trusting me with that information. It... Well, frankly it surprises me greatly."

"I enjoy keeping you on your toes, and heaven knows how many times you've returned the favor. I feel it's on far more equal footing now." He grinned at her, watching as she reacted to his words with a faint blush.

How he loved watching the color spread over her fair skin, knowing he was the one who had caused it. He had been correct in his earlier thought; this was a far-too-tempting situation.

But he had no regrets.

At least not today.

Fifteen

The secret of being a bore is to tell everything.

—Voltaire, *Seven Discourses in Verse on Man*

ELIZABETH WAS STILL MUSING ON THE DICHOT-
omy that was the Earl of Penderdale. He had
scolded her for her presence at the college, questioned her motives, and for all intents and purposes,
insulted her intelligence. Nonetheless, she wondered
if maybe she'd misunderstood half of those actions.

Who let their sister study graphology and put
it to use for king and country? Apparently Lord
Penderdale, and she was still shocked. As a student
of philosophy and human nature, Elizabeth prided
herself on sorting out people quickly, and she was
rarely surprised by them.

Not today. Today, she was properly humbled in
her assessment since many of the assumptions she'd
made regarding the earl were clearly mistaken. If he
disapproved of intelligence in women, he'd never
have let his sister do what she did. And though
Elizabeth would have sworn he considered himself her superior, since he was a man, he'd shocked

her further by stating that they were on more equal footing.

She'd fought most of her youth and adult life to find equal footing with anyone. It was always the same. Aside from Patricia, Elizabeth had always felt a step down and out of order from everyone else, as if she were constantly trying to prove herself, over and over.

Collin hadn't realized it, but he'd given her a gift in those words, even if he hadn't meant them exactly as she'd interpreted them. He had bid her good afternoon once they'd returned to her house. He'd kissed the air above her wrist, his cool breath along her skin making her shiver with a delicious feeling. It was dangerous ground, yet she kept willingly walking on it.

She wondered if after he left, he went to find Mr. Finch. Elizabeth chose a chair next to the low-burning fire in the room and sat, releasing a pent-up breath at the thought of Mr. Finch.

The truth was, she wanted to feel something for him. It would be easy, effortless, and could be done without risking her heart. But those were all the wrong reasons and a disservice to him. She'd not toy with his heart or leave him in suspense. She needed to talk to him, and soon, as much as she wished to avoid it. The last thing she wanted was to refuse her best friend's brother, but what other option did she have? Lie to him? No, he deserved better than that.

She'd check the honey's progress, read a little, and, contrary to what she'd said to Collin, she would go to visit Patricia, hoping to find a moment to talk with Mr. Finch in the process.

Drat. It was going to be difficult to spend time over there after this, she mused. Awkward, at best. But such was the price, and the sooner she addressed the situation, the sooner they could all move past it.

Elizabeth rose and took the stairs to the lowest floor where the kitchens were located. The scent of bread baking and the soft hum of the cook's and scullery maid's voices gave a welcome, homey feeling. She entered and greeted the women, her attention turning to the frame of honey in the bucket.

The golden liquid was settling down in the bottom, so it was time to suspend the frame over the bucket to remove the bottom cells, still full of honey. She laid a broken broom handle across the bucket, then threaded string through the honeycomb so it would hover over the bucket. The bottom cells of the comb began to trail into the bucket. Elizabeth nodded at her handiwork.

Next she lifted out the second comb of honey she'd brought and repeated the process of slicing open the cells with the sharp knife and allowing the honey to flow into the same bucket, now nearly half-full. She'd need to suspend the second frame this evening, but for now, it would suffice.

"Molly told us you'd given her leave to see about the tea," the cook said to Elizabeth. "We were curious and brewed some. It's not bad, surprisingly." She lifted her cup.

Tea was precious and quite expensive. It was a treat for the cook to have freshly brewed leaves that hadn't already been brewed once or twice.

"It appeared to be of good quality, so I'm not surprised," Elizabeth answered.

"If I weren't concerned about being caught, I'd happily buy it myself, but it isn't worth the trouble. I'll take the leavings," the cook said.

"Indeed, I agree," Elizabeth stated. "Enjoy your tea." She quit the kitchens and went back to her room, checking over her dress for smudges of honey. She considered changing, but the dress was none worse for wear. She made her way to the small library, picked up a copy of the latest gothic novel, a guilty pleasure she didn't often indulge, and in rather unladylike fashion flopped into a chaise.

Several chapters later, she heard the clock chime. With a reluctant heart she closed the book and set it to the side. It would nearly be time for her father to return, and then she'd visit Patricia.

No sooner had she thought of her father than the door opened and she heard his familiar voice. She made her way into the hall to greet him.

"Hello, Papa." She smiled, then halted at the expression he gave her. His gray eyes were sad, his usually perfect posture stooped. "What's wrong, what happened?" she asked, searching him over, determined to see if there were any injuries, praying it was news and not something physically wrong with him.

She could survive bad news.

She couldn't lose another parent; she'd not recover from that.

Her father set his hat on a hook and regarded her with a long breath. "Would you accompany me to the study?"

Elizabeth nodded, not trusting her voice. Following his familiar form, she waited until he sat, then took a seat across from him, watching his every move. "Papa, please, tell me what's wrong. Did something happen at the college?"

"Elizabeth, my dear…" He paused, then leaned forward, resting his elbows on his knees. "There was a decision reached, and I'm afraid there's nothing I can do to alter it."

"What decision?" Her heart was beating a painful rhythm as she waited.

Her father continued. "Cambridge is closing its doors to you."

She blinked, slid back in her chair. She'd always known it was a possibility. No, that wasn't fair. She'd known it was a probability, she corrected herself. It was bound to happen, and she'd known she couldn't stay there forever, doing her best to blend in and be invisible. However, a part of her heart had hoped that she would overcome the odds. Apparently not.

"I...understand, Papa. It was an unconventional situation at best, and I'm of an age where—"

"I tried to sway them, dear. But...the truth is, I worry about you." Her father closed his eyes. "You study more than most of my students. And it pains me to know that if you were a lad, you'd be welcome. It's unfair, I know. And yet—" He paused.

"It isn't fair, Papa. But I knew that, and I certainly know that now. It's unfortunate and frustrating. However, I can either let that destroy what I have and all I've learned, or I can use what I've been given to move on. Change is inevitable, and how we progress through it is vital, is it not?"

He nodded. "It is, and I want more for you than what you have, my dear. At the college, you're collecting bread crumbs, but you deserve the whole loaf of bread."

"Food metaphors are my favorite," she said, trying to ease her father's distress. She needed to be honest. "It's been difficult, and as much as I tried to be invisible and keep to the dark corners of the library or your office, I think I'm ready for more. I just wish I knew what 'more' was." She hitched a shoulder.

"You are so much like your mother," he said, a sad smile lifting his lips. "She never lost her thirst for knowledge, and when we traveled, she was relentlessly searching for new ideas and furthering her education."

"I miss her," Elizabeth stated softly.

"As do I, and she'd be very proud of you, my dear. Unconventional as the past years have been, I agree with you. It's time to look ahead. What that will be, I'm not sure, but life has a way of sorting it all out for us," her father finished gently.

"I'll certainly have more time to think about it," Elizabeth said dryly. "How ever will you complete all your additional research if I'm not there to assist you?"

"They delegated a student to be my assistant, but we both know that poor lad won't hold a candle to your insight." He smiled warmly.

Elizabeth's lips bent into a grin. "True." She paused before continuing. "Thank you, Papa." A sigh slipped out. "I'm thankful I was able to be there to assist you. Regardless of whether I spent the majority of my time in your office," she said.

Her father nodded, then stood. "Well, did you visit your bees?"

Elizabeth was thankful for the shift in topic and nodded. "Indeed, and we've replenished our honey stores."

"Good, I'm glad you had a good productive day."

Elizabeth thought about just how productive it had been and smiled to herself. "I'll go and ready myself for supper."

"Very well, my dear. I'll see you in a little bit."

Elizabeth went to her room and closed the door, needing a few moments to herself. It wasn't surprising, this chain of events. But that didn't mean it was welcome or that it didn't frustrate her. That they had made the decision apart from her father's input rubbed her wrong.

It wasn't fair.

However, she couldn't change it. Hiding in her father's study, trying to be invisible, and drawing as little attention as possible to herself was not enough, but if it was, did she want to keep living like that? No. She'd already reached that decision earlier… Odd how the timing had worked out. She sifted through her feelings, naming them to herself, and then grieved the change. As much as leaving hurt, it was time for something new. One thing was certain: sometimes change forced the decisions a person didn't want to make, making them for him or her.

This was certainly the case, and she couldn't help but wonder what would be next. *Small steps*, she told herself. And she knew the next one: she needed to visit Patricia and talk with her brother.

Sixteen

Doubt is not a pleasant condition, but certainty is an absurd one.

—Voltaire, Letter to Frederick William,
Prince of Prussia, November 28, 1770

"DID YOU KNOW ABOUT THE CART SELLING TEA on the way to the market street?" Collin asked Michael. They had hired a hack to take them to the place where Collin had seen the crates being unloaded by the man with the black eye.

Michael frowned. "I can ask my sister, but I don't usually purchase the sundry items for the house."

"Well, it would collaborate with our friend's story from the pub, if the tea was indeed in the crates and being sold in a clandestine manner."

Michael nodded. "I suppose we'll soon find out."

"Or so I hope," Collin added.

The hack rolled to a stop at the block just ahead of the place Collin remembered. He stepped down and paid the driver, waiting for Michael.

"How do you think we should approach this?" he asked.

Michael twisted his lips. "Show me where we're going first, and I'll try to think of the best way."

Collin nodded in the direction they should walk and strode forward.

"How did you hear about the tea sales?" Michael asked.

Collin answered quickly, "A servant."

Michael nodded in understanding.

Half-truths continued coming from Collin's lips as he kept Michael from understanding how much time he'd been spending in Elizabeth's company. Worse, he didn't want him to know; he liked that they had their own secrets. As much as it terrified him to admit, the temptation of Elizabeth was turning into an attachment that wasn't easily ignored. He didn't have time for this, nor did he have the inclination to search for a wife.

And Elizabeth wasn't a dalliance or someone with whom to pass the time. She deserved more, and shockingly, he wanted to be the man she honored with her attentions.

He cast a sidelong glance at Michael. Jealousy burned in his chest at the thought of his friend's pursuit of her. It was sobering because he'd never had to compete for a woman's attentions.

Perhaps he'd never met one worth the effort.

Until now.

"Just there." Collin mustered his attention to focus on the job at hand and paused as he came to the beginning of the street that would lead them to where an empty wagon waited.

"Doesn't appear as if anyone's around, let's go take a peek," Michael suggested.

Collin followed.

The wagon was empty, save for a few curled brown pieces of debris. Collin reached down over the side and pinched a piece in his fingers, then smelled.

"Tea," he whispered to Michael.

Michael agreed. "Indeed."

"Can I help you?"

Collin took a deep breath, met Michael's eyes, and then turned, his attention focused on the man with the black eye who had spoken. "Ah, yes, thank you." Collin thought quickly, trying to come up with a good reason why they were searching the wagon and also trying to figure out a way to ferret out information. "I'm interested—"

"The wagon isn't for sale," the man answered, then tightened his eyes as he studied Collin.

Before the other man could recognize him, Collin took action. He lunged forward, shoving the man at the shoulder and using his foot to trip him as he turned him, forcing him to face the brick wall as Collin twisted his right hand behind his back, leaning against him. The man's head made a thud as he hit the brick. Groaning, he fought against Collin's hold.

Michael leaned against the brick wall, facing the man. "We've been searching for you," he said with a smile.

"You'll not get a word—"

Collin lifted the man's arm higher, earning another groan of pain. "You see, you have something that belongs to me."

Michael nodded. "You'd better talk."

"I didn't take anything. You've got the wrong man—"

"My name," Collin ground out. "And I want to know why."

The man stopped struggling, as if surprised at Collin's words. "Name?"

"Did he stutter?" Michael asked coldly.

"Why are you using the name of a peer to smuggle tea?" Collin asked, pulling the man back from the wall, then slamming him into it again. "Why?"

Before the man could answer, the door to the left of them opened, and a man twice as broad and a head taller than Collin stepped out, his eyes taking on a flinty expression when he noticed what was transpiring.

The man in Collin's grip started chuckling. "Olsen!"

Olsen stepped forward. "What's going on?" His voice grated, as if issuing a warning.

Michael took a step back, but Collin held tight to the man in his grip.

"Your friend was just informing us why you're using the name of a peer to smuggle tea. Care to join our little party? There's room for more," Collin said with bravado.

Olsen narrowed his eyes. "There's no tea, and as for the names, that's not my business, nor is it yours." He crossed his beefy arms. "Let him go."

"No," Collin replied. "Unless this blackguard is the Earl of Penderdale, I think I have some unfinished business with him."

"Earl of Penderdale?" the man asked. "You're pissed about that? It's just a name on the list—"

"Shut up, Ray," Olsen cut him off.

Ray promptly obeyed.

"What list?" Collin asked.

"There's no list, no tea, but there will be a missing person if you don't release Ray," Olsen threatened.

Collin pressed Ray further into the brick.

"Frank, Daniel," Olsen called out, and two other men stepped into the street, each quickly assessing the situation.

Properly outnumbered, Collin slowly released Ray, watching as Michael took a few steps farther back.

The moment Ray was free, he turned and swung a fist at Collin. Collin blocked the blow and sent Ray reeling with a facer. But before he could reposition his fists, Olsen was on the defensive, sending a right hook directly to Collin's eye.

Stars erupted in Collin's vision as he staggered

back from the impact. Michael's hands steadied his shoulders as he scrambled for his footing. Blinking, he barely had time to dodge the next swing. He landed a few good jabs into Olsen's stomach, doubling the man over, but it wasn't enough. Michael was tugging on his shoulder to retreat, the movement shifting him at the same moment Olsen swung at his jaw, and the blow glanced off the bone rather than hit it fully. Collin stepped back, his eye swelling shut and the salty taste of blood in his mouth. He retreated, watching the men assist Ray and disappear into the building. Olsen watched them until Michael pulled him around the corner.

His face hurt like the devil. That facer had sent him reeling. Not an easy thing, that. He was proud of the fact he could hold his own in a fight, but when his opponent was a good three stone larger, the odds were somewhat less in his favor.

"Did you hear all that?" Collin asked as Michael helped him.

"Aye, and you lost the fight, in case you didn't notice." Michael gave a dry, humorless laugh. "At least we got away."

"Nevertheless, I've got this." Collin held out a rumpled sheet of parchment he'd taken when he spun the man toward the brick wall. "I'm not sure it's important, but usually men put their most protected items in their inner coat pocket, so when the opportunity came, I pickpocketed him."

"And got a right hook in return. But from his friend, so I suppose that's not the same thing," Michael grumbled, but he took the parchment and unfolded it. His expression registered surprise as he read through it. "Well, this may have been worth ruining your pretty face for."

He held out the paper. Squinting, Collin used his good eye and read a list of names, including his own. "I know these people..." Collin frowned. They were all peers of the realm, all men and some women, who were usually in some ballroom in London or rusticating in the country in the off-season.

"It's a criminal conspiracy, using the names of peers. But why?" Michael asked. "What good does it do? Use any different name, and it would have the same effect, don't you think?"

Collin's head throbbed and he could feel his eye swelling further. "I genuinely can't think very clearly right now."

Michael regarded him. "Understood. Let's get you back and cleaned up."

Collin dusted off his coat and followed his friend down the dark street. Every step ached, the movement sending a dull throb to his head. He'd not been hit like that since he had taken up boxing four years ago and missed a block. He'd blacked out with that one, and his sister had had some choice words when she found out. He could only imagine what she'd say if she could see him now.

It was certainly for the best that she was far away in London.

They rounded the corner and Collin spat out some lingering blood, wiping his face with an already bloody handkerchief. He must appear a mess, and suddenly it made sense why Michael was leading him through several back alleys to get to his house, as if trying to avoid as many people as possible. Collin ducked his head, keeping as much of his face from view as he could.

"Wait here," Michael said before turning the final corner, likely making sure the street was at least mostly clear of people. After a minute, he waved Collin forward. "Come."

Collin hustled from the street and into Michael's house, his head pounding at the same pace as his heartbeat.

"Good Lord." Patricia's voice brought his attention up from the floor, but it was Elizabeth's face that caught his attention. He was surprised to see her. Hadn't she said that her plans didn't include visiting the Finches? What had changed her mind? Questions pelted him, and a low burn of jealousy distracted him from the pain in his eye. Was she visiting to see Michael? Accept his suit? He studied her with his good eye. Surprise, concern, and then anger flashed across her features in rapid succession.

"Tell me the other fellow is worse off!" she exclaimed, her hands holding tightly to her skirts.

"Fellows, plural," Collin stated, opening and closing his jaw to stretch the tense muscle.

"And they don't look worse," Michael added as he walked into the room. "Pat, would you get some water and rags for Lord Penderdale?"

Patricia nodded once but didn't move. Collin noted the way her attention first locked on Elizabeth and then shifted to him.

He turned his attention back to Elizabeth, watching as she continued to study him, not sending her attention to Michael as he'd expected. Her eyes darkened with irritation. "You took on several men?"

Collin shrugged. "I did what needed to be done."

Elizabeth arched a brow, then turned to Patricia. "I'll help you get the supplies," she said, her eyes grazing over him as if categorizing his injury. "I know what to do." She and Patricia disappeared into the back room.

"I think I'd rather face that monster of a man again than her." Collin turned to Michael and smirked, but the smile quickly turned to a wince as his eye stung with the movement.

Michael grinned widely enough for both of them at Collin's comment. "Agreed."

"Whatever happened, surely there is a story," Patricia said as she followed Elizabeth back into the room. She carried a basin, while Elizabeth held a pitcher and some rags.

"Do you have any of my honey?" Elizabeth asked over her shoulder as she put her burden on the table.

"Honey? Yes." Patricia darted back down the hall and returned after a moment. "Here." She deposited the small jar beside the rags.

Elizabeth sorted through the items and glanced up at Collin, her expression brooking no argument as she addressed him. "You, sit." She pointed to him and then a chair.

Collin stiffly walked over and sat, his body relaxing. Still, his chest tightened with tension from what he could see of Elizabeth's face with his one eye. The other had swollen fully shut.

She dipped a rag into the basin of water and wrung it out, then leaned toward him. "So, you didn't win the fight, I take it," she whispered, and with a gentler touch than he expected, she started to clean the area around his eye. The scent of beeswax and lemon that he associated with her enveloped him. Having her this close was almost worth the pain.

He considered her question, and as much as he wanted to say yes, he answered honestly. "No."

"Pity. Was it at least worth destroying your face?" she asked. He watched her lips move with each word.

"Yes." He wanted to add further information, but given that neither Michael nor Patricia were privy to how familiar Elizabeth was with what was going on, he chose to stay silent.

She wrung out the rag and touched his chin with her other hand, tilting it to the side. She wiped along his jawline, the movement casting a spell over him. She paused with the rag beside his mouth, her gaze flicking up, meeting his. She quickly glanced away, but not before he saw her swallow forcibly, and she continued wiping away the dried blood. The pain forgotten, he was distracted by her perfectly bowed lips and the way her lashes framed her cheeks when she glanced down.

She wrung out the rag once more and set it aside, picking up a clean one. Her eyes met his again, and she wet the rag, then reached forward and pressed it directly on his eye.

He jumped with the pressure she used, expecting a gentle touch. "Good Lord, Elizabeth!"

There was no apology forthcoming; she simply pressed marginally harder. "Remember that there are natural consequences, Collin. You should have learned by now to pick your battles, and besides, this area is still bleeding. You need pressure. Afterward, I'll apply honey. It will help guard against infection," she answered succinctly as she removed the rag from his eye. He blinked; a blurry spot was visible through the thin slit of his puffy eye.

"I did pick my battle, and I'd pick it again." He didn't back down. "I'm not one of your students to correct."

"You're right. If I had taught you, you'd have

made better choices," she returned. "Heavens above, Collin, you could have been killed. Do you understand this? Clearly not." She tossed the rag on the table. "This is your skull, your cranium. If you get a bone fracture just at this weak point"— she pressed not so gently against his eye socket— "you can break a piece off that will pierce into your brain. There was a study done—"

"Hang the study, Elizabeth. I've been hit plenty of times—"

"All the more reason to avoid it!"

"Elizabeth?"

Patricia's voice interrupted Collin's attempt to rebut Elizabeth's argument, and both he and Elizabeth froze. Understanding washed over him. His temper had removed his rational thought, and they had been having a very intimate fight, publicly. He reviewed the words exchanged, knowing the specific word that would have spoken volumes to both Patricia and Michael, but especially Michael.

Elizabeth's name.

As he thought of her name, Elizabeth glanced to him, her expression likely a reflection of his own, then to Patricia. "Yes?"

"I… That is… Michael left." She turned to the door.

Collin closed his eyes, this time feeling the pain was a welcome punishment, but not nearly enough. He needed to talk to Michael, and it was a conversation that was going to be too little and too late.

"Excuse me." Collin stood, and Elizabeth stepped back, her eyes wide.

"Should I…" Elizabeth started.

"Let me talk to him first," Collin answered. "Please excuse me, ladies." He bowed and went to find his colleague who had become a friend.

Collin cautiously stepped out in front of the house. If Michael bloodied up his other eye, it wouldn't be undeserved, but that didn't mean he wanted it. It took a second longer to scan the street with one good eye, but he found Michael's form leaning against a stone wall in an alley not a few yards from the door. He was smoking a cheroot and didn't glance toward Collin as he approached.

"How long?" Michael asked, blowing out a puff of smoke, finally regarding Collin.

Collin didn't ask for clarification, just answered. His friend deserved that much. "Not as long as you would think. It started when she was knocked flat by the man with the black eye we were searching for."

Michael's eyes widened. "That was her? You said it was some woman."

"She asked me not to tell you," Collin answered. "She wanted to protect you from feeling guilty since you didn't walk her all the way home because you were meeting me."

Michael nodded. "That's why you were keen on splitting up while we searched."

"Yes," Collin replied.

"Do you... Are you..." Michael tossed his cheroot and regarded Collin for a long moment before asking. "What are your intentions?"

At this, Collin couldn't hold back a grin. "It's not an amusing question," he stated. "It's that I have no say in the answer."

Michael frowned. "What is that supposed to mean?"

Collin let out a long sigh and leaned against the wall with his friend, his body beginning to ache once more. "It means I don't have a choice. I mean I do, but from the first moment I met her, I cannot control my reactions. It's maddening, and at the same time, I don't want it any different. My intentions have never been dishonorable, but I've not given them much consideration since they seemed to run off without my consent."

"So, you haven't spoken to her about it?" Michael questioned.

"No. I...have not."

"Idiot," Michael muttered. "I'd have walked on the water if she'd given me leave to use her Christian name. You think that's nothing, Collin? I've known her for four years, and not once have I done anything but whisper her name to myself, never used it aloud. And yet I watch you two carry on, using each other's given names as if you're bloody betrothed, and you have the bollox to tell me you haven't asked to court her, haven't spoken to her father?" He shoved away from the wall. "I should give you another eye to match the first for being so stupid."

Collin frowned, glancing to the cobbled street. "She deserves better than someone like me."

"I doubt you can convince her to let you make her choices for her," Michael quipped.

At that, Collin barked a laugh. "Well said."

"And she'd likely give you a tongue-lashing for thinking it."

"Also true."

Michael hesitated. "I wish you had told me. It makes a man feel like a fool, Collin. You knew I had my heart set on her, and you didn't give me a warning you were fighting for her too."

"Because I wasn't fighting for her, Michael. I was fighting against her and didn't realize what was happening until it was too late," he answered honestly.

Michael took a deep breath. "I should have known, should have seen it comin'. That first time you two were here, that fight…" He blew out a breath. "That should have been my writing on the wall."

"It wasn't for me, and I'd bet it wasn't for her either. I think she would have cheerfully watched me retreat to London, never to be seen or heard from again." He paused. "Sometimes I still think that." He chuckled.

Michael gave a small, sad smile. "It's a bit of a disaster, isn't it? But thankfully, it's not much of my mine. It's all yours."

"Apparently I collect them," Collin replied, thinking of the mess over his name, the mess over others' names, and the mess he'd made with his friend. Not to mention the mess he was constantly making with Elizabeth.

"You have quite the work ahead, but I think you're equal to the task. Or not. Regardless, here's your warning, one you should have given me." Michael paused. "If you break her heart, I'll break your face and then keep her heart for myself. Understood?"

Collin's respect for the man grew as he nodded. "Agreed."

Seventeen

Love truth, but pardon error.

—Voltaire, *Seven Discourses in Verse on Man*

ELIZABETH WATCHED COLLIN'S RETREATING back as he disappeared out the door. Slowly, she turned to face Patricia, whose stare had been burning through her.

"Explain." Patricia sat and leaned across the table, her eyes sparking with interest.

"There's not a lot to explain—" Elizabeth began.

"I don't believe you. He called you by your Christian name, easily, like he's done it a million times…" Her eyes widened. "Are you betrothed? Do you have a secret romance—?"

Elizabeth gasped. "No, no." She waved her hands. "We're…" She wasn't sure how to explain it. They weren't exactly friends, or enemies, and certainly not lovers, but they were…something. Something new that she'd never experienced, however she craved and recognized and needed it.

Patricia leaned forward more, as if the movement would coax the words from her friend. "You're…"

"Complicated," Elizabeth answered.

Patricia blew out a sigh. "That was not helpful."

"It's true. I…Lord Penderdale and I…have not tried to kill each other yet, which is a success."

"This is decidedly less romantic than I was expecting," Patricia stated flatly. "Do you think Michael gave him another black eye?" she mused.

"Would he?" Elizabeth turned in her chair to study the door, as if it would hold the answer.

"Maybe, I don't know. He's not been shy about his interest in you. But you're one to be direct, yet still kind, so for you to remain his friend is answer enough for me. I'm just not sure it is enough for him."

"Your brother made his intentions known, and I am visiting today in hopes of talking to him. I…I'm unable to return his sentiments." She sighed. "It's a little late now, I'd assume. I feel terrible. My father always said my temper would be my downfall. It seems he was right."

Patricia winced. "It's a bit of a mess, is it not?"

Elizabeth turned back to her friend. "When did your brother leave?"

Patricia traced the grain of the wood table with her finger. "Well, when you called Lord Penderdale by his Christian name. I wasn't sure if it was a mistake. Your temper can be impressive," she clarified. "But when he called you 'Elizabeth,' it was clear it wasn't a slip of the tongue. I glanced at Michael then. His expression clouded over quickly, and then when you two continued fighting, forgetting both of us were present, he left."

"I see." Elizabeth took a deep breath. "I need to apologize to him. I may not have encouraged him, but I didn't discourage his affection either, and that was...weak of me."

"He'll forgive you."

"I hope so, but it's still important to ask and be humble about it. I'm sure what just happened hurt him, and that wasn't right."

Patricia nodded, then tipped her chin. "I wonder what they are talking about. I rather expected it to be an abrupt conversation."

Elizabeth glanced to the door once more. "Heaven only knows."

"Other than you as the main topic, you mean?" Patricia asked. "But in all seriousness, he hasn't asked to court you? Lord Penderdale?"

Elizabeth shook her heard. "No, nothing like that."

"Odd," Patricia mused, tapping her chin.

"Why?"

"Because it's clear he's mad for you. I wonder what's holding him back."

Elizabeth didn't answer. She was certainly attracted to him, and they sparked like flint and steel whenever they were in close contact, but that wasn't enough, was it?

"He's not mad for me," Elizabeth whispered, keeping an eye on the door. The last thing she wanted was for the two men to overhear the conversation.

"Believe what you want, but I have the distinct feeling if you applied the same principles you spoke of the last time we were in class, you'd find that your assumptions are based on emotion and not fact," Patricia surmised.

Elizabeth regarded her, blinking in surprise. "I'm impressed with your persuasive argument. Well done. It's annoyingly correct, but as your teacher, I appreciate that the lessons I've taught have certainly stuck with you."

"So, have you considered that?" Patricia pressed.

Elizabeth took a deep breath through her nose. "I have, in a way. I... It's hard to work through."

"You mean you're afraid," Patricia issued the words as a challenge.

Elizabeth straightened. "I'm not afraid."

"You are. You don't want to inspect your emotions too closely and find that you can't rationalize them with logic. Emotions involve hope, and hope is based on possible events, which means you can't control them, and you, my friend, like control," Patricia finished, casting Elizabeth a meaningful stare.

Elizabeth blinked, her brows knitting together. "I—"

The door opened, and Mr. Finch and Lord

Penderdale walked into the house. Elizabeth halted her words and watched, carefully considering what step she should take next. She needed to speak with Michael. That was only fair, but was now the time? Did he want to speak with her? Had she destroyed the friendship beyond repair? A million thoughts tumbled through her mind as she studied the two men.

As she tried to keep her attention on Michael, her eyes kept darting to Lord Penderdale, to Collin. The blood in the corner of his lip was nearly gone, but there was still some work to be done to his eye, for it was swollen shut again.

"Miss Essex, would you give me a moment of your time?" Michael asked, settling the dilemma for her.

She nodded and followed him out the door. He paused on the lowest step of the stoop. Looking up, he gave her a sad smile.

Her heart broke at the sight, knowing she was the cause and not knowing how to fix it, not when giving him what he wanted would force her to lie to him and herself.

"Mr. Finch, I—" she began and then sighed. "I'm sorry." She peeked down to her shoes, then forced her eyes up; he deserved eye contact. "I'm sorry I can't return the sentiments you generously offered," she said softly. "And I apologize further for the earlier display and wish for you to know that I never meant to cause you harm, but I did, and for that I'm truly sorry," she finished, the words tumbling out of her.

Mr. Finch glanced down at his own boots, then nodded, lifting his eyes. "I appreciate your honesty, but there's no need for an apology. You're entitled to your own emotions, Miss Essex, and you do me honor by not toying with mine."

"I would never," Elizabeth asserted.

"I know," Mr. Finch answered, and then took a deep breath. "Well, now that we've finished that…" He gestured back to the house.

Elizabeth nodded and began to turn but paused. "Thank you."

He gave another sad smile and opened the door for her to proceed into the house.

Collin was sitting in the chair, a rag pressed firmly against his eye as Patricia cleaned up the remaining bloody ones.

Elizabeth sighed, then stepped forward to Collin. "May I?" she asked, holding out her hand for the rag.

Collin removed it from his eye and slowly handed it over.

"Thank you." She dipped it back in the water, wrung it out, and then cleaned up the remaining dried blood. Her hands buzzed at the contact with his skin as she traced along the corner of his eye. Her eyes fixed on anywhere but meeting his, though she felt his attention locked on her face.

Next, she set the rag aside and lifted the jar of honey. Removing the lid, she used her fingers to gently smooth the sticky liquid along the cut next to his eye, careful to keep it safely away from his lashes. She wasn't sure if honey stung if it got in the eyes, but she didn't want to test that question this evening.

After that, she turned to the cut beside his lip. It wasn't deep, but still would benefit from some attention. She dipped a clean finger into the honey jar and turned her attention to his lips. Gently, she dabbed the honey along his cut, her fingers brushing against his light stubble. The small prick of it sent gooseflesh up her arm. His lips were faintly swollen, but with no further injury, and she struggled to force her scrutiny from them.

"Thank you," he whispered.

She flicked her gaze upward to his eyes, regretting it the moment she did. It was impossible to tear her eyes away; she was locked, trapped, and truly not fighting it at all as she drank in his expression. Even with one good eye, he was handsome.

She forced her mind to work and decided that wit would be her salvation. "Purple is a good color for you."

Collin's eye crinkled in amusement, but then he winced. "I think I'll have the guise of a dashing pirate."

"Dashing is questionable, but pirate? Certainly." Elizabeth stood and closed the honey jar, then set the rags aside.

"I'm dashing on a bad day. As a roguish pirate, I'd be devastating," he said, playing along.

Elizabeth eyed him dryly. "Hmmm, after a sound thrashing you're still full of yourself."

Collin laughed at that. "This was not a sound thrashing. It was merely a short fight."

"One you lost."

"One I walked away from," he countered.

"Actually, it was one I dragged you away from, if we're being honest," Michael chimed in. "And if you'd have stayed and received that sound thrashing, we'd be sending for a doctor, and he'd be a far sight worse than the lovely lady who attended you."

Collin turned his head fully and used his good eye to regard Michael. "It wasn't that bad."

"We clearly have different definitions," Michael replied wryly.

Elizabeth smiled to herself, thankful for the normal dynamic between them. Maybe, somehow, it would all work out.

Elizabeth regarded Collin once more. "Keep applying honey. It will help it heal."

"Yes, Miss Essex."

"And don't patronize me," she replied.

"I wouldn't dream of it," he stated in a bland tone.

"Don't lie either. I'm sure you already have enough sins to account for, so why add to them?" she challenged.

He quirked a brow, the effect decidedly awkward and not at all how he likely intended it to appear.

Elizabeth bit back a giggle. "You truly shouldn't try to appear condescending. The effect is exactly the opposite."

"Delightful." Collin groaned, then stood. "Well, on that lovely disappointment, I'm going to find my way home."

Elizabeth watched as he closed his eyes, as if waiting for the throbbing to subside. She wanted to invite him to her house, have her father inspect him, but she also didn't want to say anything in front of Patricia and Michael. Her father intended to walk her home and should arrive shortly, so she debated on how to postpone Lord Penderdale's departure for a few moments.

She followed him to the door. "Lord Penderdale," she began, but there was a knock on the door, and she paused, stepping back as Michael made his way past them to open it.

"Ah, Professor Essex," Mr. Finch greeted him.

Elizabeth released some of the tension in her shoulders. "Papa, you know Lord Penderdale." She stepped forward, then gestured to the side where Lord Penderdale waited to leave.

Her father quickly assessed Lord Penderdale and, as Elizabeth had hoped, he took action. "You look terrible. You can tell me what happened on the way to my house. I'll brook no argument."

He held up a hand as Lord Penderdale started to speak.

Mr. Finch bit back a grin, and Elizabeth noticed how his attention moved between her father and Lord Penderdale, likely thankful he wasn't in the same predicament.

"Come with me." Her father waved her and Collin forward, shooting a warning look at Lord Penderdale before he followed behind.

"We'll hire a hack. It's not far, but you don't appear as if you should be walking any of it," her father mumbled in a scolding manner.

"Professor Essex, while I appreciate—"

"Then appreciate it and do not argue about it," her father cut in.

"If I ever wondered from where you inherited your wit, I now know," Lord Penderdale said to Elizabeth as her father waved down a hack.

"Try to win an argument with him. I dare you," Elizabeth returned, grinning.

"I've had enough battles for tonight, thank you," Collin replied, wincing.

Elizabeth chuckled. "And have you won any of them?" she asked.

He regarded her speculatively, his one clear eye studying her. "Not yet, but I'm hopeful."

Something about his expression had her skin tingling, and she glanced away, overwhelmed by shyness.

"Here we go." Her father stepped into the hack

after giving the driver directions and Elizabeth followed, sitting beside her father. Collin took the seat across from them. He released a heavy sigh.

Her father studied Collin but didn't ask any questions as they were driven toward home. Collin didn't speak either, and the silence was thick, though peaceful. In a few minutes, they rolled to a stop outside Elizabeth's home. Taking her father's hand, she stepped down and waited for Collin.

"Come with me," her father said and led the way into the house. "I'm sure there's a story, but you needn't share it unless you wish." He guided them into the same open parlor that she and Collin had used that morning. "Have a seat." He gestured toward a chair and brought over a candle. As Collin sat, her father lifted the candle close to his face to study the wound. "Did you care for it?"

"Yes," Elizabeth answered. "With hot water, and I used the honey to dress the wounds."

Her father nodded. "Well done." He addressed Lord Penderdale, "Are you able to see well, nothing strange?"

Collin nodded. "It's not doubled, if that's what you're asking. I've had a broken head before, and this is far less. However I appreciate the concern," he added quickly.

"Boxing?" her father guessed.

"Yes." Collin flinched as her father gently probed the area around his eye.

"I don't think you need a doctor, but I'd not be too ambitious tomorrow." Her father leaned back, setting the candle on the edge of the table.

"I don't plan to," Lord Penderdale admitted. "Rather, I was until this happened," he amended, giving a lopsided grin. "Even I'm not that daft."

"Questionable," Elizabeth murmured, earning a single-eyed glare. "I think my new favorite thing is watching your rather entertaining attempts at facial expressions." She met his glare.

Her father glanced back to her and then to Lord Penderdale. "Elizabeth, would you go and find me some oil of calendula for the earl?"

Elizabeth nodded to her father and then caught the eye of the earl. With a saucy grin, she curtsied to him and spun on her heel to leave. As she quit the room, she was struck with how much she enjoyed seeing Lord Penderdale and her father together.

And it scared her to think of why.

Patricia's words pelted her from memory: *"You're afraid."* Was she? Did she like control too much?

As she went to the lower floor to the kitchens to check for the ointment, she considered herself, inspecting her soul without artifice.

And she didn't like what she found there.

Because deep down, Patricia was right.

She found fear.

Eighteen

The best is the enemy of the good.

—Voltaire, *Philosophical Dictionary*

COLLIN WATCHED ELIZABETH'S CURTSY, BIT BACK a retort at her playful baiting, and then watched until she disappeared into the hall. When he turned his attention back to Professor Essex, he swallowed hard.

Elizabeth's father had been watching him, likely seeing far more than Collin would have willingly spoken aloud, and now they were alone. Collin waited for the questions he knew would follow.

"Do you have anything you wish to ask me, Lord Penderdale?" Elizabeth's father said.

Right to the point then, Collin mused. Well, so much for easing into the conversation. He hadn't given how he felt about Elizabeth much thought; the feelings were still new.

Collin nodded, swallowed, and searched for the right words. "I... That is—" he started, then paused. It was all so final. He couldn't very well court her and then decide against it. It would be a scandal, and he'd hurt Elizabeth in the process, but he also couldn't very well carry on with all the flirtation, sidelong glances, and time spent with her without having a reason. And he wanted a reason. He wanted to have every right to ask her to take a walk, pay a social call, tell her more secrets, except that required a choice.

He grinned, in spite of himself. He'd already crossed that line when he'd called her by her Christian name and savored the sound of it on his lips.

"I wish to court her," Collin stated, the words ringing clearly and coming with far less difficulty than he'd ever expected.

Professor Essex nodded. "I surmised as much, but it's better to ask for permission than forgiveness. Right, Lord Penderdale?"

Collin blinked and glanced down, remembering the phrase he'd been scolded with during his time at the college as a student. "Indeed."

"You have my permission. The question is, will you receive hers?" Professor Essex mused, a grin teasing his lips and a twinkle in his eyes. "I'm the easy part of the battle."

"Of that, I am in agreement. But I accept the challenge willingly," Collin answered.

And he was assured that the battle had only just begun. He'd taken the first vital step, but that didn't mean he had won. No, it meant he had a goal in mind and a plan of action.

Sort of.

Honestly, he was making it all up as he went along. Nothing had gone according to plan from the moment he'd set foot in Cambridge. He'd been going rogue, or rather life had been going rogue for the past few weeks. He'd come to clear his name, and he'd added the pursuit of a woman who was as tempting as she was frustrating. And he still was nowhere near figuring out why his name was being used for crime.

Tea smuggling, he thought. At least he'd figured out that detail, though it did add a million more questions to the mix. Bloody frustrating, that.

"When she returns, I'll give you a moment to talk to her," Professor Essex commented.

"Thank you." Collin resisted the urge to fidget at the prospect of speaking with Elizabeth. It wasn't a proposal, but certainly implied that was the probable result. Was he ready for that?

Collin shook his head. If Rowles could only see him now, he'd be speechless. Either that, or he'd have a lot to say on the subject, too much. But Rowles had been right; Collin had been a shell. He hadn't realized how terribly he'd retreated into himself until he'd met someone who forced him out of it.

Elizabeth.

Was it any wonder he wished to court her? What she had done was damn near miraculous.

As he thought her name, she came into the room

carrying a small tin of salve. Collin stood, then took his seat once more.

"Ah, thank you," her father replied and took the tin. He eyed Collin watchfully and then leaned forward. "This will help you heal." He spread it thinly along Collin's eye and lip, then closed the tin. "Elizabeth, I'll return in a few minutes. Lord Penderdale requested a moment with you."

Elizabeth's eyes shot to Collin's, and then she turned to her father. He rose from his chair, kissed her head, and then left for the hall. The room was wide open, but with her father's absence, it felt oddly small and intimate.

Collin swallowed as Elizabeth's attention moved back to him. She tipped her chin to the side, studying him before she took a seat across from him.

There was a protocol to this situation, a proper way to ask. Nevertheless, the words failed him. For once, he wanted to be romantic, but all he could find was some dry sarcasm, which would never do, not here, not now.

"Your silence is concerning." Elizabeth narrowed her eyes. "You're not at a loss for words often." She scrutinized her lap and smoothed her skirts, her toe tapping as it was tucked under her chair.

She's nervous, Collin observed, and hope washed over him, releasing him from the tension of the situation. He leaned forward and, reaching out, tipped her chin upward to meet his one-eyed gaze.

In spite of himself, he laughed at the situation. He was about to ask to court a woman after he'd been soundly thrashed and while he was sporting a swollen black eye. It was clearly not his best moment.

And that somehow made it just the right moment.

"Miss Essex—Elizabeth," he started.

Her eyes widened as she waited, a lingering smile playing on her lips. "I've spoken with your father, and while I have his approval, your approval is what I seek."

He released her chin and regarded her. "I wish to court you, Elizabeth," he finished. "If you'll allow it."

Elizabeth swallowed, her eyes still wide as she tipped her head slightly, as if not fully believing the words he just spoke. "Why?"

Collin blinked. That was not the question he was prepared for. In fact, he was not prepared for any question, only a yes and hopefully not a refusal.

"Why not?" He turned the question around.

Her face flushed with a becoming blush. "Oh no, I asked first. And it's not such a far-fetched question. I do believe we've fought more than we've agreed, and you frustrate me to the point of vexation—"

Collin placed a finger on her lips, stilling her words.

"Exactly," he answered. "You are by far the most fascinating, intelligent, witty, and provoking woman

I've ever met. And as it turns out, I rather adore that about you. So, the question is if you can appreciate my dynamic character traits as well." Slowly, he removed his finger from her lip, caressing the line of her chin as he pulled his hand away, waiting.

His heart pounded as the moment of silence seemed to drag on forever.

"Yes," she answered, her brows puckering as she said the word. "I'd be honored, Lord Penderdale."

"Collin," he corrected gently.

"Collin," she repeated, her face blooming with color. "But that doesn't mean I'll allow you to have your way, or that I'll hold my tongue when you vex me," she added, tilting her head to the side and offering a smile.

Always challenging, Collin mused, and he rather appreciated it, usually. "I'd never expect anything less, as long as you know full well I'll be the same vexing man you provoke constantly."

Elizabeth's answering smile was brilliant, piercing him to his soul with light and warmth. He couldn't pull his attention away, merely basked in it, knowing the smile was for him alone.

And he rather liked that truth, liked it very much.

"Thank you." Collin reached out, lifted her hand, and kissed it, his eye on her becoming expressive as he did so.

Elizabeth glanced down as he released her hand, biting her lip.

Collin's thoughts surged ahead at the innocently tempting expression, and he wondered if she tasted of the honey she collected, or if it was her hair or skin that smelled of lemons and beeswax. Her lips would be soft, inviting, and before he tried anything untoward, he stood.

"In a herculean effort to be a gentleman, I'll take my leave now, Miss Essex." He bowed.

Elizabeth grinned, then stood as well. "I wasn't aware I presented that much of a temptation, Lord Penderdale."

"You have no idea, which is decidedly part of your charm. You don't use it as a weapon, but that doesn't make it any less lethal, Miss Essex."

"You're using my proper name. Perhaps you did hit your head too hard. I do remember you promising to use my Christian name as often as possible," she challenged.

Collin took a small step forward, leaving only a small distance between them. The air was charged, like the weather just before a lightning storm, and he met her eyes. Her breath came in a short gasp before her attention landed on his lips, then flicked to his eyes. It would be so easy, so natural to close the distance and taste her, to savor the soft delight of her lips, but he resisted, merely enjoyed the delicious temptation of it, the anticipation of a later time when it wouldn't be stealing a kiss, but lingering in one.

"Elizabeth," he whispered, leaning forward and gently inhaling the scent of lemons.

She gasped softly, and he noted the way her body swayed faintly toward him, as if being pulled by the same energy that surrounded him.

"Elizabeth." He whispered her name again as he leaned back just enough to see her face fully, watching with rapt attention as her lips parted.

"Someday I won't have to resist the temptation to sample every inch of you, but until then, remember this…" He lifted her hand once more, tracing her lean fingers with his touch. "The sparks that fly when we fight…are only the beginning. We, my dear, will someday burn everything down around us, and I, for one, cannot wait." He kissed her hand and stepped back.

Elizabeth released a breath, her eyes wide with wonder.

"Lord Penderdale." Elizabeth's father appeared from the hallway, nodding to Collin as he entered the room.

"Professor Essex. I was just taking my leave." Collin cast a smile toward Elizabeth, enjoying the way she still hadn't fully recovered from their close conversation.

Elizabeth blinked and then narrowed her eyes, as if seeing the interaction as a gauntlet thrown. Collin returned the expression with a small quirk of the brow.

"Please use caution tonight and take this tin. You'll likely need more of it in the morning." Professor Essex handed the tin of salve over to Collin.

"Thank you for all your kind assistance," Collin returned.

"Of course." The professor turned, then regarded his daughter, likely trying to discern what her answer had been.

"Until later, Lord Penderdale." Elizabeth gave a proper goodbye, but her eyes were twinkling with amusement, as if she were already ready for whatever came tomorrow.

Collin was certain of one thing: courting Elizabeth would never be boring. "May I call on you tomorrow?" he asked.

"Yes," she answered.

Her father nodded once as if to himself, answering that unspoken question, and then he smiled. "I'll be home in the afternoon."

"I'll come by then," Collin replied, then after saying a final goodbye, quit the room.

Footsteps behind him caused him to pause. Turning, he waited for Professor Essex to catch up. "I requested the hack wait, thus you'll have a ride home."

"Thank you for your consideration," Collin replied.

"And, best of luck," the professor said as he turned back to his parlor. "You'll likely need it."

"Of this, we are in utter agreement," Collin replied, then started toward the door. The hack was indeed waiting for him, a much-appreciated help, and he was soon on his way to the duke's residence that was temporarily his own.

It had been an eventful night, one he wouldn't forget anytime soon. He'd been beaten up; he'd almost destroyed a friendship, mended said friendship, and earned the honor of courting Elizabeth. In fact, he decided, he might have lost several battles this evening. But somehow, he'd won the war. And it turned out the battlefield was his own heart.

Nineteen

All is for the best in the best of possible worlds.

—Voltaire, *Candide*

"WELL?" ELIZABETH'S FATHER TOOK A SEAT ACROSS from her in the parlor. "Care to tell me the news?"

Elizabeth's cheeks heated as she thought over recent events. "Lord Penderdale and I are courting."

"Splendid! I will say I am not surprised. But I am curious..." Her father regarded her. "It seems you've been in each other's company more often than I realized."

Elizabeth understood the weight of the question and answered with caution. "Lord Penderdale is working in cooperation with Mr. Finch, Patricia's brother."

Her father nodded. "So, he's been present at the Finches' residence, and often?"

"Yes," Elizabeth admitted. "Which has allowed us to get to know one another"—she nearly said *to fight with each other*—"on several occasions."

"I see. Well, though we are not in London, you must take care with your reputation, my dear.

Society has rules, and they, for better or worse, must be honored," he admonished. "And I know you would like to rationalize your actions, but others won't be as generous with their logic."

"I understand, Papa," she answered, and it was the truth. For years, hadn't she tried to rationalize and use logic to argue for her place in Cambridge and then with her studies? But no argument, no logic, no sound debate would revolutionize what society had deemed right. It didn't matter if someone proved it wrong; if the majority of the people agreed, then it was as good as law.

The mind of the public had to be altered, and that was a much harder task. After all, humanity resisted change. So the rules of society applied to her as much as to anyone else, regardless of her ability to argue against their rationality.

It was frustrating, but it didn't change anything.

"I'll be cautious."

"Take Molly if you go out in his company," her father directed.

"I did today when—" She paused, earning a gently scolding expression from her father. Heat flooded her face. "Today when he stopped by to... bring something I left behind," she admitted.

She'd never been a good liar. In fact, she was terrible. He father nodded once. "Molly is a good chaperone, but he mustn't come into the house unless I'm present, understood?"

"Yes, Papa." Elizabeth nodded her obedience, chafing at the truth that though she was of age, she still was under her father's authority for the foreseeable future, and then if she were to marry, she'd be under her husband's.

In this case, possibly Collin.

The thought gave her pause, and as much as she assumed she'd resist the idea, she believed she'd still be her own person. Collin was a lot of things, but overbearing and harsh weren't among them, at least in her experience. Since her experience with him was limited, she'd need to understand him before she could accept a proposal, if indeed he thought to give her one.

"I'm trying to help you protect yourself," her father added after a moment.

"I know, Papa. Thank you." She reached over and patted his hand. "It's getting late, and it's been quite the day. I think I'll retire." She stood, and when her father stood as well, she gave him a kiss on his whiskery cheek. "Good night."

"Good night, my dear."

Elizabeth quit the room and took the stairs to her bedchamber. Molly was waiting and helped her dress for bed, stoking the fire before she left Elizabeth in the solace of her room. Her mind still busy thinking through the events of the day, she sat in the chair beside the fire, watching the flames as she reflected.

If anyone had told her two weeks ago that a peer of the realm would be courting her, she'd have laughed.

Nevertheless, that was exactly what was happening, and she was happy. It had been a blow early today when her father had delivered the news that she was no longer able to be at the college. However, the day had ended on a high note, one that was unexpected but fit perfectly.

A pinch of worry tightened her chest as she thought of how she'd need to deliver the news to Patricia, who would in turn tell her brother that Elizabeth and Collin were courting. How would Mr. Finch react? She'd already wounded him by her rejection of his affections. Hopefully this wouldn't add insult to the injury.

Or perhaps Collin would tell him. She wasn't sure, but that wasn't something she could address or fix tonight, so she set the thought aside and decided instead to bask in the glow of Collin's affections.

They were a force to be reckoned with, that was for certain. She closed her eyes and remembered how it had felt to be so close to him that she could smell the peppermint scent that clung to his skin, that she could see the hint of whiskers along his jawline, his very presence enveloping her and drawing her in. It was magnetic, addictive, and she wanted more.

Her mouth had gone dry when he'd said, "*The sparks that fly when we fight...are only the beginning. We, my dear, will someday burn everything down around us, and I, for one, cannot wait.*" She could imagine it, vaguely since she wasn't certain of the details of such a situation, but the emotion of it captured her fully, promising things she didn't know how to name but nonetheless wanted desperately.

She swallowed as she released the memory, opening her eyes and contemplating once again the low-burning fire. She understood the smoldering of the coals all too well. It echoed in her very soul and though it should have terrified her, it did not.

She recalled Patricia's words about fear once more. And she oddly felt the absence of it regarding Collin. Rather, there was deep anticipation and... expectation of fun. Because being around him wasn't difficult. It was challenging and she constantly sharpened her wits, but it was fun. There was never a dull moment, a lull in the conversation, or a hiccup that made her question herself.

In fact, she was fully, unapologetically herself around him. And for some odd reason, he found that attractive, alluring enough to wish to court her, which usually meant a proposal was forthcoming.

So much change had happened in a day. It was as if her entire future had taken a path she hadn't expected, hadn't seen, and had been put on against her will. However, as she walked along it, she saw the beauty. She studied her emotions and tried to fully understand them.

In understanding, she could master them. As she thought it, she laughed at herself. She was clearly not mastering anything, but she craved control. Maybe that was teaching her the lesson of humility.

That stung and wasn't a lesson she'd soon forget or like to repeat. Nonetheless, the fruit of the lesson was apparent, and she couldn't fault life's way of teaching the harder subjects.

She stood and crawled into her bed, nestling into the covers and pillows, sighing deeply. Her mind at rest, she slowly gave in to the deep slumber that beckoned her, anticipating the morning. Because if all this had happened in a day, she didn't want to think about what tomorrow could bring.

Elizabeth awoke the next morning with a smile, the same expectation that had lulled her to sleep alerting her to the bright prospects of the new day. She dressed and went to break her fast, greeting her father at the breakfast table.

"Good morning," she chirped, kissing her father's head before taking a seat across from him.

"Good morning, dear," he answered, then folded the newspaper. "I'm headed to the college, but I'll return this afternoon in time for Lord Penderdale's call."

"Thank you, Papa," she said as she lifted the newspaper and folded it to read.

Her father patted her head and left.

Elizabeth read through the various headlines, her attention pausing on one that detailed the arrest of a ring of criminals in London.

> LONDON: As part of a criminal investigation led by the Honorable L. Huge, police arrested several individuals involved in smuggling tea.

Elizabeth reread the article, surmising that the criminals caught were likely only a few of those involved. As she folded the newspaper, she wondered if perhaps the news would hinder other contrabandists from selling their wares. Clearly, the Crown was aware of the issue, but due to its massive size, it was difficult to conquer.

She finished breaking her fast and went to the kitchens. Her honey had all drained into the bucket, and she'd need to bottle the golden liquid and take the unneeded wax back to the hive. After that, though, she had a plan.

"Molly?" she asked as the maid was about to leave the kitchen.

"Aye, miss?"

"This afternoon when I return from the hives, I'd like you to accompany me to the market once more." Elizabeth wanted to see if the same sellers were present at the market today, or if news of the London arrests had hindered them.

"Of course, miss." Molly curtsied and then left.

Elizabeth returned her attention to the bucket and then decided a change in clothing was necessary to complete the tasks at hand. She'd forgotten early this morning about going to the hives, or else she'd have worn the same old dress that she'd used while gathering the honey in the first place.

Her mind was clearly elsewhere, and she knew why.

Collin.

A smile tipped her lips as she ascended the stairs and went to her room to quickly change into something that was thankfully easy enough that she didn't require a maid's assistance. Soon she was taking the stairs back to the kitchen. She went over to a cupboard that held small jars and removed fifteen, setting them in neat little rows. Next, she set a sieve above her first jar and, with a deep breath, lifted the honey onto the counter beside the jars.

She glanced back at Cook, who was giving her a disapproving look but held her tongue and merely handed Elizabeth a ladle.

"Thank you," she replied. Cook had been with their family since Elizabeth was in leading strings and thus was allowed more latitude than the other servants.

Elizabeth returned her attention to the honey. She slowly dipped the ladle into the golden liquid, watching as it sank in and the honey filled the spoon. She lifted it, waiting until most of the honey stopped dripping, and quickly filled the sieve, which in turn filled the jar. Each jar took two and a half ladles, and after a while, all the jars were filled, with one extra jar halfway filled as well. She scraped the bucket, then placed it in a pot of heated water from the washing and waited as the honey warmed and tipped to the side of the bucket where she'd angled it. She then poured the rest into the final half-full jar and set the bucket aside.

The honey would go to her friends, and Cook would sell the rest to other families, including the owners of the tea shop where Elizabeth taught.

As she thought of teaching, she remembered that she needed to review tonight's lesson before the evening arrived, adding it to her mental list of things to do. She quickly continued with her tasks. She cut half the honeycomb and set it inside the bucket, and took the other half and laid it in a large pot to be melted later and used.

"I'll return in an hour," Elizabeth told the cook, and then repeated the message to Molly. In short order, Elizabeth was riding Winifred back to the hives, bucket tied to the saddle so she could give the bees the wax back to use for their own purposes. A light rain fell, but as she navigated the shaded part of the path, the trees protected her from most of it.

After placing the comb near the hive, deciding it was too large to put inside, Elizabeth stepped back and watched as the bees circled, landed, and started to spread the word about the new resource.

She waited a moment, giving the bees their space as she watched them work, little by little dismantling the wax to reapply in their hive. Elizabeth loved how bees proved that small steps led to large results. It was a concept easily understood yet difficult to apply.

She returned to Winifred and began the journey home, her attention on the afternoon ahead. Anticipation filled her, tickling her senses as she thought about seeing Collin again—and soon. But it would feel different, wouldn't it? There was an... expectation, a knowing that her regard for him wasn't a one-sided emotion, nor was it merely a flirtation. It was more. And she rather liked more. It was delicious and tempting, bringing things to the surface she'd never known existed.

After she arrived at home and cared for her horse, she decided it was time to put aside the thoughts of Collin and address the more serious matter of preparing for class that evening. She'd visit the market later, she decided.

A new student would be attending, and Elizabeth was thrilled at the prospect of introducing her to the other ladies. It was a process to add a new student. With her classes not being of public knowledge, her students were mostly young ladies in families she knew and could trust to keep the secret. Patricia's family and of course the family that owned the tea shop where they had met were two examples. This new student came as a recommendation from the tea shop owner's cousin, so Elizabeth had invited her to tonight's meeting. She wasn't certain of the particulars of the new student, just that she was a few years younger than herself and had excelled in studying with all her tutors and was searching for another venue of education.

Elizabeth went to the table in the parlor that she normally used for preparing her lessons and smiled when she saw her satchel, memories lifting her spirits further. She opened the leather flap and withdrew the crumpled parchment sheets, smoothing them against the table. The first task was putting them back in order.

After an hour of study, she rang for Molly to tell her she'd be ready in a quarter hour to visit the market. On the way there, Elizabeth navigated the streets of Cambridge rapidly, her eyes scanning the faces and the darker alleyways between the tall stone buildings. As she neared the same location where Molly had procured the tea yesterday, she slowed. Addressing Molly, she spoke. "Did Cook say anything to you about the tea we purchased yesterday? Did she notice anything else?" she asked.

"Nothing of note, but she did mention it wasn't mixed with old used tea, like she would have expected of contraband," Molly said. "It's rotten, I'm sure, but as precious as tea is right now, it's not a wonder they are getting business selling it without the tax." She shook her head.

Elizabeth nodded. Cook kept the tea in a locked cabinet at night. They didn't employ many servants, and those they had were trustworthy enough to not pilfer the valuable commodity, but Cook was still mindful. Elizabeth had heard of larger households having tea stores locked by the mistress herself.

"I see." Elizabeth nodded. "Do you see the same lad?"

Molly shook her head. "No. In fact I don't see anyone who appears to be selling it." She glanced about the area. "Maybe they got caught. It is only a matter of time, miss."

"Indeed." Elizabeth nodded. "I'm going over to where you purchased the tea yesterday. Follow me."

Molly ambled behind Elizabeth as she crossed the street and paused at a slender alley between two larger stone buildings. "Do you see anything amiss?" Elizabeth asked, voice low.

"No, miss," answered Molly.

Prudence told her to walk away, but curiosity led her to walk into the alleyway to see what was on the other side of the building, what street it bled onto.

"Miss?" Molly asked, her tone high-pitched with concern.

"There's no one here. I'm going to just peek," Elizabeth replied calmly.

She followed the dirty cobbles to the end of the

alley where it opened onto a wide street with far less traffic. She examined up and down the road, searching for anything out of the ordinary.

A man was walking toward her from up the street, and she paused, finding something about him vaguely familiar. As he drew closer, she recognized him and groaned. Professor Greybeck, one of the last people she wished to see, was on a collision course with her unless she darted back into the alley. She turned to retreat, but glanced to him once more, then paused as he stopped when he saw her, his face clouding with hostile recognition, then smiling.

Elizabeth steeled herself and nodded in greeting as he continued his now purposeful approach.

His attention flickered behind her, likely noting Molly's presence. "I see you've finally taken to observing social standards. Too bad you waited so long," he said by way of hello.

"Good afternoon, Professor Greybeck. If you'll excuse me—"

"Of course." He added quickly and in a low voice, "Christ's College is finally set to rights. Those within the hallowed halls of knowledge are the ones meant to be there. Good day, Miss Essex."

He tipped his hat and left.

Elizabeth's temper flared. Of course, he'd be gloating that she was no longer welcome. It rubbed salt in her still-healing wound. "Let's return home, Molly."

Elizabeth was silent on the way home, and as she passed through the door, she was welcomed by her father.

"Good afternoon, dear," he said as she entered.

"Good afternoon, Papa." She forced a smile.

Her father paused, regarding her. "Is something the matter?"

Elizabeth twisted her lips. "Just encountered Professor Greybeck. He's quite...thrilled with certain events."

"Greybeck." Her father nodded. "He's misguided but a good educator. Most of the Fellows are, my dear. Just because someone disagrees with your application of the same methodology doesn't make them evil. It makes them mistaken."

"I'd rather think of them all as horrid, but I see the value of your words." She sighed. "Sometimes it is a very difficult thing to have a father who implements the philosophy he teaches so well," she added, though her tone was soft and had a teasing lilt.

"Try having a daughter who holds you to it with her own understanding." He winked at her.

"Very well. I won't complain."

"See that you don't," he answered. "I was going to have tea. Will you join me? Lord Penderdale will arrive soon, I'm sure."

Elizabeth nodded. "Yes, of course. I'll go ask Cook to prepare enough just in case he arrives."

As Elizabeth went to request tea be served, she thought over her father's words. It was so easy, to ascribe ill intentions to those someone disagreed with. It was simply human nature. She'd be mindful; that was all she could do.

And humble when she was wrong.

Lucky for her, it wasn't often.

Twenty

Repose is a good thing, but boredom is its brother.

—Voltaire

COLLIN HAD SPENT THE MORNING GIVING INFORmation to the magistrate at the shire house regarding the tea peddlers they'd encountered yesterday. In light of the key arrests in London related to a crime ring, Collin wasn't sure if the information he offered provided some much-needed clarification or just muddied the waters more. He wouldn't know until his missive to the War Office was answered. Until then, he waited.

Before he could visit Elizabeth, he needed to make an important communication. It was with a faintly anxious feeling that he knocked on Michael's door, waiting for him to answer.

"Good afternoon," Michael greeted him, then smirked. "Purple is your color, Collin."

Collin quirked his one good brow and entered the house as Michael stepped aside. "Thank you, I always thought I appeared quite dashing in it."

"'Dashing' isn't the word I'd use, but to each his own." Michael shrugged. "How's the headache?"

"Like a bloody army of tiny hammers. Nevertheless, it's slowly going away." Collin took a seat where Michael gestured.

"Did you talk with the magistrate?"

"Yes, and I sent a few questions to the War Office as well. I'll let you know when I hear back. I assume it will take a day or two."

"These things usually do." Michael settled back in his chair.

Collin hesitated a moment, then leaned forward. "I need to tell you something."

"Sounds serious." Michael frowned.

"Elizabeth and I are courting," Collin said without preamble.

Michael's face softened. "I see you made quick work of that." He tipped his head and blew out a breath. "Quick work. And she accepted your suit?"

Collin chuckled to himself. "While also assuring me that she is prepared to battle me to my wits' end without mercy."

Michael whistled, then smiled. "Best of luck with that."

"I'm certainly going to need it." Collin replied. "But I wanted to tell you, since before…"

Michael waved him off. "Thank you, it's much appreciated. However, I don't resent you, or her for that matter."

"You're a good man, Michael Finch."

"I bloody well am," he answered. "And my offer still stands that I'll prove it if you hurt her." He grinned, as if anticipating such an event.

"I remember." Collin nodded, returning the smile. "Did you see the article in the *Times* regarding the arrests in London?" he said, changing the subject.

"Aye, you think it's all somehow connected?" Michael asked, leaning forward.

"I'm not sure, but it's possible. Again, that is something that will hopefully be clarified when I hear back from the War Office." He shook his head. "I'm going to take the night off tonight, and I wanted to let you know. I'm a little conspicuous with the eye, dashing as I am."

Michael eyed him. "You're a frightful sight, that's for sure. It's best if you at least let it heal up enough that you're not so swollen. A fresh black eye is cause for more interest than a healing one, so we'll plan on tomorrow. I'll still see if I can find out anything from the pubs, and I'll check in with Luke, see if he's heard anything. I'll let you know tomorrow."

"Good plan," Collin replied with a smile. "I appreciate your assistance, as always."

"It's my job." Michael shrugged. "And it's been... exciting. Never a dull moment since you showed up."

"Glad I can provide entertainment." Collin stood. "Until tomorrow."

"Tomorrow," Michael agreed and saw Collin

out. When the door was closed, Collin released a pent-up breath. That could have gone much worse, but that Michael wasn't holding a grudge was a boon, and one he hadn't been planning on. Collin checked his pocket watch, then turned toward Elizabeth's house. He chose to walk, keeping an eye on each alleyway and scanning the people's faces, searching for anything suspicious.

Of course, he found nothing of note, and soon he was taking the steps to Elizabeth's house, hoping her father was home from the college.

Collin knocked, and as he waited, let the memories from the previous evening come to the forefront of his mind. He'd distracted himself from them all day, knowing that if he allowed his attention to focus on Elizabeth and just what he was undertaking, he'd not be able to give his concentration to any of the tasks at hand.

But now, now it was time to focus on the very thing he'd been anticipating most.

Elizabeth.

The door opened, and Professor Essex welcomed him into their home.

"Good afternoon, Lord Penderdale," he greeted Collin.

Collin returned the greeting, his gaze already searching for Elizabeth.

"She's in the parlor reading," her father stated, as if reading his mind.

"Thank you, Professor Essex," Collin replied, bemused. Clearly he needed to work on guarding his expressions, but there was something about Elizabeth that made him less guarded, and hopeful.

It had been a long time since he'd felt hope, and it was intoxicating.

Collin followed the hall to the same parlor they'd used the night before and couldn't help the smile that tipped his lips at seeing Elizabeth's head bent over a table with books spread over its entire surface.

When she didn't look up or notice his entrance, he stepped closer. "Good afternoon."

Elizabeth jumped, her hand resting on her heart as she gasped. "Good mercy. Lord Penderdale, welcome!" She recovered, sending him a bashful smile. "My apologies, I was... Well, why don't you take a peek." She moved to the side of the table and made room for him to see the book displayed on the table.

Collin noted the various maps, a few articles, and a maritime book all spaced out across the surface. "Are you planning a journey?" he asked, confused.

Elizabeth frowned at him. "I rather thought you were quicker than that, Lord Penderdale." She stared at him challengingly. "Try again."

He returned the challenging expression and studied the table once more. "You're researching the smugglers," he said with a hint of awe.

"I knew you'd figure it out. We'll have to work on your speed." She grinned.

Collin narrowed his eyes. "Beautiful and annoyingly brilliant, what a combination."

"I do try," she answered cheekily. "If you'll consider this…" She pointed to an article. "This is from the *Times*, a few months ago. My father keeps the newspapers. I've always wished he wouldn't, dreadful habit I thought, but it was helpful in this situation. I remembered reading several articles about the price of tea and some aspects of the tax Parliament was revisiting." She continued, "Here it names a few locations that the Hawkhurst Gang used in the 1740s, and I thought that, though that was quite some time ago, one of the places might be used again as a landing point. Then…" She pointed to another paper. "Here in the *Times* they talk about how the agricultural business is suffering because of those involved with the smuggling process. Too many people are working for the smugglers and not in farming—"

"The smugglers likely pay better."

"Perhaps but there are more than a few articles on families suffering because someone tried to exit the crime ring." She shook her head. "But I digress. So, I made a quick map of the locations, all in proximity to Cambridge, London, and several of the larger cities in England. You'll see that the transport is quite simple. Combine that with the light weight of the tea, and the smugglers would have little difficulty getting their product anywhere with a road," she finished.

"Well done. Clearly you've spent some time on this," Collin replied, appreciation and wonder entering his tone. Never would he have imagined she'd devote such effort to this; it was humbling.

Usually one to take responsibility for himself and his sister, he found it an odd sensation to have someone display care for him. And he liked it, liked it very much.

"So, if we add in the fact they are using names of the nobility to navigate… I came to two conclusions." She met his eyes, and Collin waited, watched, and tried to focus on her words, not the way her mouth formed them.

"Collin?" she said softly, then glanced to the side, as if searching for her father's presence. "Lord Penderdale?" she corrected.

"Yes?" he replied, shaking himself mentally. "Forgive me, I was just very impressed and somewhat distracted." His eyes darted to her lips and then back to her eyes.

A warm blush bloomed on her cheeks as her lips dimpled into a smile. "Thank you, but I think you'll be more impressed in a moment." She gave a crafty smile and pointed to another article.

"So, you said they were using names of the nobility, right?" she asked.

"Yes," he answered, then continued, "Actually, I can't remember if I told you this part, but when I received my sound thrashing—" He held up his hand. "No comment," he warned with a wry grin. "I was able to pickpocket a list, and my name was among several others, all peers of the realm and probably not involved in a smuggling ring. They likely are unaware, but my connection with the War Office made me aware."

Elizabeth's eyes sharpened with understanding. "That makes sense, and no, you didn't tell me. Or maybe I forgot… It was an eventful evening." She frowned. "But wait." She paused. "How many names?"

"Pardon?"

"How many names were on the list, do you remember?" she asked, her eyes bright with intensity.

Collin blinked, then mentally counted, paused, and counted again. "I believe ten."

She nodded. "During the Protectorate of Cromwell, there was a division of the land into ten regions. We don't use it today, so it wouldn't be readily noticeable…however…"

"Give every region a name, you have a territory for the smuggling ring, with a name that isn't connected, but in a location that is specific."

"Exactly."

"And the region including Cambridge is named Penderdale," he answered.

"Precisely!" She clapped. "Brilliant, when you think about it. Clearly these are not uneducated criminals." She sighed contentedly, as if the whole situation made her happy. "Brilliant plan, and I must say it was like a magnificent puzzle to unlock."

Collin resisted the urge to shake his head in bemused frustration. Of course she'd see the situation as fascinating. "Intriguing as it is, it only leads to more questions. After all, originally my name was being used in London, and that would be a different region than Cambridge."

"Indeed, it is." She twisted her lips. "Unless…"

Collin frowned, then snapped his fingers. "Unless the smuggling ring moved to new territory and kept the name."

"Maybe overtook it from a rival band of criminals?"

"Perhaps, but I'd likely think they are, unfortunately, working all together, more or less."

"That is indeed unfortunate. It's a large ring then and not easy to dismantle." Elizabeth worried her lip, frowning at the table as if the articles on it held the answers she sought.

"I…don't think it's as simple as I'd like it to be."

"On that, we agree," Elizabeth remarked. "I'm sorry. That's…frustrating."

Collin shrugged. "Indeed it is, but it's certainly expected at this point. Honestly, it has been one bad lead after another, with the only information I have been able to glean off a scrap of paper that cost me my handsome face."

Elizabeth regarded him. "Purple is not your color."

"Why, thank you?" Collin replied. "My confidence soars."

"If you expect me to lie to your face to appease you, you're sorely mistaken, Lord Penderdale."

"Oh, believe me, I don't expect anything of the sort. I'm continually humbled in your presence."

"Well, I've been the same, so I have no pity," she returned.

"Truly? Since when did I have that effect on you? Do share. It might make my wounded pride feel better," he said with a charming grin.

She sighed. "When you told me of your sister."

"Joan? Ah, turned your expectations of me on their ear, did I? Good, you needed a sound adjustment on that end."

"Why, thank you," she replied archly. "It made me…reconsider my preconceived notions."

"I admire your willingness to do that."

"Well, your words didn't give me much choice in the matter, not if I wanted to be honest with myself."

"I'll take that as a compliment."

"One of these days I'm truly going to give you a compliment, and you aren't going to know what to do with it since you're so accustomed to finding your own," she teased, her smile radiant.

Collin noted the way her dark eyes captured the light, her full lips parting across her beautiful teeth, all framed by her lovely face. Her smile was radiant, captivating him.

"I'll try to keep my composure if such an event ever occurs," he replied, his gaze roaming over her features.

She bit her lip once more, glancing down. "Don't."

He frowned. "Don't what?"

"Look at me like that."

"Like this?" He tipped her chin up with his finger, hoping her father who was reading a book on the other side of the room wasn't paying close attention.

She blinked as she glanced up, meeting his eyes. "Yes," she whispered.

"Why?" he asked, not ceasing, but caressing every inch of her face with his eyes.

Her lips parted, and she took in a shaky breath. "Because...I don't know how to navigate it."

He blinked. "Navigate it?"

She pulled back slightly, gave a quick glance over his shoulder in the direction of her father, and then turned back to Collin. "I... There's so much to feel all at once that I can't quite figure it all out, and at the same time, I don't want to. I just want more... but it's still so...strange."

Collin gave a dry chuckle.

"If you say you'll take that as a compliment—" she warned, narrowing her eyes.

"I will restrain myself. It's just...endearing," he finished. That was a simple way of saying he was quite impressed with her ability to dress him down by calling the emotional reaction to him strange while nevertheless complimenting him and his charm by saying she wanted more.

He only hoped the "more" outweighed the "strange" aspect. Maybe he'd lost his touch since leaving London. He'd never had a difficult time being charming there.

Or maybe his title was enough charm, requiring little effort on his part.

He had the sinking suspicion it was the latter.

Meaning he was possibly, faintly ill prepared to court a woman more concerned about his character than his title.

Odd, that. He'd always wanted it in a woman, but never expected to find it, and now that he had, he wasn't sure of how to secure those affections.

"You're quiet. Did I..." She frowned. "Did I say something to offend you?"

"No," he quickly answered. "Just...reevaluating. You make me do that a lot. Frustrating aspect, but a needed one apparently." He twisted his lips. "And I wouldn't have it any other way."

"Well, the feeling is mutual. I'm constantly having to figure out what I'm feeling around you, because I've never felt it before." She turned her attention back to the pages, as if her words hadn't spoken volumes.

Maybe he was charming and earning those affections after all. Hope was dangerous, but it was relentless and swelled within him something fierce.

And like with a lifeboat in the ocean, he clung to it.

Because he remembered London.

He remembered the hopelessness.

He remembered what it felt like to be empty.

And he never wanted to go back.

Twenty-one

There are truths which are not for all men, nor for all times.

—Voltaire, Letter to Cardinal de Bernis, April 23, 1764

ELIZABETH BID GOODBYE TO COLLIN, HER MIND still working on the smuggling information while her heart pounded with all the feelings he provoked within her. No wonder she was living in a confused state. It was as if her mind and heart were working independently of each other. Still, she reasoned, she wouldn't be interested or invest her time in all this tea nonsense if it wasn't important to Collin.

What was important to him was important to her, simple as that. And considering it that way cleared much of her confusion. "Papa, I'm going to visit Patricia at the tea shop this evening," she said as she entered the parlor. "After dinner."

"Very well. I'll watch you leave. Will you be back about the same time as usual?" he asked, not lifting his eyes from his book.

"Yes," Elizabeth replied, her heart pinching at the half-truth she was telling. It was better for him to not know about her teaching. If for some reason word spread regarding it, at least he could say he wasn't aware. Though now that she was no longer welcome at the college, it likely wouldn't be as big an issue if word did spread. Or so she hoped.

Elizabeth quit the room and gathered in her satchel what she needed for the evening classes. Dinner would be soon, and then she'd depart.

After they'd finished their meal, as was their usual tradition on these days, Elizabeth's father followed her to the door and watched as she walked up the street toward the tea house. It was quite close, with only a small street separating her father's view of her as she traveled, so she went unaccompanied. As soon as she arrived, she was welcomed and ushered into the closed-off room, her new student already seated beside Patricia.

Elizabeth took in a slow breath, scanned the room, and set her satchel on a side table and withdrew her book and parchments. "Welcome, everyone. It's a pleasure to be here with you tonight. Welcome to our new student." She gestured to the young lady and smiled. "I hope you'll enjoy your time here."

The young lady smiled demurely and shifted in her seat.

"Now, today we're going to start by reading and then discuss what we've read in sections. This next part of Descartes's work is one we need to separate into simple parts. After all, isn't that what he's been explaining? Break the problem down into its smallest components. In implementing this, we're not only reading the book but applying its concepts as well, which in turn will help us learn it better. Can anyone explain a time when it was useful to break down a larger problem into its most basic parts in order to solve it? Descartes uses the principle in mathematics, but it has a much broader scope," Elizabeth finished.

Patricia spoke up. "Earlier this week I began a needlepoint design that was quite difficult, and I was anxious starting it. But when I started on the smallest part of the design first, it was more manageable."

Elizabeth nodded. "Excellent example. And we can use that example to explain the concept further." She glanced to her new student, encouraged by how she leaned forward with rapt attention.

Elizabeth continued. "Needlepoint designs can be quite complex and take a lot of time and effort, combined with careful stitching to create a lovely pattern and display. Each stitch contributes to the whole and, while independent, is still part of the bigger picture that needs that single stitch to be in that place and sewn in that way. If we evaluate life, or maybe a situation in life, we can see the full picture, but there are many contributing factors that influence the way that scenario appears on the outside. Every stitch, or action, contributes to the full picture of what's taking place. So, if we take the principle of breaking down the scene—or the problem, or the picture, however you wish to apply it—to the simplest part, you'll find a smaller aspect that contributes to the whole," she finished. "This is why we study the great philosophers and thinkers. They may be writing about a particular area of study, like science or mathematics, but it all works together and often we can apply those thoughts and concepts to our lives in different ways."

She watched as her students nodded silently. "Now before I digress more, let's begin to read." Elizabeth retrieved her book, opened it to their last page read, and began.

As the class progressed, they took turns reading and discussing. Before long, the class time was finished, and Elizabeth lingered to say goodbye to her students and to see if the newest member had questions.

Sure enough, the young lady waited until most of the students left and then approached Elizabeth.

"Thank you, Miss Essex, for allowing me to join your class," she said with a sweet tone. "I'm Rebecca White."

"A pleasure, Miss White. I was thrilled you were interested and could attend," Elizabeth returned.

Rebecca continued, "It's far different than any sort of study I've had before, and I sincerely appreciated how you explained about applying various concepts to everyday life. It was delightful. I can hardly wait to implement your teachings."

Elizabeth flushed at the praise. "Well, they aren't my teachings. I'm merely introducing you to the books and great thinkers who wrote them, but thank you all the same."

"I'd love to attend the next meeting."

"We'd love to have you," Elizabeth remarked, thankful the new student was going to return.

Rebecca gave a quick smile. "I'll see you soon, Miss Essex. Thank you again." And with that, she departed from the room, leaving Rebecca with her parchments, books, and a lingering Patricia.

"Hello, Patricia," Elizabeth said as she placed her things back in her satchel, a smile playing at her lips as she remembered when Collin returned that very satchel.

"You've been smiling frequently," Patricia said with an arch grin. "One must wonder why."

"Am I?" Elizabeth relaxed her smile and went back to fastening her satchel.

"Yes, you are. And I won't leave until you tell me why," Patricia whispered intensely, her expression determined.

Elizabeth resisted the urge to roll her eyes. "Oh, is that so?"

"Yes, it is." Patricia placed her hands on her hips. "So, the sooner you tell me, the better off we both will be. We can't exactly spend the night in the tea house." She grinned.

"No, we can't," Elizabeth answered but avoided the first question. Part of her was bursting to tell her friend about Lord Penderdale, but the other part wanted to have a delicious secret, something that only she and Collin shared. Well, she, Collin, and her father.

"Did he ask to court you?" Patricia asked softly. Nonetheless, the intensity in her voice was unmistakable.

Elizabeth glanced up, blinking in surprise that Patricia had guessed it so quickly.

"He did! I knew it. I thought…when he came over…I thought I heard something of the sort, but I didn't want to eavesdrop too much… Oh, this is so exciting!" Patricia gushed, then glanced to the door, making sure they hadn't drawn attention.

"Wait, Lord Penderdale came over to your house today?"

Patricia nodded. "It was earlier this afternoon. He stopped by and spoke with my brother, which is not out of the ordinary." She paused. "I was walking upstairs but I thought I heard your name mentioned so I crept closer. I couldn't hear much, but it made me wonder if maybe the events of the night before had led to an important question…" Her words trailed off and she arched a brow suggestively.

"Well, you'd be correct in all your many

assumptions," Elizabeth replied, unable to keep the smile from spreading across her face.

"I knew it!" Patricia said, then whispered more softly, "I knew it."

"Clearly you did, which begs the question, why ask?" Elizabeth hitched a shoulder and then started to leave the room.

"No, don't leave. I want to know all the details." Patricia followed her.

"Why don't you come over for tea tomorrow and we can talk then?" Elizabeth turned and gave her friend a meaningful glare.

Patricia pouted but nodded. "I'll see you tomorrow then."

"Very good," Elizabeth replied, then thanked the Smiths, who owned the tea shop, and started out the door. Her father would be waiting for her outside their house, anticipating her arrival, and she didn't want to linger any longer and risk causing him concern.

She quickly crossed the street and soon could see her stoop, her father smoking his pipe while he waited. It was a comforting sight, and she slowed her walk just slightly, taking time to enjoy the moment. For the first time in a long time, she felt like her life's trajectory had an arc she understood, and she reveled in it.

For however long it would last.

Twenty-two

Common sense is not so common.

—Voltaire, *Philosophical Dictionary*

Joan,

My apologies for not writing sooner. I received your letter and set it to the side, then promptly forgot, but I trust you'll forgive me when I tell you why I forgot. However, first I will tell you I haven't made much progress on my reasons for visiting Cambridge, which is a source of frustration and disappointment. I wish I could send you some interesting details from my adventure, as you put it, but aside from a small altercation that gave me a roguish black eye, I have little to say. And yes, I did look like a dashing pirate. And please tell that to Rowles so that he may disparage me. I'm not around to hear it, so give him full leave to entertain himself.

I miss you as well. As it turns out, I have met a young lady with whom I think you'd be fast friends. In fact, I shudder to think about if and *when you two meet. The world will likely never recover. Though I will give you some credit, just not much. Her name is Miss Elizabeth Essex. The moment you read the name to Rowles, he will likely question if it's Professor Essex's daughter, and the answer to that question is yes. He will then ask many more questions. For all those details, I'm afraid I must leave you in suspense.*

I'm not certain when I'll return to London, but I'm sure it is carrying on well without me. Thank you for sparing me the on-dits. It's much appreciated.

Sincerely yours,
Collin

Collin finished the letter, sealed it with his wax and set it aside to have a servant dispatch it in the morning. He glanced at his timepiece. Normally he would be preparing to meet Michael, but he was taking the night off, and it felt awkward to be aimless. Though, if he were honest, that had been the tone of his life for nearly a year before he came to Cambridge. Which was likely why it chafed so much now.

He didn't want that anymore.

It didn't fit.

And he was thankful, because that season was finished and he was ready and waiting for something new. Something more. If only he could get this blasted name problem solved. He shook his head. Elizabeth had gone to great lengths to assist him, all without him asking. Taking a deep breath, he leaned back against the soft leather chair and thought over all the details of this afternoon. It was all good information, but it didn't solve anything.

And he was tired of going in circles, rather than finding solutions. It felt too close to the restless, aimless feeling he'd abandoned in London. Uncomfortable in his own skin, Collin decided he needed air. He stood from the desk and quit the study. Shrugging into his greatcoat, he took to the streets of Cambridge. He didn't have a place in mind, but he walked toward the River Cam. He took the stone bridge over the river and paused at the top, watching the water lazily swirl under the bridge. He passed along the other side of the river, navigating around several college buildings, and took another bridge back over to the other side, ending up near the shire house and tea shop where he'd seen Elizabeth for the second time. The place was closed, the windows all dark as he passed and moved on.

He wove between smaller streets until he paused by a familiar alley. He walked down it and came face-to-face with the apothecary that wasn't an actual apothecary. Leaning against the stone wall, he kicked up a leg. Some London apothecaries sold tea. In fact, it was common to buy used tea in a cheaper apothecary since they'd add willow, licorice, or sloe to the used leaves to be resold to poorer families for as much as one to two shillings a pound.

Collin's face twitched in disgust at the thought of how that tea must taste. Still, it was a far sight better than some of the other additives he'd heard found in used tea. He gave a shudder.

He watched the shop, noting that the few people walking up and down the street didn't glance in the windows. It wasn't wise, what he was thinking, but fortune favors the bold, he told himself. With a shove off the wall, he walked up the road to the next crossing, took it, and then started back along the side of the apothecary shop. As he got nearer, he wondered just what his plan of action should be. When he was a few steps away, he decided to test his fickle luck and opened the door, hoping his black eye would give him an excuse to seek a remedy.

"Well, look who it is."

Collin swore under his breath. The man who had delivered his black eye now stood behind the apothecary counter.

"I won't pretend you're here for a remedy, but I'm certainly happy to perhaps make your other eye match," the man stated, leaning against the counter and eyeing Collin.

"I want in," Collin said, his mind working rapidly to spin the story. Inspiration hit him, and he relaxed his posture. "Whaleford, the area just north." He waited to gauge the man's reaction. A small pause in his challenging glare was all the encouragement Collin needed to continue. He had selected a name on the list, the list that this guy likely didn't know he had, and furthermore had guessed on the location. They were currently south, so north was an easy lie that would fit most scenarios. If Elizabeth was correct about the shire division according to name... Well, he was putting that theory to the test.

And praying it worked.

"What of Whaleford?" the man asked, narrowing his eyes.

"I didn't like how he ran things. Parliament is passing legislation against the smugglers and has his name on a list. I don't want mine next to it." He shrugged, playing off the lie as smoothly as possible. "So I moved, and I want in."

"I thought you said you were the Earl of Penderdale," the man replied, the words not a question but an accusation.

"I am, how the bloody hell do you think I chose this place? It's perfect. Any involvement I have will be assumed to be under a false identity. It's diabolical, really."

The man frowned. "You'll need to meet with McKensie." He pushed back from the counter.

"Wait here, and you better not be wasting my time, or you'll run out of time to waste, if you gather my meaning."

Collin released a breath when the man stepped from the room, his head spinning with the thought of gathering any other useful information. This was as close as he'd gotten to any answers in the past several weeks.

Of course, he was all alone, no one knew where he was, and he was lying through his teeth about speculative information that, if mistaken, could get him killed.

Brilliant.

"Come back here." The man waved him forward.

Collin breathed in a silent breath and strode forward. The hall was dimly lit, and a door was opened where the man held it wide. "McKensie, this is who is asking for you."

Collin turned the corner, keeping his expression neutral as he studied the older man with salt-and-pepper hair and a tidy beard. "You've come from the Whaleford district?" he asked without putting down his parchments.

A few candles sputtered as Collin came farther into the room. Well, the suspicions about the shire's names were correct. One piece of information assured, he simply nodded. Then replied, "Yes."

"I see." The man glanced up. The expression was dry, edged with ill humor. "You're a piss-poor liar.

You're from London. I've seen you there. That's not the Whaleford region, so now you have the opportunity to explain yourself." He folded his hands and leaned back. "Besides, one of my informants has been trailing you. Taking up residence in a duke's Cambridge lodgings?" He clicked his tongue. "Not usual for the business, but you may have reasons. I'm a patient man. I'll wait to hear them before I make a judgment."

Collin's mind worked quickly. "I was sent to London, and I am...old acquaintances with the Duke of Westmore. That's common knowledge. What you don't know is that my business partners are only willing to work with someone of their own class, as I'm sure you are more than willing to understand," Collin replied. "So, your informant, whomever it may be, is merely giving you information that I want to be known. Consider that."

McKensie frowned, then shrugged. "Maybe, maybe not. But I'll give you the opportunity to prove yourself." He handed a note to the man still standing at the door. He took it, tucked it in his breast pocket. "Send that to Whaleford." The man nodded.

Collin's spine prickled with sweat as he considered what the man was implying.

"Whaleford will either collaborate your story or deny it. Either way, I know where you're staying and, if that is not enough"—he stood and leaned across the desk, his hands spreading across the top—"I know who keeps you company, a delightful strawberry blond who is far too smart for her own good, and likely yours. Good day."

The man standing in the doorway grabbed onto Collin's arm and ushered him out the door and to the front of the apothecary. "We'll find you, no need to return." The man gave a wicked grin and slammed the door in Collin's face.

Collin nodded, adjusted his coat, and walked calmly up the street as if he had no concerns at all, just in case he was being watched. But he was uttering words he'd rarely spoken aloud.

What a bloody disaster.

He had three, perhaps five days before there was a reply to the message. He could try to confiscate it, but that wouldn't work. When no reply was forthcoming, they'd merely resend it.

No, he needed a forgery, and to steal the real letter. If that was possible. He didn't know how they communicated, and it likely wasn't through the bloody English post.

He took the road home, keeping his pace careful, his demeanor unremarkable, in case they followed him to where he was staying.

Which they already knew.

And they knew about Elizabeth too. How in the bloody hell did they know all of this?

He took the steps to the duke's residence and,

once inside, walked directly to the study. He needed to think, he needed a plan, and it needed to be quick.

Twenty-three

Work keeps at bay three great evils: boredom, vice, and need.

—Voltaire, *Candide*

ELIZABETH AWOKE THE NEXT DAY WITH A BRIGHT sense of purpose. Perhaps there was some way she could turn her classes into something that was more socially acceptable. It would be a great relief to have her desire to teach be an outlet she didn't have to constantly keep under lock and key. But she was a gentleman's daughter so taking on a paid position of any sort would be an insult to her father, as if he were unable to provide, and since she was still of his household, she would be expected to operate under his rules—and he wasn't familiar with the fact she taught her classes. These were two large issues to be overcome.

And then there was the problem of the subject material. It wasn't as if she'd laid open the pages of graphic biology of the human anatomical form— which would be scandalous at best, but the material she taught wasn't something any governess would consider primary or secondary education. She was teaching women to be as smart, or in some cases, smarter, than most men. Being bested in intelligence by the woman he courted wasn't exactly high on any gentleman's list. She blushed as she considered how Collin had found that an attractive trait. Why couldn't there be more men like him?

It was still a considerable obstacle, convincing both parents and young women to further their education into the deeper sciences, mathematics, and philosophy than a regular governess would be educated enough to teach. It wasn't done.

Not only was it not done, but it was frowned upon, greatly. These were not small issues, and the earlier feeling of purpose and lightheartedness faded away like steam from a hot cup of tea.

Elizabeth quit her rooms and approached the breakfast table, fully expecting to see her father waiting for her, as was their usual routine. When he wasn't at his usual position at the table, nor was the *London Times* anywhere in sight, she frowned.

"Molly, where is my father?" she asked as the maid walked past the room.

"Ah, miss, there was a visitor earlier this morning for him. Still here, I believe."

Elizabeth tipped her head. "This morning? Already? That's uncommonly early." What she didn't say was *impolite*. She held her tongue and waited for Molly to reply.

"It's not my business, miss. I'm sure your father will be here shortly." She nodded and went on her way.

Elizabeth's curiosity piqued, she leaned out into the hall, listening intently. Sure enough, she could hear the muffled voice of her father through a closed door somewhere down the corridor, and the voice of another she didn't recognize. She breathed quietly, hoping to catch any words or hear the other voice more clearly in case it was someone she knew. After a few moments of disappointment, she went back into the breakfast room to satisfy her morning hunger.

As she sat down to eat, she glanced to her father's place and then to the empty table. The visitor must have been rudely early if her father hadn't brought the paper into the breakfast room. Her lips twisted as she glanced to the hallway. She *could* go and fetch the paper from her father's study, but that was likely where her father was conversing. However maybe it wasn't, so she stood. If she moved toward the study, she could maybe hear more clearly and then she could maybe determine what was so important it couldn't wait until a decent hour to be discussed.

She took a step toward the hall, then paused.

No. She wasn't going to eavesdrop. She was better than that—wasn't she?

She took another step, and then forced herself to go and sit down at the table. No, her father would discuss whatever it was with her, if it was her business. If it wasn't, then she didn't need to know. She wouldn't be like those busybodies who were constantly searching for that delicious tidbit of gossip. No, she was above that. She valued education, philosophy, intelligence.

She worked hard to convince herself to stay as she ate a rasher of bacon. While she was pouring a second cup of tea, she heard voices in the hall. She froze, listening intently. Her father's voice was bidding someone goodbye, and as luck would have it, the other gentleman didn't talk.

While she waited, she listened intently as her father's footsteps traveled the hall toward the breakfast room. Her back was to the door, and she turned as she heard him grow closer. She prepared a welcoming smile for him, but the moment she saw his face, a cold chill froze her expression in place.

"Good Lord, Papa, what is the matter?" She stood quickly, nearly knocking over her chair in the process.

Her father held up one hand, halting her movement. His gray eyes were weary and mournful, a look that brought back memories of when he spoke of her mother's passing.

"Papa?" she whispered. "Who—what happened? Are you ill?" she asked, scanning his face, his body for injury that she may have missed. Any clue as to what tragedy had cut him so deeply that his expression would be so broken, so hurt.

"Elizabeth." He sighed, then glanced down. "I had a guest this morning."

Elizabeth swallowed, then nodded, waiting, impatient for him to continue.

"He works under the provost of Cambridge University," her father continued.

Elizabeth blinked. The provost was the head of Cambridge, and her thoughts immediately flew to her father's position as professor and her heart clenched.

"He was given some information, regarding you, and…and at first I assured him it couldn't be accurate information. It couldn't, wouldn't be true. It would mean you…have been less than honest with me, and that wasn't something I was willing to believe." Her father's mouth pinched as he looked down, folding his hands.

Elizabeth's breaths came in short gasps. However, they made no sound, as if her breathing wasn't giving her body the air, just sucking it in and out, not doing any good. *No, no, no!*

Her father continued, "Then he told me the subject material that his daughter had learned last night…and I recognized it. It was some of the same material you helped research a few months ago. And I knew." He shrugged. "I knew he was speaking the truth. And that, as you can imagine, was very difficult." He met her eyes, his contemplation spearing her heart.

"Papa."

He held up his hand again and took a deep breath. "Seeing as I'm quite certain you know to what I am referring, I'm going to give you the opportunity to explain yourself."

Elizabeth nodded, tears brimming in her eyes. Soon they were spilling over and trailing down her cheeks. Was it worth this? Heartbroken, she questioned all the decisions that had led her here, measuring them against her father's broken expression as she glanced up. Was it worth this price?

She took in shaky breath. "It was...difficult for me to study and have no way to apply it, aside from my own life." She paused. "Patricia listened when I needed to somehow get the information out of my head, and it wasn't anything she'd ever learned before. It...made me think. Certainly, there had to be more women like me, Papa. Women who wanted to grow, and learn, who had this insatiable need for diving into why things work the way they do and read, read for days. And I thought that perhaps it was that they had never been given a chance to learn, as I had." She paused, calmed herself, and then continued, meeting her father's scrutiny with a direct one of her own. "So, I spoke with the Smiths, asked if I could use their tearoom for a ladies' club, just a few evenings. Their daughter had been the bane of every governess they'd hired, and I offered to take on their daughter in the club for women's education. They agreed, and in hindsight I can see I exploited a need they had. But I will say it worked well for their daughter, and—" She paused. "No, no excuses, I'll continue with the story." She nodded to herself. "I began with two ladies, and the word was spread very carefully so that it wouldn't be well known—to protect you, and to protect me. I knew it wasn't exactly proper—"

Her father scoffed at this.

"It was scandalous for a woman to be teaching the material I brought to the ladies, and I wished to protect you from that. So, though I grew the club to several students, I deliberately chose not to tell you, thinking I was protecting you from the scandal I could potentially cause, so that if it was discovered, you could deny ever knowing. Foolishly, I thought that would protect you, and I can see now it was far worse and hurt you more deeply than any other choice would have done." She finished, "And for that, I'm sorry, Papa."

Her father nodded once, then took a deep breath. "Elizabeth, this must stop."

Elizabeth's heart fractured at his words. It wasn't as if she'd deluded herself into thinking it was something she could do indefinitely, but she'd been lying to herself as much as she'd been lying to her father. "I know."

"This was a dangerous game, Elizabeth. And I don't understand why you thought it could be played without a consequence." His white brows furrowed over his eyes. "You are far more astute and intelligent than this suggests."

Elizabeth took a slow breath. "I'm sorry."

"It's not enough," her father replied, softly, gently, making the words all the more powerful. "It's not enough to be sorry, Elizabeth. There are consequences."

"I know."

"But do you? Honestly, Elizabeth, do you? Did you truly consider the consequences before you started, or did you just disregard them? Because let me tell you the real ramifications." He paused, then speared her with his gaze. "Because I don't think you did consider all the possibilities. I think you were blinded by what you wanted and only saw what you wanted to see."

Elizabeth blinked back tears.

"Elizabeth, dear child, as much as we may not agree with social conventions and how unfair they may be, they are still alive and present, demanding respect, and when we disregard them fully, we invite the repercussions that accompany that. In this case, you're teaching material that is not part of a lady's education, which is seen as vulgar, scandalous, and not respectful of your social standing. It puts you in the same position as a bluestocking, and not in a cavalier way, but in a way that disrespects the privilege to which you were born and which I've given you. Which leads me to the second ramification. Elizabeth, did you consider how this could hurt me? Not just the dishonesty, though I'll say that is certainly what hurts the worst at the moment, but the fact that it undermines not only my integrity as a professor of Cambridge, but also my respectability. And if I cannot be respected, do you think I can remain doing what I do? Already I'm known as an eccentric. I'm at peace with that since it's quite true. However, I am not so unconventional that I'd throw all social protocol out the window, not for your sake, because it would reflect poorly on you. Yet you denied me the same respect."

Elizabeth's tears flowed freely, streaming down her face in quick succession as each of her father's words hit her soul like sharp arrows, hitting true and sinking deep.

"You can excuse your behavior. Nevertheless, you cannot do it well because your arguments are weak and based on what you wanted rather than what was socially acceptable, which is the context of the world we live in. You've studied enough to know this."

"Yes, Papa," she answered, her voice nothing more than a whisper. It was all she could do; he was right. Every part of his argument was correct, and every part of hers was…selfish.

Not because it was wrong to educate women.

But because she wanted it and did whatever it took to see it through, damn the consequences.

The moral was right. The actions wrong.

And that meant the whole thing was corrupted.

Her father let out a slow sigh. "Now, I believe I've chastised you thoroughly, and I need to tell you something that is a boon in the middle of this mess, regardless of how it may be mistaken as approval of your behavior." He narrowed his eyes. "The gentleman is not going to tell anyone else about your... class. As it turns out, his daughter was a new student last night, and that is how he learned about it and came to tell me. However, his daughter was also so impressed she begged him not to disclose the information. So, your secret is safe, for now. But that is only under the condition that you stop."

Elizabeth nodded, her tears slowing only slightly. "I understand."

He shifted on his feet. "I understand that you need an outlet, a way to share what you've learned, my dear, so we'll find a way that won't destroy your reputation, or mine. I have a few ideas, and when I'm less frustrated, you and I can discuss them. Because I don't fault you for wanting to do what you're doing, Elizabeth. However, I do fault you for the way you went about it." He nodded, as if finishing in gesture what he finished with words.

"Thank you, Papa," Elizabeth replied, her heart rallying faintly at her father's last words. "I love you."

"I love you too. Since I didn't get a moment to break my fast before I was interrupted, I'm going to do that now." He moved into the room and took a seat. Elizabeth studied her cold tea.

"Will you sit?"

Elizabeth glanced to her father, then to her chair, and nodded. But her belly was in a tight knot. As soon as it was polite, she excused herself to her rooms.

She had some heart searching to do.

And some amends to make.

It was always easier to solve mathematical problems or ask the deep questions that didn't need to be fully answered than to search and unlock one's own heart and fix what lay beneath all the lies a person told oneself.

And that were believed.

Twenty-four

I have always thought the actions of men the best interpreters of their thoughts.

—John Locke, *An Essay Concerning Human Understanding*

COLLIN KNOCKED ON PROFESSOR ESSEX'S DOOR as soon as it was a polite hour. He needed to speak with Elizabeth and her father. It was a matter of safety, though he wasn't sure how he would approach the conversation. Because it was all his fault. He'd put them in danger, and it was his job to save them from it.

If they'd answer the bloody door.

He knocked again.

Stepping back, he waited, staring at the knob, willing it to turn and open.

"Yes, my lord?" Molly, the maid who had accompanied Elizabeth on their tea escapade, asked with a polite tone.

Collin released a deep breath. "I… That is, is Professor Essex home?" He wanted to merely barge through the door and call out for Elizabeth, but they were courting so certain expectations would need to be observed. And as he'd already put her and her father in a certain amount of peril, he'd not cause damage to her reputation as well.

"My lord, my apologies, the master isn't at home," Molly said regretfully, then eyed him cautiously, as if sensing his agitation.

Collin mumbled a word under his breath. "Is Miss Essex at home?" he tried, thinking that perhaps he could escort her on a short walk, with Molly accompanying them. Certainly that would be allowable.

"Miss Essex isn't taking callers," Molly said stiffly.

Collin let out a tight breath. "Would you please let her know who is requesting her company? I believe that might make a difference." Or so he hoped. Why was she not receiving callers? It seemed off, like a puzzle piece missing from a picture that inhibited the viewer from understanding the picture.

Molly debated, switching her weight from foot to foot before she nodded once. "But please wait here." She closed the door.

Collin twisted his lips. He couldn't very well just come in, not with her father gone, though he'd done it before, but that was…different. Damn and blast how this courting changed things.

He took the steps of the stoop down to the street and scanned the faces of those walking on the road. Was there someone here now, watching him? He narrowed his eyes as he thought about it, fury building in him, even as an errant thought tickled his mind. If Elizabeth refused to see him today, he could use that to her benefit. At least for the moment. For if someone was keeping an eye on her residence, then the servant not allowing him entrance might make the tea smugglers think that she had severed a connection with him. That would make her safer for the moment. He hated the thought, resented thinking it, but it could work, at least in theory. He glanced back to the door, half of him wishing to see Elizabeth open it, half wishing to get a refusal so he could have the chance to keep her somewhat safer.

The door opened.

Collin took the step up and then paused as Molly shook her head. "Miss isn't feeling well. She gives you her apologies, Lord Penderdale."

Collin nodded. "Please give her my deepest regards." He smiled wanly, then waited for the door to close. With a flair of drama, he took off his hat and swung it in a deliberate expression of anger and frustration. He stomped down the final step, huffed, took on a grim demeanor and all but stomped away. As he finished his performance, he hoped that it wasn't in vain, and that someone of import saw it and would report it back to McKensie.

It was the least he could do.

But in the meantime, if Professor Essex wasn't

at home, that meant he was at the college. Collin started toward the River Cam, determined to find the professor, one way or another.

He took a bridge over the water and navigated along the cobbled street until he came to Christ's College. He opened the door to the building holding the professors' private offices and nodded to a few students who gave him curious stares. He traveled the hall, then paused in front of Professor Essex's door, knocking.

"Enter."

Collin twisted the knob and walked into the room.

"Lord Penderdale," Professor Essex said with some surprise, and stood in respect. He gestured to a chair and then took a seat himself.

Collin nodded his thanks and took a seat, memories of the first time he'd visited the professor upon returning to Cambridge flooding his mind. It was here he'd met Elizabeth, already captivated and irritated by her beauty and wit. Reflecting, he could see how he had already been fighting a losing battle regarding her, and he smiled in spite of himself. He leaned forward, resting his elbows on his knees and forcing his attention back to the task at hand.

"Professor Essex, first I hope that Elizabeth feels better. I stopped over at your house before coming here and was informed that she was feeling poorly."

Professor Essex glanced to the desk, shifting

in his chair. "Yes, well, I'm sure that she will work through it," he replied cryptically.

It was an odd reply, and Collin frowned. "Work through it?"

Professor Essex released a tight breath, as if bearing a heavy load. "There was some news that came to us early this morning...rather, came to me." He drew a deep breath. "And as you are courting my daughter, I think you should be aware. However, I also want to give my daughter the opportunity to speak with you about it, so I'm facing an odd question of what is best at the moment—whether you should hear it from me, or from her." He leaned back, closing his eyes.

"Why don't you give me a small amount of information and go from there? If I believe it is something that should come from Elizabeth, you have my word that I will wait to hear it from her and give her the benefit of the doubt," Collin answered.

"You're very kind, Lord Penderdale," Professor Essex replied. "Very well." He paused. "It was brought to my attention today that Elizabeth has been holding a ladies' education club that has garnered the attention of those that would see it ended."

Collin nodded. "I see." He wasn't sure if he should divulge that he was aware or merely leave it alone until he was able to speak with Elizabeth. But with her father's words, much of the morning's situation made sense. Elizabeth would be distraught, knowing her father's displeasure not only at her activities, but that she'd been dishonest with him. The rejection he'd suffered earlier seemed quite insignificant, and he wished she'd shared her burden with him rather than suffer alone.

"Your reaction makes me think two things," Professor Essex stated as he leaned forward. "One, that you already knew. Or two, you understand that this could hinder her respectability, especially as the wife of an earl."

Collin wasn't going to be dishonest with him, so he merely nodded. "I was aware."

"I see," Professor Essex said. "I will say that gives me some relief. I was concerned this would potentially ruin her in your eyes."

Collin chuckled without mirth. "Professor Essex, I'm inclined to find her more desirable because of her actions." He shook his head. "Believe me, I know what game I play with fate regarding Miss Essex, and I will say I'd not have it any other way."

Professor Essex gave a soft chuckle. "Good, at least there are no surprises there."

"Elizabeth is likely flaying herself for her dishonesty," Collin observed.

Her father answered, "Yes, and rightfully so."

"There is…one other matter I came to discuss with you." Collin sobered, leaning back in his chair as he thought about how best to approach the topic.

"Yes?"

Collin glanced down to his hands, folding them as he considered his words carefully. "Do you remember when I disclosed my reasons for returning to Cambridge?"

Professor Essex nodded.

"Well, I made some progress, but that turns out to be the problem. And while I've been exceptionally cautious"—*except for last night*, he amended mentally—"the rogues I've discovered have unfortunately connected me to Miss Essex as well."

At this, her father stood up straight. "Oh, well that presents a problem, doesn't it?"

"It does, and so you can see that safety is a concern."

"It is indeed."

Collin had toyed with several plans, but continued to come back to this one and decided to test it out. "I have an idea."

"Oh?"

"Yes, it's probably a little abrupt, but would you and your daughter consider taking a holiday to London?"

Professor Essex quirked his brows; they truly had a language of their own. Collin deliberately had to disregard them to keep his focus from straying. "It would take a few days to find a replacement for my classes, but I believe it might be a good option. With the current situation with Elizabeth, removing ourselves from here for a few days might help."

"Then we are in agreement?" Collin asked.

"Yes, I'll speak with Elizabeth when I return home, and perhaps you can take dinner with us. Or do you think that will be a risky choice?"

Collin shook his head. "If we remove you from the area soon, then I think the risk will be minimal. The benefits will far outweigh it, and by this evening I can have most of the arrangements made for you."

"There's no need. I can—"

"I insist," Collin interrupted. "My apologies, but in this I'm determined. I created the problem, and it is upon me to make amends. Besides, you'll be far more comfortable traveling in my carriage than if you traveled post."

Professor Essex paused, then agreed. "Very well. I'll anticipate hearing all the particulars tonight."

"Until this evening." Collin stood and then, with a bow, quit the room.

Before he closed the door, Professor Essex's voice bid him pause. "Thank you, Lord Penderdale."

Collin gave a nod and a small smile. "Thank me when I've made sure your daughter is safe. Until then, I am the one in your debt."

He didn't wait for the professor to say anything more, merely closed the door and walked back down the hall. There were plans that needed to be made, and with any luck, they'd be twofold.

Protect Elizabeth.

And have her meet his sister.

Twenty-five

*He that judges without informing himself to the utmost
that he is capable cannot acquit himself of judging amiss.*

—John Locke, *An Essay Concerning Human Understanding*

ELIZABETH WAS STILL CHIDING HERSELF WHEN her father came home and told her that Lord Penderdale would be joining them for dinner and, more surprising, that they would be traveling to London.

London.

She hadn't been there for years, and then it had been seen through the eyes of a child. There was so much she wanted to see, to experience, and yet she was also fighting the oddest sense of fear.

Of the unknown.

This time, she wouldn't be going just as a visitor. She would be making connections and introductions, and while she prided herself on being socially adept, her recent failings were making her question herself.

When Lord Penderdale's arrival was announced, she stood from her place in the parlor and waited.

She grasped her skirts, trying not to wrinkle them by twisting them in her anxiety. Her father had also said that he'd disclosed the day's events to Lord Penderdale, which gave her further reason to fret.

He knew about the ladies' classes because she'd told him. However, knowing was different than others knowing and, as her father had stated so clearly that morning, the consequences of others knowing. It was why she kept referring to him not as Collin, but as Lord Penderdale to remind herself of his position and title.

When they'd first met, he'd called her selfish.

And it was bitter to know he was right and that she'd have to eat those words he'd fed her. Their truth had sunk deep this afternoon, and she still hadn't quite recovered.

That deep soul-searching, sincerely seeing herself not as she wanted to be seen or to see herself, but as she actually was, had been excruciating.

And the night was young, and she wasn't sure what it held.

She didn't think his affections would be compromised. Nonetheless, she wasn't going to hold him to anything. It wouldn't be fair.

She'd done this to herself.

She'd take the consequences.

"Ah, Miss Essex, lovely as usual." Lord Penderdale came into the room, his expression soft and welcoming as he spoke.

Elizabeth's knees weakened slightly as relief flowed through her. And the realization she had expected him to put her aside.

"Lord Penderdale." She curtsied.

He blinked and paused. "Well, I certainly enjoy your graceful movements, but I'm quite certain the only time you've curtsied in my presence before was in sarcasm, so there's no need to start now. Unless that was sarcasm, in which case, I approve," he said. "I certainly deserve it."

She blushed, feeling a little more like herself at his words. "I do nothing that's not deserved. On both counts," she added with a small smile.

"Ah, that's the spirit," he replied, his gaze warm as he came a few steps closer.

Elizabeth's father came into the room and greeted them both with a smile. "Dinner will be soon. Until then, let us sit and discuss the next few days."

Elizabeth's lightened mood was short-lived, her heavy disappointment in herself weighing her down immediately as she studied her father. He'd been so kind, forgiving even, but the person she couldn't forgive was herself.

"Elizabeth, none of that," her father chided her.

"My apologies, Papa," she whispered softly.

Her father glared at her.

She forced a small smile.

"That's not much better," he replied, then took a seat beside her and picked up her hand. "My dear, if we never recover from our mistakes, then they continually have power over us. So, grow from them, and then you'll make me far prouder than if you merely rake yourself over the coals inside your mind."

Elizabeth nodded.

"And you're not the only one offering apologies today." Lord Penderdale seated himself across from them. "I assume your father told you of the plan to remove you to London for a short time?"

Elizabeth glanced to her father. "Yes."

"Did he tell you why it is important?" Lord Penderdale asked.

Elizabeth's heart clenched. "No, I... Well, I didn't consider why. I've...had a lot of other things on my mind."

Lord Penderdale shared a look with her father, increasing her anxiety. "What is going on?"

"Well, the criminals I'm trying to ferret out did some ferreting of their own and connected you to me, putting you and your father in a certain amount of peril. For that reason, it's quite desirable to remove you from their locale and have you take up residence with the Duke and Duchess of Westmore, my sister and brother-in-law."

Elizabeth frowned. "We're going to be the guests of the duke and duchess? I... That is, certainly we don't want to be an imposition—"

"Oh, it's not an imposition in the least. In fact, if you tried to take lodgings anywhere else, my sister would find you and make it impossible for you to refuse her hospitality. Then she would promptly hunt me down and fillet me alive."

"Oh."

"Yes, oh." He grinned from ear to ear, as if the whole idea brought him deep joy.

Elizabeth studied his face, her insides unwinding and warmth seeping into her very soul. His eyes twinkled; his lips invited her attention as she openly stared.

His attention dropped to her mouth as well, and her lips buzzed as if the look were a touch.

Her father cleared his throat.

Elizabeth jumped slightly, and Collin glanced away, then continued speaking about their plans.

"I've arranged for my carriage to pick you up the day after tomorrow to take you to London."

Elizabeth held up a hand. "Wait, are you not coming?"

Collin shook his head. "No, I have unfinished business and, since I've made some important headway, want to stay the course. So far, my plan is dependent on how I'm able to address the problems here in Cambridge. If they resolve quickly, I'll come to London and you can have the pleasure of watching my sister and brother-in-law harass me endlessly. Or, if fate is kind, the process here will take a while and you'll return once I've tied up loose ends, saving me from my sister."

"If I ever need to blackmail you, I'll just tell your sister what you've said," teased Elizabeth.

"Ah, dear Miss Essex, my sister is already fully aware of my feelings," he returned playfully. "And while I tell her it's part of my charm, she doesn't believe me. Perhaps you can put in a good word for me? I wrote her a few days ago regarding you. In fact, the one I should be pitying is you."

Elizabeth's face flushed. "You wrote to her about me?"

"Of course. Now that I'm courting a lovely young lady with more than half a brain who is able to humble me with the precision of a skilled archer, I won't ever have to give her a birthday present again," he replied with a wry tone.

"Aren't you generous," she replied dryly. "Am I to take that as a compliment? Half a brain?"

"I am the giving sort, and yes, I rather do think it's a compliment. If you had spent any amount of time in London and seen the ladies there, you'd understand."

"Your humility is endless."

"I've been told as much, but it never hurts to be reminded," he replied.

"I'll be sure to ask your sister for every story she wishes to share about your childhood. Since you've had such a legacy of humility, I'm sure the study of your past behavior will be a boon to my education."

Collin's eyes narrowed. "You wouldn't."

"I would, and I will," she replied with a soft chuckle.

"I need to rethink this plan. Clearly there's a fault I didn't foresee," he remarked.

"Too late. Think of it as me honing my skills on keeping you humble."

"I certainly wish you wouldn't work on those particular skills. There are so many others…" He paused, glancing to her father and then not completing the sentence.

Elizabeth blushed but let out a burst of laughter at Collin's regretful and faintly chagrined expression.

"Apparently you humble yourself as well."

"Just when I'm in the presence of those who make me forget myself. Remember, use the power you wield wisely."

"Understood." Elizabeth nodded sagely. "I'll endeavor to be trustworthy of it all."

"Why do I feel like I just signed a deal with the devil, and when is dinner so I can extricate myself from this situation I don't know how I created?" He turned to the door, as if trying to conjure up a servant to invite them to the table.

"Is this that charm you were talking about?" she asked, teasing him.

"Yes," he said tightly, turning back to her, his eyes daring her to continue.

"Noted. It's a good thing you're handsome." She giggled, then pressed her fingertips to her lips.

Her father coughed as if choking on a laugh. "There are few places more entertaining than this room right now."

Collin turned a dry expression on her father and then turned back to her. "You're enjoying this too much."

"I am, and I don't regret it."

"I've said it once, and I'll say it again. When you meet my sister, the world will shudder that you two have joined forces."

"I'll probably like her more than I like you," Elizabeth dared to say.

Collin eyed her suspiciously before answering. "Challenge? I accept. You've been warned."

"I have been. However, I don't foresee this being a problem. I rather like the idea of your constant effort for my affections," she replied saucily.

"As if I haven't tried already?" he asked, crossing his arms over his chest, an amused expression in the twinkle of his eye.

However, Elizabeth could see what he was doing, and she was deeply thankful he was drawing her out, helping her to move past the earlier events of the day that had left her so empty. He was giving her a distraction, a bit of fun, and she fell a little more in love with him for it.

As she thought the words, she paused and swallowed, glancing down and away from him.

Love?

That's what this was, wasn't it? She took a few seconds to collect herself, to think, to evaluate. She'd read a million books, seen it displayed in millions of ways, yet…it was something one couldn't merely read about.

It had to be experienced.

And as she glanced up to meet Collin's curious gaze, she knew.

It was, indeed, love.

Well, if it was a day where her soul was to be laid out naked, then it would be only fitting to add this truth to mix. She offered Collin a reassuring smile, speaking that same reassurance to herself.

It wasn't one-sided.

He was courting her, seeking her hand. It wasn't one-sided, she repeated to herself. Because the only thing more terrifying than realizing she was in love was the fear she was in it alone.

Twenty-six

COLLIN ESCORTED ELIZABETH TO THE DINNER table, her hand resting on top of his as he walked with her through the hall, her father following behind. When he'd first arrived, he had hardly recognized the subdued woman that Elizabeth had become. It had jolted him, and his one goal from that moment was to tease her out of the shell into which she'd retreated. He was surprised to see that aspect of her character. He'd rather expected her to be fierce and defiant, which she was, unless it was against those she loved. It was an aspect of her character that spoke deeply to him: loyalty.

It was a rare commodity, and all the more precious because of that. He offered her a playful smile as she walked with him, and jostled against her shoulder lightly, earning a playful glare in response.

"Problems walking straight?" she quipped.

"I'm merely drunk on your presence," he whispered softly.

"Is that so? I'll make sure my father removes the wine from the table before we begin dinner, if I'm merely enough," she teased.

"Oh, you're enough," he whispered back.

"You're quite sure of yourself tonight."

"When in our acquaintance have I not be self-assured?" he asked.

She twisted her lips as he paused just before her chair and pulled it out for her. "Well, never."

As she sat, he whispered, "Exactly, and I don't plan to change now. So, we'll just say it's part of that charm." He stepped away to find his own chair.

"Well, now that you've taken a small pause from your banter, are there any other details in the travel plans, Lord Penderdale?" Elizabeth's father asked as the first course was served and the wine was poured.

Collin lifted his glass and met Elizabeth's eyes as he took a sip.

She blushed and turned her eyes downward, then toward her father, but not before Collin watched her swallow forcibly and take a deep breath.

He loved the way she reacted to him, even in the little things.

"Lord Penderdale?" Elizabeth's father spoke his name, bringing him back to the conversation.

"My sister will address any other needs, since she will be the one with whom you are staying. My carriage will be here the day after tomorrow, as discussed, and until then, if you have need of anything, please don't go anywhere alone or, better, send a note to me and I'll procure whatever you need and have it delivered to you. The more we can limit exposure, the better."

"I understand," Professor Essex replied. "I don't foresee any needs, but I'll be sure to keep you informed." He took a sip of his wine, then continued. "My classes are being overseen while I'm away, and I can imagine the only other person who needs to be informed is perhaps your friend Patricia Finch?" He turned to his daughter.

Elizabeth set her spoon down and let the bowl be removed. "Yes, I'll send her a note to invite her to call on me tomorrow." She turned to Collin. "Or should I have her stay away, since we don't want her involved?"

Collin considered her question. "I don't think it will be a great risk. She's not a connection to me, which eliminates the risk for her." Though as he said the words, something seemed off about them. If they knew that Elizabeth was connected with him, then they would also know about Michael, and if they knew about Michael, they should also think of Patricia as means of a threat against Michael.

He needed to stop by their house, and soon. Michael needed to know so he could protect his sister.

"If you think it's safe, I'll continue with the plan," Elizabeth replied.

"Very well, then I think we have everything settled," Collin replied, glancing to Elizabeth. She was exquisite, and he watched her mouth curl in a secretive smile. He wanted to share all her secrets, have all those expressions of her beautiful mouth memorized so he could read them as quickly as her words.

She shook her head and smiled, returning to their meal.

Collin enjoyed the conversation, and as they adjourned to the parlor after dinner, Elizabeth's father took up a book and went to a far corner of the parlor, giving them a small semblance of privacy.

God bless the man.

"So, I heard about what happened," Collin said, sitting beside Elizabeth and resisting the urge to reach across and grasp her hand.

Elizabeth gave a shaky sigh. "It was terrible," she said as she glanced up to meet his gaze, only to look back down at her lap as she twisted her fingers together slowly. "I should have known. I knew better…which makes it so, so much worse."

He nodded, not sure what to say. So he just listened as she continued.

"I… Do you remember the first time we met when you returned to Cambridge?" she asked.

Collin chuckled. "Yes, I think I rather made an impression, didn't I?"

"If my memory serves me correctly—"

"It no doubt does."

"You asked why," she said, her forehead puckering slightly. "Why I wanted to be in a place where everyone pretended I didn't exist."

"Ah, yes, that question." He widened his eyes and shook his head. "I really know how to make an impression, don't I?" He shrugged.

"Oh, you certainly made an impression," she said, some of her earlier tension releasing from her expression.

Collin nodded.

"Do you remember my answer?" she asked, studying his face.

Collin nodded, then quoted her. "'One, because I enjoy learning, and this is the ideal place for it. Two, because I wish to be with my father, and three, because I can.'" He shook his head. "It was the way you answered me that made you unforgettable. You spoke to me like I was a five-year-old schoolboy."

"Clearly I made as much of an impression on you as you did on me," she replied dryly. "I was a little irritated with you."

"A little?" he asked, aghast. "Your expression would have cheerfully set me on fire."

She blushed, chuckled, and then nodded. "Very well, I would have done just that."

"Honestly, it's important." He smiled archly. "But I digress. Pray continue."

She shrugged. "You answered me and said—"

Collin interrupted her. "'All noble reasons, minus the third.'"

"In what way?" Elizabeth asked, repeating her own question from what seemed like forever ago.

He gave her that same patronizing expression that she remembered so clearly and continued with the memory. "'Come now, Miss Essex. You're clearly an intelligent woman. Your third reason is purely selfish. You care not for how your presence impacts others, or if it makes them uncomfortable. It's for your own enrichment, and let's be further honest… That enrichment is noble, but at the same time…'"—he paused, truly not wishing to finish the words he remembered so clearly—"a dead end." He winced.

Elizabeth sighed. "You…were right."

Collin met her eye. "While I adore hearing those words from your lips, as a man of honor, I can't accept them, as much as I'd like to. Because they weren't true or accurate. It was spoken with a fast judgment that wasn't fair to you or your integrity. For that, I sincerely apologize, Miss Essex."

Elizabeth shook her head. "No, I was being selfish. And was further selfish with the class that I taught, not telling my father and brazenly going against convention. I love to teach. I want to give my knowledge and study to those who haven't had the same opportunity as I have, but I need to do it in a way that doesn't compromise that same education or undermine those I love."

Collin grasped her hand, carefully, tenderly, stroking the top of her fingers with his. "I…" He paused, not sure how to turn the words of his heart into the words of his lips. "We'll find a way," he answered simply.

She gave a slightly confused expression.

"We'll find a way. Because you have far too much to offer, and you are, from what I hear, an excellent teacher, so—" He shrugged. "We'll find a way to make it work, so that you do what you love without feeling like you're betraying the people you love with a bit of scandal." He patted her hand. "I will say, though, as much as going against the social convention can be uncomfortable and frowned upon, your kind is my favorite."

"Is that a compliment?" she asked, glancing down, though she smiled.

"It is. It speaks of your courage, determination, and loyalty. Your willingness to risk exposure and ridicule to educate women in deeper subjects than were considered necessary speaks of your tenacity, and that is a rare character trait. And I, for one, appreciate that about you."

She met his gaze. "Thank you... I'm glad since I won't be changing that."

"Don't change a thing." He patted her hand, then clasped his fingers around hers, squeezing. "Not one thing." He studied her fingers, then regarded her once more. "Elizabeth." He gave his head a slight shake and smiled, not sure how to continue but knowing it was necessary. Like air, like water, she was necessary for his soul. And he wasn't going to wait any longer. He didn't need to. His heart had made up its mind when he first met her.

"I love you," he whispered softly, watching as wonder spilled over her face in a warm expression. "I love your wit, your candor. I love the way you are relentless in the pursuit of understanding and ideas. I love that you…" He laughed. "I love that you did hours of research on tea smuggling, not only because you knew it was helpful but because you also can't resist that endless curiosity that you always have circling in your mind." He squeezed her fingers gently.

"I love that you are fiercely loyal and unapologetic about who you are and what you think. I love that you are fearless, sometimes to your own detriment." He gave a wry twist of his lips, his expression endearing. "But practical as well. I love that you care enough for the small things, the small creatures, that you'll use honey sparingly out of respect for the bees." He met her gaze, all bravado, everything except his heart stripped away. "I love you because you are the most amazing, unique, and strong woman I've ever known. Your beauty keeps me awake at night, and your heart humbles me each day. Will you do me the immense honor of becoming my wife?"

Collin couldn't breathe. He'd said everything that was on his heart, and all he could do was wait.

Elizabeth's expression was glorious, her eyes wide with wonder and delight and, if he could name one emotion, love. But she hadn't said a word. She glanced down at their folded hands, then back up, nodding once, then nodding with enthusiasm as she pulled away her hands and covered her mouth as if holding back laughter and tears at the same time.

"Yes?" Collin asked, just making sure. He wanted the word, the promise, the vow.

"Yes," she whispered.

"For my part, I approve," Professor Essex said from his corner. The sound of a page turning punctuated his statement.

Collin glanced up to the older man, and from across the room, the professor gave a wide smile, then returned to his reading.

"Well, I must say I was not expecting that tonight." Elizabeth took a deep breath, smiling, laughing between words.

"I like to keep you guessing. It's part of that legendary charm," Collin replied, lacing his hand through hers tighter, as if fusing them together.

"You certainly do that." Elizabeth pulled her hand away and wrapped her arms around him in a tight hug. "I love you too," she whispered against his neck.

Collin's skin erupted in gooseflesh, his body catching fire with the words that had the power to send him over the edge. He breathed in the scent of lemon and beeswax that clung to her skin, memorizing the moment. His lips burned with the need to kiss her, but with her father looking on, it wasn't the ideal moment.

But soon.

As he inhaled the sweet and fresh scent of her, he vowed it would be soon. "I love you so much," he whispered. "I never knew a love such as this existed until I met you." He spoke softly, pouring his heart into the words.

Elizabeth pulled back, a frown puckering her face. "And we're leaving the day after tomorrow. That's…disappointing." She squinted her eyes at him, as if he were at fault.

Which, of course, he was. "It's only for a short time and for the benefit of keeping you safe."

"I understand, but that doesn't mean that I like it." She leaned back into his shoulder. He wrapped his arm around her, holding her close. "I know. I'll miss you too."

"I would hope so." She gave a small laugh. "If not, we have a larger problem then the tea smugglers because I will not settle for less than your whole heart, Collin Morgan, Earl of Penderdale," she replied, honesty ringing in her tone.

"Then we are in full agreement, because I'll not settle for less either." He kissed her hair.

Collin was hoping for an opportunity alone with Elizabeth before he departed that evening, but her father was ever vigilant, more so than during their short courtship, as if reading Collin's mind.

After bidding Elizabeth a drawn-out goodbye, his heart burning with the lingering touches and looks with which she favored him, Collin left their residence with a full heart and very impatient spirit.

Perhaps he'd procure a special license.

Or maybe he wouldn't. No need to make a scandal of it. There would already be some talk back in London, but then again, London would create talk about nearly anything.

Indecision warred within him, so he'd not make the decision today. And furthermore, he would ask Elizabeth her preference, since he was certain she'd have an opinion on the matter. He grinned in spite of himself. Life with her would certainly never be boring.

Collin was tempted to stop by the Finches' residence to speak with Michael, but the late hour had him second-guessing himself. He decided a morning visit would be in order. It would give him and Michael the full day to make headway on the situation at hand as well. With the decision made, Collin headed home, his heart full and his future sealed with the most important things: hope and love.

Twenty-seven

At the touch of love everyone becomes a poet.

—Plato, *The Symposium*

COLLIN AWOKE THE NEXT DAY FULL OF PURPOSE and with a plan. As soon as it wasn't unforgivably rude, Collin visited the Finches' residence. Knocking once, he stepped back, rocking on his heels.

The door opened, revealing a quite disheveled Michael. "Good Lord, man, did I wake you?" Collin asked with more feeling than politeness.

"Aye, you did. I'm well though, and if you're here this early, you've got something to say." He opened the door wider, and Collin followed him inside.

He took a seat at the table in the parlor, watching as Michael rubbed a hand down his face and then took a seat as well, slouching with fatigue.

"So, what has you here so early?" Michael asked, leaning forward.

"Well, there are several things to discuss, actually. I'll start at the beginning." Collin sighed. "The other night, I told you I'd stay home and rest."

"Let me guess… You didn't?" Michael asked dryly.

"No."

"Shocked."

"You're not, but I digress."

Michael waved for him to continue.

"Miss Essex had made an interesting connection with the names on the list and the original regions from Cromwell's day. The list divided them into districts with a peer of the realm's name as the code for that district," Collin said.

"How did she figure that? Wait, you know? It doesn't matter, and it doesn't surprise me. She's too smart for her own good. Continue."

Collin wanted to argue his words. "She's not too *smart* for her own good. Too brave, maybe, but her intelligence is an asset."

Michael blinked at him. "Very well, I take it back. Continue."

"Well, I visited the apothecary—"

Michael groaned. "What did you do?"

"I went in and said something about the other districts, and I named one, saying I wanted that district." Collin shrugged.

"Oh. How did that work for you?" Michael asked skeptically.

"Well, it worked a little too well," Collin replied, twisting his lips. "Here's where it all went to hell."

"You're clearly alive so they didn't kill you…so it could have gone worse?"

"Maybe," Collin replied.

"Oh, good Lord, just tell me." Michael rubbed his face again. "It's too early for this. Gah! Go on! Tell me."

"Well, I was taken back to a man named McKensie."

Michael's face went blank. "Who?"

"McKensie. Apparently he's the person in charge of this district—"

Michael stood. "You're a dead man, Collin."

"Well, not quite." Collin shrugged. "But he did send a message to check my credentials, which of course, will return and implicate me as a liar—"

"Bloody hell," Michael swore.

"And they also connected me with Elizabeth—"

Michael stopped. "They did?"

"Yes, but I'm sending her to London before they can receive word about my made-up tale."

Michael's body sagged in relief. "Very well, that's the one good thing you've done. The rest, horrible. You've single-handedly put yourself and others in danger. For what, Collin? Tea?" Michael tugged his hair and kicked a chair.

"No. Not for tea." Collin stood. "For my name, Michael."

"Hang your name!"

"No! It's the name that my father gave me, and that someday, God willing, I'll give to my children. It's the name..." He paused. "It's the name that Elizabeth will have when she marries me. It's the name of my past and all the hope of my future. I'll not just let it be used carelessly. Right now, the War Office and Parliament believe that my name and others are not connected, but what if someone compromises that?" He leaned forward, splaying his hands on the table as he regarded Michael. "What if someone gets greedy and decides he might as well benefit from the use of my name and then it all goes to hell? That's not the legacy I want to leave, and it's sure as hell not the legacy my father left to me. I'm on borrowed time to make this right, to clear it up so that it's not an issue for any future generations. I could care less about the tea smuggling. Though it is wrong, it is not my problem. But when they started using my name to do it? They made it my problem." He released a deep breath.

Michael shifted on his feet. "We need a plan."

"I have one," Collin replied.

"No, you are no longer trusted to make plans. You made a mess out of this one."

"It's a good plan," Collin tried.

"To hell with your bloody plan." Michael lit a cheroot.

"You don't want to hear it?"

Michael paused. "Fine, what is this plan? And when it's horrid, I'm going to remind you that you no longer get to make plans. You compromised everything."

Collin sat down. "Once Elizabeth is out of town, we approach them."

"Already it's terrible. And the 'we' aspect? Bloody awful. Because I'm the one part they don't know about, apparently. Unless you failed to mention that you've exposed me too?"

Collin shook his head. "That's the one thing I can't quite figure out."

"What? A hole in the plan?" Michael said with sarcasm. "So, start again. You go and approach them. I'll stay behind and cover your bloody ass."

Collin laid out the plan carefully, hitting each detail. "I'll approach them and tell them I lied. Offer them a bribe to keep it quiet, since I was trying to get a cut of the business, and see if they walk away. If they know my name is attached to their smuggling, they will have to change the name because the whole operation only works if no one has solved the puzzle of the names. But since it's solved, they'll have to change the name again to keep their anonymity."

"That's a lot of possibilities that all have to go right. And you're still not catching these guys. They are still smuggling tea, which is quite illegal."

"They are, and they'll get caught eventually, but it's too big an operation for me. Hell, it's too big for the War Office and the entirety of Parliament. I'm cavalier and brazen, but I'm not stupid, and I know this isn't a war I'd win. So, I'm picking my battle."

"Your name."

"Exactly."

Michael twisted his lips. "It might…*might* work. However, there's a lot of risk."

"Riskier than them finding out the hard way that I lied to their faces?"

"Point taken," Michael replied. "When do we take action?"

"Elizabeth leaves in the morning. So, midafternoon tomorrow. Hoping they haven't received the news that I lied by then."

"You better pray they are slow in receiving that information."

"I am," Collin assured him.

Michael sighed. "This is not what I expected."

"I know. But you've been an asset and a friend." Collin extended his hand to Michael.

Michael took it, shaking it firmly. "That's the only reason I'm following this through and not leaving your rich arse to the local sharks."

"Thank you for that. Turns out I have a lot to live for."

"That's assuming you survive this."

"I've been in worse situations."

Michael chuckled. "Of that I have no doubt. It's a wonder you're still alive."

"Thanks, friend."

"You're welcome," Michael returned, smiling. "It's what friends are for: honesty, even when it hurts."

"Lucky me."

"And me. Now, you better make sure you have the funds for that bribe."

"I already started making arrangements."

"About time you did something right," Michael replied with an exasperated chuckle.

Collin smirked. "Turns out, I think I'm finally starting to get a lot of things right. Took me a while, but you know what they say, 'Better late than never.' Chaucer was brilliant."

"I think it's 'For better than never is late…'"

Collin blinked. "I'm impressed."

"I'm more intelligent than you expected, and you're less than I expected. Brilliant day."

"At that charming insult, I'm going to take my leave." Collin laughed as he shook Michael's hand once more. "I'll keep you informed of any changes, but let's plan on tomorrow afternoon."

"Good. I'll see you then. Try not to do anything else foolish. Please?" Michael chuckled and waved goodbye.

As Collin left, he thought of the rest of the quote from Chaucer, "For better than never is late…" It was the ending that Michael left off that spoke deeper. "Never to succeed would be too long a period."

Never to succeed would indeed be too long a period.

His life had been marked by lacking success in what mattered most.

But no more.

Better late than never, but it was time to succeed on the things that mattered, like his future.

Twenty-eight

Wonder is the beginning of wisdom.

—Socrates, quoted in Plato's *Theaetetus*

ELIZABETH AWOKE WITH A BRIGHT SMILE, HER body tingling with joy as she remembered the evening before. She was betrothed, and to Collin. It was wonderful and hilarious at the same time, since she was certain they'd argue as much as cats and dogs, but she'd never felt more secure and loved than when she was with him, never more confident about being herself.

For so long, she'd lived a dichotomy, feeling like she didn't belong and brazenly unapologetic about it. And that he loved that about her, why, it was more than she had dared hope or imagine. And that he didn't want her to change, to be a subservient wife with no thoughts of her own… Elizabeth shuddered at the thought. She couldn't do that, she wouldn't. It would go against every bone in her body. But that's not what he loved about her. She leaned in to her pillow and imagined his face. He had been so tender, yet fierce in his words. He'd even mentioned her bees. She laughed at that memory. He didn't leave anything out of the proposal, and it was humbling to be known so completely.

The good.

The bad.

The big things.

The little things.

The vulnerability of it all was unsettling, new, but she also loved the feeling of having her soul laid bare and being loved for it. Who didn't want that?

A life, a future, a new name, and a joined heart. And as if that wasn't enough, a constant companion who pushed her, challenged her, teased her, and wasn't offended when she did the same.

If she had any reservations, it was about meeting his sister. While Collin had assured her that theirs would be a fast friendship, she still was concerned. She knew she wasn't like most—or really any—of the ladies in London. She was a nobody as far as her pedigree. Her father was knighted; however, Collin was an earl and was expected to marry someone of equal social status, not a bluestocking from Cambridge who had nearly caused a scandal.

She sighed. It would be difficult to be herself and not compromise or dilute who she was but also follow all the social conventions well enough not to cause talk. She wasn't sure if they'd leave the house while she and her papa stayed at the home of the duke and duchess, but if they did, she'd be mindful.

After dressing and breaking her fast, she sent a note to Patricia, inviting her for a visit. Molly had already started packing, and Elizabeth was hoping Patricia had some advice to offer.

It wasn't long before Patricia came and all but bounced into the room. "London?" Her smile was bright. "I'm burning with jealousy! What dresses are you bringing?" she asked, then began searching through piles of fabric on the bed.

"Good morning to you too," Elizabeth said with a grin.

"You can't take this one." Patricia lifted a gown and set it on a chair. "You're staying with a duke and duchess, so dress accordingly!" she chided, though she kept her bright smile. "Ah, this will work, and then where's that yellow muslin..." She answered her own question and lifted it up, brushed it and set it aside. "Of course, all of these will need to be pressed before you can wear them anywhere, but the staff will take care of that in London."

"Yes, I'm sure we will be well cared for." Elizabeth covered her mouth with her hand to keep from giggling at Patricia's enthusiastic behavior.

"Your nicest gown is a little outdated." Patricia lifted a white frock from the pile. "It will do, I suppose."

"I'm not going to meet the Regent or attend any balls, Patricia. It's not even the season."

"More's the pity." Patricia sighed.

"I'm quite thankful it's not the social season." Elizabeth gave a soft shudder. "I know, in theory, how to act and what to do, but I've exercised the skill very little recently."

"You'd do well. I wouldn't worry. You have quite the social grace when you wish to use it."

"I find that laughable."

"You do! You just choose to disregard it most days." Patricia gave a wink. "Shoes! You'll need to bring slippers and boots—"

"Molly already packed those," Elizabeth explained.

"Good, good. Now that we've got that settled…" She took a seat in the chair beside the low-burning fire. "Why are you going to London in the first place?"

Elizabeth had debated about what to tell her friend. She didn't want to raise alarm, but she also didn't want to be dishonest. "Well, for several reasons," she hedged.

Patricia gestured to the chair across from her. "You appear nervous. Sit and tell me everything!" She clapped her hands.

Elizabeth shook her head with amusement. "Very well. Last night I accepted Lord Penderdale's proposal." She bit her lip, her smile almost painful, it was so wide.

"What? And you didn't tell me that the moment I walked into the room? Shame! I'm so thrilled for you! I knew it the moment you two were bickering and fighting like mad. An emotional response like that…" She wiggled her eyebrows. "I'm very happy for you, Elizabeth."

Elizabeth glanced at her hands. "Truly? Though you had other plans…" She regarded her friend.

Patricia waved the words away. "I did have other plans. However, these are better! Now I get to visit you in London, and you can introduce me to all your husband's interesting unmarried friends…" She grinned.

Elizabeth frowned for a moment. She hadn't thought that far ahead. She'd be leaving Cambridge behind. Not until they were married, but afterward. His home was in London. Not Cambridge.

"I… If you'd rather I not visit…" Patricia started, a cloud of hurt flickering across her features.

"No! It's not that! Of course, you'll be welcome, and I'll likely beg you to stay longer than you'd like," Elizabeth answered, earning a relieved smile from her friend. "It's just that, well, it shouldn't come as a shock, except it sort of does…the fact that I'll be moving to London."

"Ah, I understand that."

"Yes, but I'm not opposed to it. Rather, the more I think of it, the more it sounds like an adventure. And there will be museums and ways to study that Cambridge doesn't offer."

"I'm sure you'll be quite busy." Patricia blushed and studied the fire, hiding her smile.

"Stop that." Heat rushed to Elizabeth's face. "I am nervous to meet his sister though," she confessed.

"She'll love you. Don't worry."

"I certainly hope so. If not, that won't bode well."

"Lord Penderdale isn't the sort to let his sister dictate anything in his life," Patricia observed.

Elizabeth sighed. "Yes, but I'd hate to cause a conflict."

"You won't," Patricia said calmly. "So don't borrow a worry that isn't a real one."

"Wise words. Thank you."

"I had an excellent teacher." She winked.

At the mention of teaching, Elizabeth's chest tightened. "About that…"

"You'll have to quit. You're going to be married. It's only logical." Patricia waved off the explanation and turned back to the bed, as if studying the dresses laid out.

Elizabeth took a breath and was about to tell her the whole story, then stopped. Why? What benefit would it have to Patricia to know? Let the events take their natural course. The fewer people who knew, the better, right? She released a breath and stood. "How do you think I should wear my hair?"

Twenty-nine

There are many wonderful things, but none more wonderful than man.

—Sophocles, *Antigone*

COLLIN ARRIVED EARLY THE MORNING OF THE scheduled departure to London. He'd spent the day before arranging everything for his afternoon plans with Michael, but in the middle of the plans, his thoughts had never been far from Elizabeth.

Molly opened the door and ushered him in. The hall was lined with several trunks, and the footmen he'd brought from the duke's residence had begun lifting and loading everything Molly indicated. Collin left them to their work and found Elizabeth and her father in the parlor. Elizabeth was scribbling something on a parchment, and her father was patting his coat pockets, as if assuring himself that he'd not left anything important behind.

"Good morning," he greeted Collin.

Elizabeth's eyes shot up and her welcoming smile filled his heart. "Good morning," she answered softly. She folded the piece of parchment and set the quill down.

He withdrew a small letter from his coat pocket and walked over to her, offering it to her. Elizabeth smiled shyly and took the note, and then lifted the one she'd just finished and offered it to him.

"Ah, I see we had the same plans."

"For once," she returned with a teasing grin.

Collin tucked the paper in his coat and offered her his hand. "Will you sit with me a moment?"

"Of course." She took a seat beside him on the settee where, only a short while ago, he'd offered her his heart and hand. Memories flooded him as he regarded her. "I wanted to say thank you for leaving somewhat abruptly for London and also for trusting me."

Elizabeth nodded. "Of course, and it was the most practical and reasonable option. Part of me desperately wants to stay behind to make sure you're safe...but I won't delude myself into thinking I'm in any position to save you."

"You saved me." He touched her chin softly. "You saved me from a life of apathy and hopelessness."

She grasped his hand as it held her chin and speared him with her gaze. "No. You allowed yourself to see the beauty, the potential, and seized the opportunity to live it," she said with a smile. "That's courage, bravery, and much harder than letting someone do the saving for you."

"Wise and beautiful... I'm a lucky man."

"Very, very lucky." She arched a brow, and as her attention dipped to his lips, he had to pull back before he kissed her for the first time right in front of her father. Truthfully, he had no reservations about it, but he rather thought that Elizabeth might. And the first time he kissed her, he wanted her full attention, not sharing it with some distraction like her father's presence.

"Joan is expecting you," he said, forcing his thoughts in line. "She will have received my letter before you arrive and will possibly accost you when you get there." He chuckled.

"Should I be afraid?" she asked playfully.

"Yes," he said, his expression serious. A smile spread across his face. "No, Joan is all I have for family, and it's giving me great joy to know that marrying you will give her a sister. We've lost much of our family. It's time to add back to the numbers." His face twisted as he said the words.

"Do we have a moment? Can you tell me what happened?" Elizabeth asked, touching his face lightly with her gloved hand. He leaned into her touch and nodded once. "My parents passed—my father, then my mother. My twin brother—"

Elizabeth gasped, her expression puckering in sorrow.

"He was lost in a fire, as was my brother-in-law's brother. In fact, several of London's families lost their heirs in that fire."

"They were all together?" Elizabeth asked, tipping her head, her expression deeply sympathetic.

"Yes, it was a party for one of my brother's closest friends. I didn't attend. I was on a mission with the War Office, or else I would have perished too. I still carry guilt over that." He shrugged. Admitting something he'd never said out loud was easier than he'd expected. He continued. "Joan and I were left alone after that."

"That's...a lot of loss." Elizabeth brushed her thumb against his cheek.

"It is. And still life moves on, which I think is harder," he admitted.

She nodded. "It is. When my mother died, that's exactly how I felt. How I still feel. And there's the crippling fear of losing my father...or anyone else I love." She glanced down. "It's not something you get over."

"It's not," he answered, wonder filling his heart that in talking about the most painful moments of his life, he was experiencing real comfort and understanding. Elizabeth had known loss as well, known it deeply. It changed a person, and he loved her even more for her compassion.

"So Joan, she'll likely tell you I was a tyrant— which I sort of was—but you understand why now. She was all I had left." He shrugged a shoulder.

"I understand." Elizabeth nodded, then with a twinkle in her eye, she added, "In efforts to befriend your sister, I may not defend you…" She gave a soft laugh. "But I understand, Collin."

"Those are terms I can accept." He grinned.

Elizabeth released his cheek and smiled shyly.

"Thank you," he said softly, lifting her hand and kissing it slowly.

She inhaled a shaky breath, her lips blooming with color and tempting him beyond what he thought he could endure.

"For?" she asked breathlessly, her gaze darting between his lips and his eyes.

He groaned. Blast her father for being so vigilant.

"For listening, for understanding. It's not something that's easy to speak of, but when you talk with the right person, that makes all the difference."

"I'm honored," she replied, her face a well of deep emotion.

"I sincerely don't want to watch you leave," he whispered softly, caressing her hand with his fingers.

"I truly don't want to go," she responded, her voice low and raspy.

"And yet…" He studied her, every nuance of her expression burning into his soul. "You must."

"I must," she agreed. "But only for as long as necessary."

"Yes."

She pulled away her hand and pointed at him. "And you'll write and let me know how you are faring." It wasn't a question.

"Yes," Collin replied, grinning.

"And you'll—"

"Are you always going to be this demanding?" he asked playfully, kissing her hand again just for the pleasure of it.

"Yes," she whispered breathlessly.

"I'm sure I'll find my own ways to be demanding as well," he said with a wicked grin.

Warmth suffused Elizabeth's face.

A footman entered the parlor. "My lord? The carriage is ready."

Collin stood and helped Elizabeth to her feet as well. He nodded to the footman and then to Elizabeth's father, who had taken up another book in the far chair.

Collin gestured to the door and followed them out into the hall and then to the front stoop. Gently, he aided Elizabeth as she stepped into his well-sprung carriage and then stepped back as Professor Essex shook his hand, said his goodbyes, and followed his daughter into the conveyance.

There was something deeply personal about having her ensconced in his carriage. Seeing the Penderdale crest painted on the side and having her watch him from the window made his heart pinch with how right it felt. If he was having this much of a reaction with her merely using his carriage, he couldn't imagine what it would be like to see her interact with his sister. He made light of how much they'd overtake the world once together, but truly he couldn't imagine a better friend for Joan, or for Elizabeth. Both were women before their time, women who weren't afraid to be unconventional, women who were far more intelligent and witty than most. They were unique.

He was only deeply regretful that he couldn't be there to watch their first interactions. Rowles's face he could imagine, and he likely would hear a very specific, detailed account from his sister about the whole thing, but it was different, not being there.

But Elizabeth would be safe.

And that was what mattered.

He lifted a hand in farewell as the carriage rolled forward. Elizabeth's eyes were on him, not wavering until he couldn't see her any longer and the carriage had disappeared around the corner.

It was done.

And now came the hard part.

Finding the end of the maze of lies that had been woven around them.

He took a deep breath and began the short walk back to the duke's residence. He had a little time before he would meet with Michael, and then so much of his future would be decided—as in whether he had one at all.

Because he hadn't shared with Elizabeth that there was a real life-or-death risk. If working for the War Office had taught him anything, it was that life was fleeting. And fate had punctuated that lesson with the untimely deaths of his family. He only hoped it was the beginning of something new, not the end. Regardless, he'd made provisions for Elizabeth.

He'd spent time yesterday contacting his solicitor in London, giving instructions in case the worst were to happen. If all went well, those plans were to be disregarded. He'd also sent along a letter to give to Joan, and one to Elizabeth, if the worst-case scenario took place, so that his final words were delivered to the two women he loved.

There was peace in that, though he hoped it was all for naught. And he'd find out soon enough. He arrived back at the duke's residence and went to the study where he'd hidden the funds he'd be using as a bribe. Dear Lord, he'd never thought it would come to this. Nevertheless, what other option did he have? None, and he'd spoken the truth to Michael yesterday. He wasn't about to delude himself into thinking he could single-handedly take on the tea smuggling ring that provided more tea than any of the legal channels.

He tucked the bribe money in his coat pocket, making sure it was secure and didn't appear obvious to someone inspecting his coat closely. The last thing he wanted was someone to think a bulge in his coat was a pistol. Dear Lord, that was a fast way to get killed and then robbed. He sighed.

Collin quit the duke's lodgings and headed toward Michael's house, his heart pounding as his mind continued to spin along all the details of the plan to be enacted shortly. There were far too many variables for him to be assured of any success, but he had to try nonetheless. Avoiding the problem would only lead to a greater drawback.

Michael answered the door before Collin knocked. "Are you ready?"

"As I'll ever be," Collin replied, sighing. "This is going to work."

"Are you convincing me or yourself?" Michael asked.

"Both?" Collin replied, then gave a lopsided grin. "I don't know. Let's get this done before I have any more time to think about it."

"One of the smartest things you've said in a long while." Michael gave him a dry smile and closed the door. "Now, let's review the plan once more on our way."

Thirty

One word frees us of all the weight and pain in life. That word is love.

—Sophocles, *Oedipus at Colonus*

ELIZABETH'S HEART HAMMERED AS THEY approached the Mayfair district of London. They had just passed by Hyde Park and were entering into the cloistered luxury of the London elite.

She did not belong here.

But she took a deep breath and forced herself to notice the small details: the perfectly clipped hedges, the last blooming flowers of fall, and the light rain that cleaned the otherwise smoky air.

The carriage paused before a gate, the gray stone town house rising up after a short stone walkway that led to the steps. The stone home was magnificent, not like anything she'd seen before, except for illustrations in books. Her heart pounding harder, she forced deep breaths.

"There's nothing to fear, my dear." Her father's words comforted her. And she gave him a weak smile.

Just as Collin had predicted, the moment the

carriage pulled in front of the home, a fiery red-headed woman bounded down the stairs, a gentleman following her at a much more sedate place, an amused smile on his face. The duke and duchess, she presumed. Her attention went back to the woman and her face lit in the most welcoming smile.

Elizabeth had barely stepped from the carriage when the duchess welcomed her. "You must be Elizabeth."

Elizabeth curtsied.

"Your Grace." She lowered her head in respect as she rose. The moment she was standing, she was pulled into a tight hug.

"You have no idea how happy I am to meet you, dear Elizabeth," the duchess whispered fiercely.

Elizabeth returned the hug, her earlier stress melting away. "I'm truly happy to meet you as well."

The duchess released her and smiled wide, and Elizabeth wondered if perhaps Collin wasn't exaggerating when he said his sister was unconventional. Because ladies were only to give small, coy smiles. Yet the duchess was unapologetically warm.

And Elizabeth immediately loved her for it.

"Allow me to introduce my father, Professor Essex," Elizabeth said as she stepped aside for her father.

"A pleasure, Professor," the duchess replied kindly after his bow.

"Professor!" The duke reached them, his expression wide and welcoming. "It's been too long."

Her father bowed, and the duke offered her father his hand.

Elizabeth turned to her father with curiosity.

"He's an old student and also was a fellow professor at Cambridge until recently."

Elizabeth's eyes widened. She hadn't been introduced so she waited.

"Miss Essex, please meet my husband, the Duke of Westmore."

Elizabeth curtsied again, showing her respect.

"Please, call me Rowles. We're all family, or soon to be, are we not?" he said significantly.

"Please, come in. We are so pleased to have you at our home," the duchess said, pulling Elizabeth's arm and tucking it in her own as she led them up the stairs. "I'm sure you're tired from your journey. Would you prefer tea first, or to freshen up?" she asked.

Elizabeth glanced to her father.

He replied. "A moment to freshen up would be most appreciated."

"Of course. A maid will show you to your rooms, and the footmen will bring up your things shortly. I'll have tea ready in about an hour. Will that be satisfactory?"

"Delightful. Thank you very much for your hospitality," Elizabeth said with heartfelt appreciation.

"We have been anticipating your arrival the moment we heard the news of it," the duchess said. "And as Rowles said, we don't hold with convention around family. Please call me Joan." She squeezed Elizabeth's arm and released it.

"Thank you, and of course please call me Elizabeth," she said to both of them.

Joan gestured to a maid, who led them up a beautifully crafted walnut staircase. Elizabeth finally gave her attention to her surroundings and was thankful she'd ignored them at first, or else she'd have been fully distracted by their beauty. Light flooded the antechamber before the staircase; the warm wood was highlighted by freshly painted cream-colored plaster walls. The marble floor at the base of the staircase was brilliantly polished, reflecting the light from the windows. She followed the maid upstairs to a wide hall lined with rich, dark wooden doors. Large paintings in elaborate frames lined the halls, accented by slender tables that held various vases with autumn flowers. Elizabeth took in the color, tasteful and understated with an undeniable wealth that she'd never seen firsthand. "Here are your rooms, miss." The maid opened a wide door and ushered Elizabeth in.

Light spilled into the room, highlighting a four-poster bed piled high with pillows and a writing desk at the window. The room led to a washing station and likely a dressing chamber. It was larger than any room Elizabeth had stayed in before. Still even in its grandeur, it was welcoming and inviting.

"The footmen will be up shortly with your things. Until then, may I be of assistance?" the maid offered.

Elizabeth declined her assistance, wanting just a moment to herself to think. Dismissed, the maid left and closed the door, and Elizabeth sat on the bed, sinking deep in the luxury of it as she closed her eyes and relived the past few minutes.

The duke and duchess were nothing like she'd expected. Though Collin had told stories of his sister, Elizabeth hadn't quite believed him. However, she was so thankful that Joan, Duchess of Westmore, was exactly as her brother had described her: unconventional, quick-witted, kind, and delightful.

The duke was even more surprising. He clearly doted on his wife and didn't appear the stuffy, self-important type that Elizabeth had associated with the title. She'd heard that one of her father's fellow professors had inherited a title and resigned his post at the college, but she hadn't paid much attention to the story. How unbelievable that the same man was to be her brother-in-law! She blushed, still unable to believe she was betrothed to Collin.

Betrothed, nevertheless, and here she was, meeting his family without him. Because he was in a certain amount of peril, and she would have no word from him for a few days.

Her heart sank and her belly felt sick at the thought. She said a fast prayer for his safety. Heaven knew he needed all the help he could get.

The hour passed rapidly and soon Elizabeth made her way downstairs to take tea with the duke, the duchess, and her father. A footman escorted her to the parlor where Joan was waiting, teacup in hand.

"Ah, welcome. I hope you are refreshed?" she asked, indicating a chair. "Please have a seat. May I offer you some tea?"

Elizabeth thanked her, choosing a wing-backed chair across from her hostess. "Yes, please."

"How do you take it?"

Elizabeth blushed slightly as she thought of honey and how that had led to one of her first conversations with Collin. "Nothing added, thank you."

Joan handed her a teacup and studied her a moment. "The only downfall to being a redhead, or of the strawberry blond variety," she said with a nod of her head toward Elizabeth, "is that our emotions tend to be reflected on our faces, like in that delicate blush you just tried to hide." She offered a smile. "So, either I've made you slightly uncomfortable, or you were thinking of my brother..." She grinned. "And I sincerely hope it was the second option."

The duchess sat and lifted her teacup, a wide smile teasing her lips.

"Ah, so you must not have the temper that

I inherited with my hair," Elizabeth said, then belatedly hoped she'd not spoken out of turn.

The duchess laughed, unapologetically vibrant. "Ah, well, we don't mention the lesser qualities, my dear." She added, "And I prefer to think intense, not quick-tempered."

"I'll remember that," Elizabeth replied.

"But you never answered my question," Joan reminded her.

Elizabeth scrunched her nose. "Well, it's a bit of a story."

"We have time."

"It's likely not what you're expecting."

"Even better." The duchess was leaning forward with an expectant look on her face.

Elizabeth took a sip of tea, building up her courage. "Well, I'm not certain how much your brother has said concerning how we first…interacted with each other." She winced. "Honestly, not much has changed on that front, but I like to think I'm less likely to jump to conclusions about him than I did originally."

"You've certainly piqued my curiosity," Joan stated, offering a good-natured smile. "He hasn't said much, only that you and I have some similar character traits. He was disappointingly vague." She flicked her fingers. "Men and their lack of detail."

"Well, I must admit that our first interactions were not pleasant. I believe I insulted him fully, and he returned the favor." Elizabeth bit her lip.

"I'm sure he deserved it. What was the argument about, if you don't mind me asking?"

"Which time?" Elizabeth replied with a grin.

"I think I understand why my brother couldn't resist you." Joan returned the smile.

"I, for my part, did try to be quite resistible, prickly, in fact."

"Yet he won your heart…" Joan let the question linger, as if wanting Elizabeth to confirm it.

"Yes, against my will, and I rather like that. It wasn't something I forced; rather I resisted. He…" She paused. "I can be rather unconventional, and rather than wish that to be something he can change, he appreciates that, encourages it. I never thought I'd find that." Elizabeth hitched a shoulder.

Joan sighed softly. "You have no idea how happy I was when he wrote of you. He'd been going through a bit of a rough patch of late." She frowned slightly. "I've been concerned, but there was little I could do other than badger him relentlessly."

At this, Elizabeth chuckled.

"I did—badger him, that is. But it wasn't enough, and when he left for Cambridge, I wasn't sure whether it was the best idea or the worst. There was little for him here in London, besides me and Rowles, and of course our dear friends Catherine and Quin. You'll meet them later," she interjected. "He was quite lost and needed a purpose."

"Well, he did make some progress related to the

reason he came to Cambridge, a little too much progress in my opinion. Regardless, it's unfortunate that I can't do anything about it."

Elizabeth nodded. "The waiting is the hardest."

"It is."

"He's quite capable. He's been trained well, but I'll admit that I don't like the idea of him being alone there."

"He has Mr. Finch," Elizabeth told her. "So at least he won't be attempting anything alone."

"Ah, is that the gentleman who was referred to him by the shire office? He mentioned that in his last letter, the one informing us of your arrival."

"Yes, his sister is one of my greatest friends." Elizabeth offered a gentle grin. "She compared the interaction between your brother and me to the fireworks at Vauxhall Gardens."

Joan regarded her, blinked, then started to giggle. "Oh, I wish I could see it."

"You will. We still have, er, heated discussions."

"Good. He needs that sort of penance in his life."

"I don't plan on changing."

Joan smiled softly. "He was right, much as it pains me to say that out loud."

Elizabeth winced. "Painful indeed. I'll not tell him the words left your lips."

"Thank you. He said we would be fast friends, and I can see that we will truly get along famously, Miss Essex."

Elizabeth blushed and thanked the duchess. "I truly hope so."

"I'm already assured of it."

"Assured of what? Or should I not ask?" The duke entered the room followed by Elizabeth's father.

Elizabeth stood and curtsied.

"Thank you, but not necessary." He gestured back to her chair and took a seat as well. Elizabeth's father took a chair beside her and accepted the duchess's offer of tea.

"To answer your question, just saying that we're going to be fast friends. Beware." Joan quirked a brow at her husband.

"I see. Well, at least when you two join forces, I can retreat to billiards with Collin."

"Capital idea," Joan replied. "And I have a brilliant idea of my own. When my wayward brother returns to London in the next few days, Lord willing, I believe a party is in order."

Elizabeth glanced up.

"A party?" Elizabeth's father asked politely.

"Indeed, a ball. You, Miss Essex, need to let the world know that my brother has met his match. And a party is just the right way to announce it."

Elizabeth forced a smile.

She'd studied social protocol, rarely followed it, and now was going to be the highlight of a London ballroom where the strictest social protocol was not only expected, but any faux pas would be a scandal.

What could go wrong?
She was quite certain she had the answer.
Everything.

Thirty-one

*It is one thing to show a man that he is in an error, and
another to put him in possession of truth.*

—John Locke, *An Essay Concerning Human Understanding*

COLLIN SHARED A LOOK WITH MICHAEL AS THEY
parted ways, he to the apothecary, Michael to the
rear entrance at the back of the building. It was
the closest exit to McKensie's office, and if things
went badly and Collin needed to run, Michael
would be close by. If there was no one guarding the
back door, Michael could possibly sneak in as well.
Although he wouldn't try that unless Collin took
too long. It was risky regardless, but at least Collin
wasn't alone.

As Collin walked down the street toward the
apothecary, he thought over what he was going to
say and how he'd persuade them to take his offer.
Any sort of bribe went against his grain. However,
he'd gone over the scenario time and time again,
and he didn't see another way out when he was
dealing with a crime ring as large as this.

He paused in front of the apothecary, took a deep

breath, and entered. The door closed behind him, and Collin took in his surroundings. The candlelight flickered from the gust created by the closed door, but there was no other movement. The man who had been behind the counter the first time was absent. After a few moments, Collin heard steps.

Olsen came out from the hall, his regard quickly sharpening with recognition as he studied Collin for a moment. "I thought we said not to come back."

"I have something I think you'll be interested in." Collin left his hook vague, hoping greed would whet their curiosity enough to gain him an opportunity.

"I doubt that." Olsen cracked his knuckles. "But lucky for you, it's not up to me. Wait there."

Olsen stepped back, keeping an eye on Collin as he rapped a few times on the door that Collin recognized as belonging to McKensie. Olsen waited a moment, then opened the door, speaking in hushed tones to the man before waving Collin forward.

"Slowly now, I'd hate to bloody up that pretty face." His tone suggested otherwise.

Collin moved forward slowly, keeping his hands visible.

"You have three minutes, so you'd best make them the most convincing three minutes of your life," he challenged.

Collin nodded and stepped inside McKensie's office. It was now or never.

"You again. Interesting. I was going to send Olsen

after you today. I received an interesting letter from Whaleford." He lifted a piece of parchment and set it down on the table. "And the little English flower you've been sniffing around has now vacated the city, so you've left me with limited prospects for punishing your dishonesty." He leaned back in his chair.

"How about I pay for my debts?" Collin asked, then slowly, so both Olsen and McKensie could watch his very deliberate movements, withdrew the funds he'd procured and set them on the table.

McKensie's eyes darkened. "What's that?"

Collin gauged his reaction to the stack of notes on the table. "For your silence on the matter. I figure I needed something, which I believe you can finalize for me, and in return, you are reaping the benefits. I'm leaving Cambridge on the morrow anyway."

"So you think," Olsen said with a dark chuckle.

"What is it you need?" McKensie flicked his eyes up, then back to the bribe.

Collin breathed out slowly. "Your names for your…operation's locations…have been compromised. You know this. It's not new information, but I'm just making sure they get changed with alacrity and don't involve themselves with me."

"Didn't like our little trick?"

"No more than you'd like me to pull one on you," Collin replied tightly.

"I'll consider it." McKensie pulled the notes toward him.

Collin reached forward and placed a hand on the funds. "This is not an amount that buys possibility, but action," he replied darkly.

Olsen spoke up. "You're not in a position to be making demands."

Collin didn't release his hold but met McKensie's flinty stare. "You harm me, and it won't be something you can cover up. Do you honestly think that the death of a peer of the realm will go unnoticed? You're more foolish than I anticipated." He released the money and straightened.

"Very well." McKensie tucked the money in his front pocket, then nodded to Olsen.

"My appreciation," Collin replied, then made to leave.

Olsen stood in his way. "Not quite." He grasped Collin's arm and swung with his other.

Collin ducked out of the way, wrenching his arm free as he headed into the hall, toward the back door. He kept his back to the wall, maintaining an eye on Olsen. "Nimble, you are not," he replied.

Olsen's grin darkened.

"Olsen, don't kill him. As he said, it won't go unnoticed, but…rough him up a bit. Remind him that peers of the realm bleed just as much as the rest of us," McKensie said from his desk, not pausing his work to study them.

"We had an agreement."

"We did, and I'll uphold my side, but I never said I'd stop Olsen from exacting his justice. You lied to him. He takes that personally." He waved his hand as if telling Olsen to hurry up.

Collin groaned.

Olsen started toward him, his corded arms flexing as he fisted his hands. When he reared back, Collin ducked, landed a right hook into the man's stomach, and rushed to the back door.

Olsen's footsteps came rapidly.

Collin was nearly to the back door when it opened, revealing Michael.

"Ah, you here to join the fun, Finch?" Olsen's voice stopped Collin cold.

Collin paused and regarded Michael with a frown.

"What, you didn't think we noticed you were working with Finch here?" Olsen's voice grew closer, but Collin didn't move. Regret and defiance flickered across Michael's features.

"Michael?" Collin asked.

Olsen's voice was right behind him. "He didn't tell you that he's our eyes and ears in the shire house and with the local magistrate? Keeps us informed when the law comes sniffing too close."

Collin turned back to Olsen. "He failed to mention that."

"Must have slipped my mind." Michael's voice was dry and full of sarcasm as he addressed Collin.

"Sorry, friend, but I was being honest when I said your plan was bloody awful. I just didn't tell you why." He shrugged a shoulder. "Olsen, take him out back and let's get him somewhere where the blood won't stain the floors." He jerked his head to the open door.

Collin glared at Michael as Olsen's beefy hands wrapped around his shoulders, shoving him forward. Michael was outside in the street when Olsen pushed him through the door.

The unmistakable click of a pistol filled the street, echoing in its lethal threat. Collin's shoulders were abruptly released, and he stepped forward.

"McKensie is in his office. He's the contact for this area. If you search his desk, you'll find all the information you need for this locale," Collin said to the officers all lined against the wall of the building, holding their position. One had a pistol against Olsen's back.

"Yes, sir." One of them nodded at Collin, and then carefully they filed into the hall. There was a scuffle and swearing as McKensie was drawn out next. Collin stepped aside as a carriage with bars came around the corner toward them. Both Olsen and McKensie were loaded up inside, then sent off.

"Well, that went much better than I expected." Michael clapped Collin on the shoulder.

Collin released a tight breath. "You, my friend, are a terrible actor."

Michael chuckled. "I'm excellent. You're just jealous of my clear talent. I've been working with these guys for the local magistrate for months, and they didn't suspect me once."

"Because they aren't that intelligent."

"Yeah, well, neither are you."

"I orchestrated all the additional men needed for this scenario."

"Yes, and I made sure you didn't die," Michael replied.

"Fair."

"It was a cooperative effort," Michael stated, then offered Collin his hand.

"Agreed."

An officer from the War Office stepped out from the building, his expression direct. "Thank you. Turns out there's plenty of information in the office that will lead to several more arrests. You did good work, my lord, Mr. Finch."

"Thank you," Collin replied at the same time as Michael.

The officer nodded to both and then directed several others to come with him to begin the removal process of all the information for later study.

"Well, what is the plan now? You've done what you've set out to do."

Collin shrugged. "In a way, yes. They will have to change the names of the smuggling areas, so my name will no longer be linked. That's good. It will take some time; it won't be immediate. However, I'm no longer concerned that it will affect my family poorly in the future."

"Bloody hell, they forgot to take the bribe from McKensie, or did he leave it in his desk?" Michael turned to glance toward the hall.

"Oh, don't fret. It wasn't all real." Collin shrugged.

Michael frowned. "It was fake?"

"I put several high-value notes on the front and back, then used discarded parchments in the right size to fill in the rest. If he'd inspected more closely, he'd have noticed, but greed tends to blind people, so I took my chances. I'll retrieve those larger notes later, but even if I don't, it's not a deep loss."

Michael stared at him. "You're braver than me, or stupider. Yeah, we'll go with the latter."

"Probably," Collin replied. "Probably. Nevertheless, at least it's done. Parliament will have new evidence to make the changes to help prevent the smuggling, and I, among others of the *ton*, will no longer have our good names used for nefarious reasons."

"All in a day's work," Michael replied.

"Indeed."

Michael turned to the men taking information from McKensie's office. "I'm going to stay and make sure they get everything. Check the unusual hiding places, make sure nothing is left behind." He slapped Collin's shoulder. "And you, I believe, have a trip to plan for."

"Indeed, I do." Collin slapped Michael's back as well. "Indeed, I do."

Thirty-two

A sound mind in a sound body is a short but full description of a happy state in this world. He that has these two has little more to wish for; and he that wants either of them will be little the better for anything else.

—John Locke, *Some Thoughts Concerning Education*

COLLIN STEPPED AWAY FROM THE DUKE'S Cambridge lodgings while the carriage was being loaded. He had a half hour or so before it would be ready to embark, and he had a very important errand to run beforehand. He took the now familiar road toward Michael's house, a smile tipping his lips at the events of the day before. In truth, he'd been unaware that Michael had been working both sides until two days ago, but it had worked out brilliantly. Michael had gleaned all the information he'd needed from both Olsen and McKensie, and likely the man who had received the black eye from Luke would be arrested soon enough. Michael needed more assistance in arresting them, and Collin was able to procure it, and quickly. After they'd discussed their plan, he'd dispatched a messenger to the War Office in London, and they'd sent a small group of officers to assist. Everything from then on went to design, at least mostly.

Collin had one regret: not being able to see Olsen's face when he realized he'd been double-crossed. Beautiful.

As he approached Michael's door, he knocked twice and waited.

After a moment, the door swung open. "Ah, miss me already?" Michael asked, stepping aside for Collin to enter.

"Desperately," Collin replied with sarcasm. "Actually, I just had a little unfinished business." He withdrew the final payment, plus a generous bonus, from his pocket and handed it to Michael.

Michael's eyes widened, then smoothed in understanding as he tucked the money into his front pocket. He grinned. "All actual money, right? No cut-to-size parchments in between?"

Collin chuckled. "All authentic."

"Good, thank you."

"No, thank you. I can say that this was a successful endeavor because of you and your insight and expertise…even if you did wait until the eleventh hour to tell me what you'd known all along," he added with a wry tone.

"Sort of known, it wasn't all pieced together." Michael shrugged. "But you did the piecing, so for that, thank you. We certainly made a good team."

"We did. If you ever want to dabble further in the War Office's work, let me know." Collin extended his hand. "I can't think of a better man, or friend, Michael Finch."

Michael took his hand. "Thank you, it's been mostly a pleasure, my lord," he teased.

"Mostly," Collin agreed.

He took his leave and headed back. The carriage was ready when he crossed the street, and he took a final moment to study the building, the street, Cambridge itself. It was time to say goodbye. But what a hell of an experience it had been. He approached the loaded carriage and soon was on his way to London and Elizabeth.

Nearly seven hours later, the carriage turned in at the Westmore residence. Collin hadn't sent word ahead of him, but Joan knew he'd arrive as soon as the loose ends were tied up in Cambridge.

It was a lovely sight, even if it wasn't his own home. It was where the people he loved were, and that was enough. As the carriage rolled to a stop, he glanced out the window toward the door and grinned as the butler opened the door and Joan, followed by Elizabeth, came rushing out.

Collin grinned wildly, his gaze flicking past his sister and landing on Elizabeth. Dear Lord, he'd missed her. As the footman opened the door, he stepped out and, before saying hello, strode toward Elizabeth and, propriety be damned, pulled her into a tight embrace.

"Good God, Elizabeth, I missed you."

"You're well? Not hurt? It's over?" she asked, her voice muffled against his coat as she melted into him.

He'd never felt anything more right, more benevolent and true, than Elizabeth in his arms. "It's over. I'll tell you all about it later. Just let me hold you for a moment. I need to feel you in my arms."

"I need to feel you in mine, safe and sound." She sighed softly. "Drat you for making me worry so much."

"I'm sorry. It was unforgivable of me."

"It's forgivable, but only barely," she replied as he released her, needing to see her face, study her features, and get lost in the expressions of her eyes.

"I'll take barely." He grinned, lifting his hand to cup her chin. "I'll take whatever I can get."

His finger brushed against her lip and her eyes darkened, flicking down to his own. She swayed forward, her lips parting ever so slightly as she tipped her chin just a fraction.

Collin breathed in the sight of her, his body tightening, his heart pounding as everything around him faded, his entire soul focused on Elizabeth and how much he wanted to taste her lips. He leaned forward, angling his head slowly—

"Collin!" Joan's voice jarred him as much as her hand on his shoulder did, pulling him from the spell Elizabeth had woven around them.

"Not here, not now, not her first kiss. For pity's

sake, you're more romantic than that," she chided him. "Besides, you haven't said hello to me, and I'd like to think I matter just a little." She cast him a wicked smile, as if proud of her timely interruption.

"Hello to you too, sister." He sighed. "Wait." He flicked his attention back to Elizabeth. "What do you mean, I haven't kissed her yet... Just how much have you two been talking?"

"Far more than is good for either of us," Rowles said as he came down the stairs, joining the party. "And I suggest leaving it at that."

Collin studied his friend, then grinned. Shaking his hand, he released more of the stress of the past week. He was home, among his family. It was done.

And yet, it was also the beginning. A beautiful beginning full of hope.

"So, was I right?" He turned to Elizabeth. "I do love hearing I'm right. They may be the sweetest words in the world."

"Those—those are the sweetest words?" Joan asked, huffing. "You're decidedly unromantic, even worse than I expected."

"You clearly set the bar too high," he said to his sister, then returned his attention to Elizabeth. "I'm waiting."

"Yes, we're fast friends, just as you expected. But I don't think that will operate in your favor," she replied with a saucy tone.

"I'm right, and that's truly what matters in this

situation. I knew I'd be on the losing end, so this is my consolation."

"Because you're so often wrong?" Elizabeth replied, grinning unrepentantly.

"Did I say that?" Collin asked, pulling her hand and tugging her close once more.

"No, but you implied it. Just as good as admitting it."

"Not exactly," he said, his attention captivated by the way her lips moved when she spoke.

"Dear Lord," Joan interrupted. "Well, shall we at least move this tête-à-tête into the house? Or shall we have tea brought out here to your carriage, not that we'd all fit."

"Someone has a sour disposition," Collin teased playfully as his sister moved past him toward the stairs.

"No, you're just being exceptionally dense," she replied good-naturedly.

"Your words pain me!" Collin pretended that an arrow pieced his heart.

Beside him, Elizabeth pretended to pull it out. "Better now; you'll live to fight another day."

"Brilliant, I do love a good fight. It clearly entices me." He offered his hand to her, giving her his most roguish grin.

Elizabeth blushed. "Well, I can't exactly say anything in response since I'm the same way."

"Ah, another point to agree on. I should make a list."

"It may be a short list."

"Regardless." He shrugged, then sobered. "I'm so happy to be with you once more."

Elizabeth regarded him through lowered lashes. "It was a very long few days."

"But it's over."

"Yes, it's over and I need to hear all the details, and then I'll tell you about all the particulars of our upcoming event."

Collin frowned. "Event? Why does that sound ominous?"

"Because you're clearly fatigued from your journey, no other rational reason," Joan said.

"Maybe I should have stated the question differently. What event?"

Elizabeth shared a look with him, one that said she was both excited and terrified. Neither of which made him feel better about the question.

"A ball."

"A ball," Collin repeated.

"Yes. Was I too quiet?"

"No, I don't think that's ever been an issue for you."

"There's a first time for everything," Joan quipped. "Yes, a ball."

"In the autumn?"

"Why not?"

"Haven't most people left for the country already?"

"Yes, but that won't stop us from having a party. It just might not be as well attended. Are you offended by that?"

"Heavens no."

"That's what I thought. In fact I rather anticipated you'd appreciate it."

"I do."

"I don't see the problem."

Collin blinked. "There isn't one. I am just surprised."

Joan regarded him. "Oh, I was expecting more of a fight. Well, no matter. I have it scheduled for this weekend. Now, tell me what happened in Cambridge."

"Wait a moment. You didn't communicate that the ball is to be so soon," Collin replied, spearing Elizabeth's amused expression with a disgruntled one of his own.

"I figured you'd be back by today or tomorrow. How else did you think we ran out when you arrived? I've had servants watching for you."

"You are terrifying."

"Delightfully terrifying," Rowles replied, giving his wife an enticing smile.

"Not now." Collin gave a shudder.

"If you could have seen yourself on the steps earlier, you'd have little to say about passionate displays, my friend. I merely said something, and your expression could have burned down my house."

"It's made of stone."

"You get the point."

"May I have your attention. Please?" Joan interrupted as they all took a seat in the parlor, Elizabeth's father joining them.

"Now, I will admit I took a risk in sending out invitations, but clearly it paid off, and this weekend we will have a delightful little—"

"You don't do 'little' anything," Collin broke in.

"Ball," Joan finished. Then she turned to Elizabeth. "Do you see why he vexes me?"

"Yes, I understand," Elizabeth replied, earning Collin's scrutiny. "What? You knew this about me already."

"The two of you, stop working together on everything. Give me a chance to settle down for a moment. I just arrived."

Elizabeth patted his arm and smiled. "Forgive me."

"You're the lesser problem here." He studied his sister.

She ignored him. "So, this weekend, as I was saying, will be the ball and it will be lovely and you can announce your engagement," she finished.

Collin grinned as suddenly it all made sense. "Brilliant idea."

Joan beamed. "I knew you'd see it that way."

"I assume you've taken Elizabeth shopping?" He regarded Elizabeth with a warm gaze. A ball he could take or leave, except a ball in honor of his engagement to Elizabeth, informing all of London that he was ending his bachelor days? That was indeed a ball he'd love to celebrate.

"Yes, however I'm not to tell you any details of the dress." Joan gave a wicked smile. "As your penance for making me worry so."

Collin regarded her. "I suppose I won't harass you for the details then."

"You're going to be quite pleased."

"I have no doubt." And that was the truth. He had questioned many things weeks, even days ago. But there was one decision he hadn't questioned once: Elizabeth in his life.

As he met her eyes and reached over to grasp her hand, he felt the truth of it anew.

"No doubt at all," he whispered for her ears only. "Now, if you please, what happened in Cambridge?"

Collin took a slow breath, and told the tale, leaving out a few names and details to keep the questions to a minimum. Also, he could read the worry in Elizabeth's eyes, and there was no need to make it worse. All was well.

Finally.

All was well.

Thirty-three

The thoughts that come often unsought, and, as it were, drop into the mind, are commonly the most valuable of any we have.

—John Locke, Letter to Samuel Bold, May 16, 1699

THEY HAD JUST FINISHED DINNER THAT EVENING when, rather than adjourning to separate rooms for the men and ladies, Collin had suggested an evening stroll in the small courtyard. To Elizabeth's great delight, her father had declined, along with her soon-to be brother- and sister-in-law. Collin ushered her out into the cool evening.

"Finally." Elizabeth breathed the word out with feeling.

Collin broke into a laugh, pulling her close as he kissed the top of her head. "My sentiments exactly."

"You know, before we were betrothed, we had more time alone." She smiled up at him, giggling softly.

"I do believe you're right."

"Say that again," she teased, leaning in to him teasingly.

"No, once is enough for your greedy heart," he scolded with a grin.

Elizabeth sighed softly. "I can't wait until it's just the two of us."

Collin chuckled. "My family already getting irritating?"

"No! That's not what I meant." Elizabeth stopped walking and regarded him. She'd loved spending time with his family. It had exceeded every expectation she'd dare imagine.

"Oh, well I find them annoying, so we'd be in agreement." He tapped her nose playfully. "But I knew you didn't mean it that way. I was just teasing you. If anything, you may like my sister more than you like me."

"She is delightful," Elizabeth said. "And every bit as kind yet truly funny. I've never met her equal." She was being honest. She and Joan had become fast friends, and she was thrilled with the prospect of such a sister-in-law.

"Believe me, God broke the mold after He made her, thank goodness." He glanced heavenward.

Elizabeth shoved him flirtatiously. "Some would say the same about me."

"Yes, but in your case, God merely made perfection and didn't need to replicate it," he replied softly, his regard roaming her features and making her feel beautiful down to her toes.

Elizabeth blushed, then followed him as he led

her around the corner of a wide tree. "I'm glad you feel that way, I'm inclined to see all my many faults."

"I like to think of them as opportunities to grow," he said. "'Faults' is such a negative word." He tightened his grip on her hand, tugging her close.

"I have many opportunities to grow," she amended.

"As do I, and we'll improve together. Sound like a plan, Miss Essex?"

"Indeed, Lord Penderdale," she replied with a cheeky tone.

He grinned. "Using my title without sarcasm… I'm not sure I know what to do with that."

"Don't get used to it," she quipped.

"I would never dream of it," he replied and placed his free hand on his heart.

"Good. Now, tell me all the things you didn't tell your sister when you gave your account of all that transpired." She speared him with a direct look.

"How do you read me so well? It's quite frustrating," he said.

"You can read me as well. Therefore, it's fair. Tell me," Elizabeth entreated him. She grasped his arm and closed her eyes for a moment, savoring his presence. She'd been beside herself with worry, hoping she wasn't making too much of the situation and then fearing she was making too little. It was a mess, and it wasn't until she'd seen Collin that she was able to take a full breath.

Collin shrugged. "I didn't tell her that Olsen had tried to beat me into submission, or that Michael was the one playing both sides."

"Mr. Finch?" Elizabeth started. "No." She was shocked, trying to imagine Mr. Finch in such a situation. Eagerly, she waited for Collin to continue the story.

"Indeed, he didn't tell me until a few days ago. Nevertheless it worked in our favor, leading to all the arrests." He shrugged as if the news wasn't astounding at all.

"Well, that was a turn I didn't expect," she murmured.

"You and me both, and I like to think I'm quite astute." He waved his hand.

"You are, but clearly Mr. Finch had to be quite cautious or else he would be in greater danger than you." Elizabeth frowned. "Poor Patricia, I hope she didn't know. Now that it's all taken care of, I hope she wasn't worrying." Elizabeth's heart pinched for her friend, and she made a mental note to write her soon.

"I don't think she knew. I didn't ask Michael directly. That's simply what I'm assuming." Collin traced the length of her arm comfortingly.

Shivers of pleasure ran up her spine at his touch, but she forced herself to focus on the conversation. "Good, well, anything else?"

"No, not that I can think of. It was, when all's said

and done, quite quick. And then I headed home to you," he finished.

"Yes, to me." She squeezed his arm. "I love you," she whispered, her heart still raw from concern.

He paused, turning and touching her chin with his fingertips. "I'm sorry I put you in a position where you were so worried." His brows furrowed with the intensity of his words.

"You're here now; that's what matters," she replied, her face darkening with emotion.

"Indeed, but it still leaves a mark," he whispered softly, his eyes darting between hers, then down to her lips, and then back.

Elizabeth had never been kissed, and she'd never wanted it more. As a lady, she should wait for Collin to begin the kiss, to lead her down that path to passion. But her impatient heart fought against the constraints of society's rules.

"Collin," she murmured, and then before she could talk herself out of it, she slowly rose onto her toes, and as her eyes fluttered closed, she met his lips. Warmth coursed through her, her body tingling with acute awareness that was almost painful in its pleasure as she slowly leaned away, ending the kiss.

As her eyes opened slowly, her heart pounding an unsteady rhythm, she met Collin's surprised and approving smile. In a moment, it shifted to something dangerous that had her belly flipping over with anticipation. "Not enough."

His words were low and deliriously passionate as he leaned forward and captured her lips. His kiss was inviting, playful, and passionate all at once as he angled his head just enough to take her lower lip between his teeth, caressing it with the velvet of his tongue. Elizabeth forgot to breathe, devouring every sensation. Over and over, he coaxed her lips to blend with his, nipping, playing, and, true to her nature, she learned rapidly. It was a new sensation, to initiate the passion of the give and take of the kiss. His arms trailed up hers, leaving goose bumps in their wake as he rested his hands on her shoulder, then along her back, pulling her in close, tightly until there was no space between them. His fingers teased up her neck and she shivered, her breaths coming in short pants as she devoured kiss after kiss, never wanting to stop.

She splayed her fingers up his neck and into his hair, the sensation of it setting her further ablaze inside as she caressed his lips with her tongue. Collin groaned, the sound like surrender and restraint at the same time, and a moment later, he gentled the kiss, then after lingering against her lips a moment, withdrew.

Elizabeth's heart was racing as if she'd run across the countryside, still her body wasn't tired, but exhilarated and needy, wanting more, and she wondered if she'd ever get enough. It was a delightful sensation, and she craved more of it. She leaned up and kissed his lips, remaining there, stroking the smooth skin of his lower lip with her tongue, teasing him.

He kissed her back, then withdrew again. "I... Good Lord, Elizabeth, if I'm to maintain my honor...or yours..." He released a tight breath, then chuckled. "I never thought I'd be so easily undone by a woman, but you, my dear, are proving me wrong." He kissed her softly but didn't deepen it. "I could happily ravish you right here, but I won't. However, when we are married..." He kissed her again, slowly, deeply, and then retreated as if toying with her, a delightful game she immediately loved. "However, when we are married," he said again, "you won't leave my bed for days."

Elizabeth grinned against his lips. "Promise?"

"Absolutely," he whispered. "Which does bring me to another important question and thankfully will distract me from the delightful temptation you present."

"It sounds serious."

"It is." He turned them around and headed back toward the house. "Speaking of marriage, the question now is when?"

"When?" she asked.

"Yes, when. The convention is for the banns to be read for three weeks in succession, the announcement in the *Times*, and of course, holding the wedding at St. James's."

Elizabeth nodded. "And the unconventional way?"

Collin shrugged, but the movement was significant, as if he was trying to disregard this option too much. "A special license procured at Doctors' Commons."

"Which would allow it to be in a few days' time, instead of weeks, correct?" Elizabeth asked.

Collin nodded. "But it can cause gossip that there's a…need…for an immediate wedding."

Elizabeth blushed at his implication, but also had a thrill run through her at the prospect of such…activities. "What is your preference?" she asked, distracting herself as well.

Collin turned to her. "Marriage. One way or the other. That is my preference."

"That's certainly good to know, since we'd have much to discuss if that were not the case," she said. "But which of the two options for timing would you prefer?" she clarified.

Collin answered. "For my impatient nature, the latter. For the sake of your reputation, the first."

Elizabeth twisted her lips. "You didn't answer the question." She looked up at the stairs, pausing as she regarded him.

"I'm learning from the best." He bent down and kissed her softly.

"And I'm learning from you," she murmured against his lips. "So, in that spirit, I'll leave the decision up to you."

He groaned. "You can't. I'll choose wrong."

"Or right." She nipped at his lip.

"We're eloping," he growled against her lips and kissed her deeply.

She pulled back and giggled. "I'll clarify. You choose from the options you mentioned before. Gretna Green wasn't on the list."

"Damn the list." He kissed her quickly.

"Your choice."

"You're a menace." He chuckled against her skin as he pulled her close into a warm embrace.

"And don't you soon forget it."

"You won't let me. And I wouldn't have it any other way. What's that quote…" He arched a brow.

She quirked one brow in question.

"'All is fair in love and war.'" He kissed her lingeringly and then tugged her hand as he led her up the stairs.

Elizabeth laughed. "Certainly words we will live by."

Thirty-four

New opinions are always suspected, and usually opposed, without any other reason but because they are not already common.

—John Locke, *An Essay Concerning Human Understanding*

THE EVENING OF THE BALL, COLLIN WAS BREATHING epithets aimed at his sister. He'd tried all day to see Elizabeth, but his pest of a sister had kept her cloistered under the guise of preparing for the evening.

He didn't buy that lie for a moment. It was about making him wait. But the hardest part was admitting that she was right because waiting for Elizabeth was always worth it.

"Why does this seem familiar?" Rowles handed him a glass of champagne, eyeing him over the glass before he took a sip. The party was well attended, for the end of the season, and he'd been given many questioning glances. It was, after all, his engagement ball and his betrothed had yet to make her entrance. Collin swore under his breath once more at the person at fault, his sister.

"I was going to ask you the same question." Collin took a sip of the chilled champagne, its bubbly flavor teasing his senses, although it was nothing compared to Elizabeth's kisses. Waiting be hanged, he wasn't going to practice patience while the banns were read and announcement in the *Times* all took their time. No, one kiss and he'd made up his mind.

Because he wasn't a patient man, and Elizabeth was too tempting for his sanity and for his honor.

Yes, it was certainly the wiser choice to get a special license. Of course, it helped to have a duke or two—he raised a glass to Quin who was grinning at him from a few yards away—in his pocket to help motivate the clerk at Doctors' Commons.

"What has you all serious?" Rowles asked, regarding him curiously.

"Just thinking about the quickest way to the altar," Collin replied with a wicked smile.

"Ah." Rowles chuckled. "That." He grinned. "That is certainly a sentiment I can understand."

"Yes, well, remember the 'sentiment' you're referring to is my sister, and I'd rather not think about that…at all…ever." Collin grimaced.

"What a lovely sentiment it is…" Rowles took a sip of champagne.

"And may I offer a change of subject?"

"I will. Consider it an early wedding present, not discussing your sister's finest qualities."

"Dear Lord, save me."

Rowles continued. "I find it delightfully amusing that you're searching for the quickest way to the altar, when only a few weeks, maybe a month ago, you were doing everything in your power to keep away from one."

Collin speared him with a glare. "It makes a difference when you meet the right person."

"Yes, that I can agree with. But it's still amusing, the complete change in you. Except that's not all. Your sister and I—"

"Again, I'd prefer not discuss any subject that starts with those four words."

"Have been talking about the other changes in you," Rowles finished.

Collin regarded him. "What changes?"

Rowles sipped his champagne. "There are several."

"Enumerate them for me then."

"Cheeky tonight, are we? Or are you just impatient until your sister brings in Elizabeth?"

"Both. She's taking bloody forever."

"She wants to be dramatic."

"Heaven help us all."

"Regardless, allow me to enumerate your changes," Rowles told him. "Before you left for Cambridge, we were worried about you. You'd been surly—and not your usual sarcastic self, but dark and depressed. You didn't come out from that hard shell of cynicism. You didn't anticipate the future with any hope, and there was no real joy in your life."

"I sound like a pleasure to be around."

"You weren't. You were bloody awful."

"So, I take it I've improved."

"You've...changed. You are who I remember you to be...before..."

Collin swallowed and regarded his friend. "The fire," he finished.

Rowles had lost a brother in that fire too. They shared the burden of the loss.

"Yes. It was almost as if...the loss had slowly been spiraling you downward and you finally hit the bottom. That was a few months ago, then when it was the anniversary—"

"Of my father's death, the one time I forgot because I was so bloody despondent I didn't notice what day it was anymore."

"Exactly, that was when we knew something had to happen. We just weren't sure what. Or if there was anything we could do."

Collin sipped his champagne, reliving that evening.

How could he have forgotten?

He remembered the feeling of icy-cold shock as realization hit him.

"Next thing Joan and I knew, you were off to Cambridge. It was a little terrifying, not knowing how you were."

Collin shrugged. "I left the party and made some decisions. Turns out it was one of the best things I could have done."

"I agree."

"Talking about me?" Joan's voice interrupted his thoughts and he turned, but before he could offer a smart remark to his sister, his breath was stolen away.

Elizabeth's shy smile captivated him, body and soul. It warmed him from the inside out, her eyes only for him. She walked forward and took his extended hand. He lifted her gloved fingers to his lips and kissed them, pulling her in slightly closer than was socially acceptable as he lost himself in her dark gaze. "Stunning, intelligent, and ravishing my self-control every moment... How did I get so lucky?" he asked, whispering the words for her ears alone.

"Handsome, witty, mostly intelligent and brave... How did *I* get so lucky?" she countered, her words teasing but her expression fiercely passionate as she locked eyes with his. She was indeed worth the wait, in every sense. The green silk clung to her body, the color enhancing the creamy hue of her skin and the brightness of her strawberry hair, contrasted with her dark eyes. Her long, lean fingers grasped his tightly as if needing a lifeline.

"You're exquisite."

"Everyone is staring." She swallowed but held her head high, every inch the queen of the moment.

"Because they are as captivated as I am, dear Elizabeth," he whispered softly.

"Or they are just curious," she said with a grin, relaxing a bit.

"Think of it like your beehive."

She frowned slightly, and Collin continued. "In a room full of bees, everyone all the same, there's only one queen, and without her, the rest of the hive wouldn't survive."

"I think London would survive without me, as it has for centuries." Smiling in challenge, she waited for a response.

"But I wouldn't, and they can see that. And they want it too," he finished, meeting her gaze with all the love in his heart.

"The waltz is about to start," Joan murmured.

Collin led Elizabeth to the dance floor as the music started and pulled her in close as he began to lead.

"You know, this is the first time I've ever danced with you."

"We've danced around arguments for weeks now," she teased, her wit just as sparkling as her expression.

"And here I thought since it was our engagement ball, there would be a cease-fire."

"Never." She tempered the word with an easy grin. "I rather like accosting you." Her attention darted down to his lips.

"If you keep looking at me that way, I assure you, sweet Elizabeth, we are going to scandalize all of London as I devour you right here," he whispered softly, temptingly, as if challenging her.

"That is one challenge I'll have to decline, out of respect for your sister. I, for my part, wouldn't mind. No, that's not true. I would. I would…tomorrow."

Collin chuckled. "Is that to say you'd not regret it tonight?"

"Likely not. You tend to distract me."

"That's only fair, since I feel the same way."

"Equals."

"Did you ever consider yourself anything less?" He raised the question.

A blush bloomed in Elizabeth's cheeks. "No. That is one of the many reasons I love you." She didn't glance away shyly when she said it; she merely met his gaze with a direct and frank one of her own. "Because as *your* wife, I'm also still me, with my own thoughts, ideas, plans…"

"Future, your own opinions," he added. "All of it, and I wouldn't change that about you at all. I only ask that when you disagree with me, you do it gently to make sure I'll recover some day."

"Agreed, same. Because I've been known to be wrong a time or two."

"Only once or twice though."

"Maybe more."

"About me? You were wrong about me."

"You were... You didn't present yourself accurately."

"So, it's my fault?" he asked provocatively.

"Yes," she returned.

"You know, if you smile any wider, the whole of London is going to think you're entirely too happy."

"Then they will be correct in their assessment."

"Say it again," he ordered softly, his eyes flicking between her lips and her gaze.

"That I'm happy?" she asked, her expression serious as her eyes lingered on his lips.

"Yes. Tell me I make you happy."

"You make me happy. Happier than I ever imagined being, and I love you," she finished.

"Not as much as I love you."

"We can't possibly make that into an argument."

"We likely will."

"I'll win."

"Oh, my sweet Elizabeth, when we fight over that...we both win."

Epilogue

ELIZABETH STRAIGHTENED HER HAT AS SHE stepped from the carriage to the Thomas Coram Hospital for Foundlings. Taking a deep breath, she squared her shoulders and tried not to think about the reasons she was running late.

Married life was delicious, and Collin was as insatiable as she was, which led to many hurried arrivals for appointments and various other events. It had become a problem, yet not one she had any desire to fix.

But today was special. Every Tuesday and Thursday were. As she crossed the courtyard to the entrance of the hospital, Joan met her halfway, a bemused expression on her face. "I can make my own assumptions on why you're late, and they will be the ones I want to pretend are true. You're married to my brother, after all." She gave a slight shudder, then grinned.

"As you wish. I still have plenty of time before class starts," Elizabeth said, defending herself.

"You do, which is why I told you a half hour earlier than is necessary."

"You didn't." Elizabeth turned shocked eyes to her sister-in-law.

"I did, but it's for the best." Joan gave a saucy smile. "You have several new students today, and after the first class we are going to meet with several of the older ladies who wish to be governesses."

"Very good, and like last time, they've all had the same educational background?" Elizabeth asked as they entered the building.

"Yes. One moment, I'm going to ask Miss Vanderhaul if they are ready." Joan stepped away and spoke to one of the directors of the hospital, giving Elizabeth time to consider what was ahead.

Before Elizabeth had married Collin, Joan had explained the work she did volunteering at the Foundling Hospital. Elizabeth's curiosity had been piqued, and after she asked further questions, Joan invited her to visit and see how the orphans' education was addressed.

The moment Elizabeth set foot in the Foundling Hospital, she knew it was her new purpose. As Joan had just mentioned, the older girls were always seeking employment, and becoming governesses was one way they could seek gainful work. But to be a governess, one had to be educated, and sometimes the hospital's curriculum wasn't enough, not for positions that paid better.

Seeing an opportunity to help, Elizabeth spoke with Miss Vanderhaul, and together they had developed a plan to educate young ladies who wished to be governesses. So, Tuesdays and Thursdays, Elizabeth met Joan at the Foundling Hospital, and Elizabeth would teach for hours.

And she loved every single moment.

"The younger students are in the library," Joan interrupted Elizabeth's thoughts and gestured down the hall.

Elizabeth followed her. The children they passed in the halls gave shy smiles and polite nods as they passed. The others who worked with the children gave respectful nods or bows as they smiled in welcome and gratitude. Elizabeth paused for a moment, just before she entered the library.

The contrast stole her breath.

Cambridge, Christ's College. The library where she'd hidden, where she'd tried to blend in and be invisible—where she wasn't wanted or respected. And now, here at the Foundling Hospital, where her teaching was making a real difference in children's lives, where she could teach and cultivate young minds with the basics while adding touches of philosophy or science, and have it matter. Where her assistance could truly make their life after the hospital better, more secure, more profitable. It was overwhelming.

"Elizabeth?" Joan called, beckoning her in warmly.

Elizabeth smiled and walked into the library, her forever place of sanctuary.

What had begun in pain had ended in beauty.

Some lessons only life could teach.

And she was always a willing student.

*Read on for a look at the latest title in the
Duke's Estates series from New York Times
bestselling author Jane Ashford*

One

CHARLOTTE DEEPING WALKED ALONG A COUN-
try footpath, partly shielded from the brisk October
wind by a thorny hedge. The month was almost
over, and she was glad of her warm cloak and thick
gloves. Yellow leaves rustled at her side, under
scudding clouds, and wizened berries hung on the
branches. The air brought the scents of the waning
year and thoughts of endings. She told herself she
was not lonely, but she couldn't help wishing for
her three best friends. Ada, Harriet, and Sarah had
been her constant companions since they had met
at school at thirteen. They'd been the sisters she'd
never had, and she missed them with a wistful mel-
ancholy that was unlike her. She was the acerbic
one. Nothing depressed her spirits.

A clutching briar snagged her cloak. Charlotte
pulled it free. Her friends were all far away and
married now. She had turned twenty. It was time
to think of the future—a topic as thorny as the
hedgerow.

With only a flurry of hoofbeats as a warning, a rider hurtled into sight above the shrubs on her left, jumping bushes, path, and all. More than a thousand pounds of horse surged past a few feet from her nose, so close that it seemed gigantic.

Charlotte threw up her arms and jerked backward. Her bootheel caught in the hem of her cloak. She staggered, lurched, and fell flat on her back with a thud that drove the breath from her lungs. Her bonnet tipped forward and covered her face.

"Oh my God!" exclaimed an appalled male voice. There were subdued hoofbeats as the rider turned his mount. "Are you all right?" he called.

Charlotte concentrated on catching her breath. She knew she would, eventually, but the struggle was frightening. Her chest wouldn't work, which goaded her toward panic. That and the fact that one more step and the horse would have hit her, breaking bones at the very least.

Feet hit the ground nearby. Then two knees in riding breeches thumped down at her side, just visible from under the skewed brim of her bonnet. "Miss? Are you all right? Oh lord. Can I…? What shall I…?"

At last, Charlotte's lungs started functioning again. She drew in a welcome deep breath, and then another. She pushed back her hat and glared up at a figure silhouetted by the sun. "What the deuce did you think you were doing?" she asked.

The man drew back. He was holding the reins of a dancing, snorting hunter, who clearly objected to Charlotte's incursion into their ride. "I didn't realize there was a path along here," he said. "I was just hacking cross-country, you know."

She knew all too well. The area around the Deepings' Leicestershire home filled up with hordes of hey-go-mad young gentlemen as the fox-hunting season approached each year.

"My friend Stanley Deeping told me the country was good in this direction."

"Oh, Stanley." The second of Charlotte's four brothers had the brains of a huge friendly dog. In her opinion.

"You know Stanley?" He seemed pleased by this fact.

"He's my brother."

"Oh." The sun-dazzled figure cocked his head. "You must be Charlotte then. Miss Deeping, that is."

His tone had altered. Charlotte didn't know what her brothers had told their cronies about her, but she doubted it was completely flattering. She sat up and adjusted her bonnet, insofar as that was possible. She suspected the back was irreparably crushed.

"Let me help you." He offered a hand.

"Is your hand shaking?" she asked him.

"What? No."

It definitely was. She decided to take it. He rose and pulled her to her feet in one smooth motion with an excess of casual strength.

Charlotte looked up and up. She was thought tall for a girl, but this man overtopped her by six inches. He...loomed. Though she didn't think he was doing it on purpose. He was bent forward, his forehead creased with worry.

Height was the only thing they had in common. He was well muscled, while she was often judged too slender. His hair was light brown, while hers was black. He had guileless blue eyes, and she an acute dark gaze. Handsome, yes, he was—very. A bit too much to be comfortable. And possibly well aware of it. She couldn't quite tell. He was probably around Stanley's age of twenty-six. She realized she was still holding his hand. She dropped it.

More than likely, he had the brains of a flea, Charlotte thought. Stanley didn't cultivate intellectual friends, while she was known for her sharp mind. It went with her sharp tongue and angular frame.

"I really am sorry," he said. "Are you all right? Shall I take you home?"

"Throwing me over your saddle like young Lochinvar?"

His eyes widened. "Who?"

"It's a poem. Never mind." It was foolish to quote poetry to Stanley's friends. Even Walter Scott.

"Oh, a poem." He said the word as if it explained any amount of strangeness.

"I'm quite all right," Charlotte added. "You should continue your ride." She wanted him to go. She needed to collect herself. Far more than should have been necessary, even considering the fall.

He looked uncertain. "I'm Glendarvon, by the way," he said. "Not a proper introduction, but I know your name, so…"

Charlotte searched her memory. She didn't think Stanley had ever mentioned anyone named Glendarvon. By the way he said it, she suspected it was a title. Her mother would know. She was a compendium of such information.

"It's too bad you don't have your horse. You could show me the best fox runs hereabouts." He said it with the air of someone offering a treat.

It never occurred to him that she wouldn't have a horse. Which was reasonable. Of course she did. In her family, it was unthinkable not to ride. The Deepings had been breeding racehorses and hunters since the time of Charles the Second. That racing-mad monarch had knighted her ancestor for his out-standing efforts. The family had grown increasingly prosperous because they didn't keep a racing stable themselves but rather sold to those who indulged in that expensive pastime. And the hunting season was her family's glory. Her father and brothers were all dead keen, even Cecil the dandy. And her mother enjoyed their happiness. "I'm sure Stanley will take you around," Charlotte said.

He nodded, not looking particularly disappointed. "Don't suppose you hunt."

She could have. She certainly rode well enough. But she didn't. Charlotte had no interest in being spattered head to toe in mud while chasing foxes who didn't deserve that level of organized aggression. In her opinion. She started to say so. But this topic was the subject of fierce arguments with her brothers, in a family that specialized in loud debates over the dinner table. She didn't care to begin one here, with a stranger.

"If you're sure you're all right?" he asked.

"Perfectly."

"Well, then I suppose…"

"Go on." Charlotte made a shooing motion.

Moving with loose-limbed grace, he mounted the horse.

"Do watch where you jump," she added.

"I will." He gave her a small salute and rode off.

Charlotte watched him go. He had an admirable ease in the saddle, but any friend of Stanley's *would*. He didn't look back. Why would he?

She resumed her walk but found her steps turning back toward home rather than onward. And when she reached the house, she went in search of her mother.

"That's Laurence Lindley, Marquess of

Glendarvon," Mama replied when she inquired. "Stanley knows him from Eton. He's staying with us. He arrived this morning."

"Here?" asked Charlotte. Their house was spacious, but the family nearly filled it when they all were at home. It couldn't accommodate many of her brothers' cronies who came up for the hunting. They usually stayed in nearby inns.

"I thought we would put up a few of the boys' friends."

"The most 'suitable' unmarried ones?" Charlotte asked drily.

Her mother looked furtive. They resembled each other in the face, with dark eyes and angular features. Mama was smaller and more rounded, however. Ladies were supposed to be softly rounded, Charlotte thought. As well as sweet and biddable. And pure as the driven snow. She'd often wondered how these traits were to be reconciled. Biddable and pure could so easily conflict.

"You didn't take to any young men during the season," her mother replied. "I thought this would be an opportunity to become acquainted in easier circumstances."

"I've told you I don't intend to marry," replied Charlotte.

"You have." Her mother's tone had gone acerbic now. "A number of times."

"Yet you don't listen to me."

"Because it's nonsense. What else will you do? All your friends have married."

"I could help Papa breed horses. Henry doesn't wish to. He wants to be a diplomat. And Cecil is too fashionable to run the stables."

"And Stanley and Bertram?"

It was true that these brothers were deeply involved in the breeding schemes. And they were far better at it than Charlotte. Her liking for horses didn't stretch to the smallest details of their pedigrees and temperaments.

"You will be happy with a husband and family of your own."

As Mama was. And so she wanted that for Charlotte. But they were quite different people. Oddly, Charlotte thought she was probably most like her brother Cecil, despite her tepid interest in fashion. He would be horrified by the comparison, she thought with a smile.

"That's better," said her mother. "You have such a lovely smile."

No one seemed to realize how infuriating that remark nearly always was, Charlotte noted.

◆

Laurence couldn't believe the level of noise at the Deeping dinner table. Shouting seemed acceptable, even de rigueur. Passionate debates raged in several spots, competing for attention. The other two houseguests, old friends of Henry Deeping, had plunged right in, seemingly accustomed to the din. One of them pounded on the table now, rehashing a controversy from past hunting seasons with obvious relish.

He supposed it wasn't really shouting. Just lively argument. But Laurence had been reared by dutiful, correct, and very *quiet* people. Orphaned at four, the last of an eminent family line, he'd been put in the hands of subdued caretakers whose faces had continually changed. He'd scarcely had time to know one before they were gone. Later, when he came of age, his trustees had explained that they hadn't wanted him to become too attached to any caretakers, lest he be taken advantage of. They'd seemed to expect praise and gratitude for their efforts. Laurence hadn't provided them.

The kind of mayhem surrounding him now would have meant disaster in his early life. A voice somewhere deep in him cried, "Fire, fear, foes!" He didn't show that, of course. He'd learned very early to keep such feelings to himself. And since he'd attained his full growth and musculature, no one seemed to expect emotion of him, which made things easier. People who looked like him were not supposed to be anxious.

"Fop," said Bertram Deeping to his older brother Cecil.

"If you think being fashionable makes one weak, I am happy to take you outside and thrash you," replied Cecil.

"What, beat me senseless with your masses of fobs?" asked Bertram.

"With my punishing left," Cecil replied. "As you may remember from the last time."

Bertram grimaced. Then he laughed, which Laurence found inexplicable.

Laurence was still getting Stanley's brothers straight. They all had dark hair and eyes and a similar sharp cast of features. The eldest, Henry, was three years older than Laurence's twenty-five and seemed a pleasant, polished fellow. Apparently, Henry was set on the diplomatic corps as a path to make his way in the world. He was also, according to Stanley, a devil of a marksman, the envy of Manton's shooting gallery in London.

Stanley threw back his head and laughed at something his father said. The tallest and bulkiest of the four Deeping brothers, Stanley was the most open, accepting fellow Laurence had ever known. They'd met at Eton when Laurence first arrived, fresh from the strict, austere preparatory school he'd detested. Thirteen years old, Laurence had been wary and reluctant and nearly sick with nerves. And then Stanley had happened along, discovered they lived in neighboring counties, and greeted him with metaphorically open arms.

Stanley had just assumed they'd be friends, with no guile whatsoever, and he'd guided Laurence to his quarters and the classrooms and past the potential perils of the place with kindness and unfailing good humor. Laurence would always be grateful to this least self-conscious of human beings.

Perhaps the third brother, Cecil, had absorbed all the self-consciousness available in the family, Laurence decided. Cecil was unmistakably a dandy. His waistcoat was bright enough to hurt one's eyes. And he couldn't wear all those fobs hunting, surely? The clatter would scare off the foxes. Yet, unlike many of his ilk, there was muscle under Cecil's exquisite coat and a hint of laughter in his eyes. "Puppy," he said to Bertram.

The youngest brother at eighteen, Bertram stuck out his tongue, earning a reprimand from his mother and ignoring it with all the exuberant bravado of his age. He seemed a bit unformed. Like Stanley, he was horse mad and involved in the Deeping breeding farm. Laurence had already discovered that those two could talk horses for hours. Literally. Fortunately, they didn't insist on it. Bertram didn't appear to have many other topics of conversation, however.

His gaze moving on, Laurence encountered the dark, sardonic eyes of Miss Charlotte Deeping, the lone daughter of the household. He'd nearly killed her earlier. He shuddered at the memory—the slender figure suddenly beneath his mount's hooves, falling backward. Catastrophe avoided by inches. Really, mere inches. He couldn't bear to think of it.

Miss Deeping's lips turned down as if she could read his thoughts. Which she couldn't, of course. Thankfully, that was impossible. She was a creature of angles, striking rather than pretty, dark and... spiky. The word came to him out of nowhere. It felt as if she had more spines than a hedgehog. Did hedgehogs bite? He wasn't sure. She looked as if *she* might.

Her dark eyebrows rose, and Laurence quickly looked away. He drank some wine and ate some of the excellent roast beef before continuing his examination of the company. Miss Deeping was one of only three ladies at the dinner table with eight men, which was unusual. The other two were his hostess, an older, softer edition of her daughter, and a sturdy square-shouldered lady of perhaps fifty. The latter had been introduced as Mrs. Carew, and she resembled their host, Sir Charles Deeping. Both of them had hair more dark-brown than black, and hazel eyes rather than the deeper brown of the rest of the family. Laurence hadn't quite figured out Mrs. Carew's position in the household. She'd said very little, but she did not have the air of a timid companion.

Acknowledgments

I'd like to thank my amazing family, who constantly supports me! Of course that especially includes my tall, dark and handsome husband who gives me a Happily Ever After every day! I'd also like to thank my fantastic editors, and everyone at Sourcebooks who have been amazing through each of these books!

About the Author

Kristin Vayden has published more than a dozen titles with Blue Tulip Publishing, *New York Times* bestselling author Rachel Van Dyken's publishing company. Kristin's inspiration for the romance she writes comes from her tall, dark, and handsome husband with killer blue eyes. With five children to chase, she is never at a loss for someone to kiss, something to cook, or some mess to clean, but she loves every moment of it! Life is full—of blessings and adventure. Needless to say, she's a big fan of coffee and wine…and living in Washington, she's within walking distance of both.

Follow Kristin online:
facebook.com/kristinvaydenauthor
Instagram: @kristinkatjoyce